Vida looked down at their hands, wrapped gently in their own harmless embrace. She took Kirsten in her arms. "Please don't cry," she said, wiping her tears away. Kirsten looked so sad. "I'm sorry I hurt you. I don't mean to hurt you. I just can't stand what we do to each other."

Kirsten nodded and kept crying while Vida kept wiping the tears away.

Vida softly kissed her eyelids and her cheeks, whispering, "Shh . . . it'll be all right."

It would have been all right if Vida hadn't kissed her, softly at first, then harder, their tongues finding each other. Remembering other, better days, Vida reached for Kirsten's breast, rubbing her finger around her nipple, remembering how soft her nipples were, and then wanting to taste them. She unbuttoned Kirsten's dress and took a nipple in her mouth, feeling Kirsten kiss her neck. She reached up under Kirsten's dress spreading Kirsten's legs, going inside deeper, feeling Kirsten just as eagerly reach for her until they were both holding each other tight and coming within seconds of each other.

Visit

Bella Books

at

BellaBooks.com

or call our toll-free number

1-800-729-4992

HIGHER GROUND

SAXON BENNETT

Bella
BOOKS

2004

Bella Books, Inc.
P.O. Box 10543
Tallahassee, FL 32302

Printed in the United States of America on acid-free paper
First Edition

Editor: Christi Cassidy
Cover designer: Sandy Knowles

ISBN 1-931513-69-4

To my beloved partner, Lin,
for being so understanding about the process of book making

Acknowledgments

To my furry family for helping out in their own unique ways: Sarah, the sassy calico cat, for sitting on the manuscript, which is always a good sign, it is like a cat blessing that everything will work out and Gunter, the biggest cat in Texas and we don't live in Texas, for stoically helping with the office work, this means he naps in the sun while I toil and to Annie and Jane, the new, lively puppies, who play babushka with me when I'm on the verge of going stark, raving mad from sitting in front of my computer for so long.

Part One

Chapter One

Vida Sumner watched her young counterpart move in front of the camera. She smiled shyly up at Vida. Vida smiled back with a glance at Sid the photographer. Mercedes LaFontaine blushed and lowered her eyes. Sid took the shot and then gave the thumbs-up signal to Vida, one of the veteran models for Vanessa's Closet.

"That was perfect," Sid said.

"I'm sorry. I'm still so nervous in front of the camera," Mercedes said.

"Hey, you're new. Give it some time and you'll be just like the others. Baby, you're going to have a long career with us. I can tell," he said.

"Thanks," Mercedes said, putting on her robe.

"Go change and we'll do the next shot," Sid instructed.

Mercedes went to change.

"She's hot for you," Sid told Vida.

"Yeah, right," she said, watching the comely figure of her coworker walk away.

"Girl lust, I'll never get it. If the straight world only knew that half you gorgeous babes were dykes, they'd just shit."

"You're jealous," Vida said, taking off her robe, thinking this was a benefit of being a lesbian and hanging around attractive women all day. Underneath she wore a set of bra and panties, part of a new line Vida liked.

"Damn right. She stands a chance at your stunning breasts, long legs, golden hair and stunning blue eyes. Who wouldn't be jealous?"

"That's right, boyfriend," Vida said, squeezing her breasts together.

Sid fell to his knees and said, "Please God, make me a lesbian in my next life."

Vida laughed.

Mercedes came back into the room. "Sid, what's wrong? Are you all right?" she asked, concern etched into her face.

"It's my heart." Sid clutched his chest.

"He's all right. He is just disappointed that he wasn't born a lesbian," Vida replied.

"You know, Sid, that could be arranged. A little surgery and some hormones and you could become your dream," Mercedes quipped.

"And a haircut and a shave," Vida said, referring to Sid's unruly mop and goatee.

"Yeah, that too," Mercedes agreed.

Sid grabbed his crotch and said, "No way."

"You have no sense of sacrifice or dedication to the cause," Vida said.

Mercedes laughed.

"All right, you two, let's get back to work. Now stand together and let's get some of that sexual energy you girls are so good at generating," Sid said, getting up and grabbing his camera.

❦

After the shoot Mercedes sauntered over to where Vida was standing with her friend Eva Lewis, another model. Eva and Vida had started modeling together after college and had become fast friends, dealing with love lives and modeling careers over the years.

"Here she comes," Eva said. "Third time's a charm."

"I've already got more than I can handle with Kirsten. I don't need anymore complications," Vida said, her gaze blurring with the consternation of a failing love affair.

"Live a little. We're in Key West, girlfriends are at home, beach, moonlight, flings . . . think about it."

"You're going to get me in trouble," Vida said.

"No, *she's* going to get you in trouble."

"Hi, Eva," Mercedes said.

"Hi, sweetie. Is everything going okay? Now, if Sid's being nasty you just let me know and I'll set him straight for you. He's kind of rough on the new girls sometimes," Eva said.

"No, he's okay."

"Vida and I were just going to go for a stroll along the strip. Maybe do a little shopping and grab lunch. Do you want to come along?"

"Sure! I need to change," Mercedes said.

"We'll wait," Eva replied.

They watched her go off to change.

"Nice hind end, eh?" Eva said.

"We're models. We all have nice *hind ends*." Vida smiled.

"Is it nicer than Kirsten's?"

"You tell me."

"I can't. Kirsten always has her butt concealed in that stuffy, albeit well-tailored, suit of hers," Eva said, doing the swing-around thing with her neck.

"Teach me how to do the neck thing," Vida pleaded.

"Honey, I done told you it's a black girl thing," Eva said, her eyes shining.

"You are not the ordinary black girl. English citizen, Oxford-educated with wealthy parents, does not create the average American black girl."

Eva smiled. "Maybe later," she said as Mercedes approached, looking more like a home girl in her loose-fitting jean shorts and baggy shirt tied up at the waist than a Vanessa's Closet cover girl. Mercedes asked shyly, "Ready?"

"Girlfriend, we're always ready," Eva said, doing the neck thing again.

"What are we waiting for?" Mercedes asked, mimicking Eva's neck movements and flipping her long brown curly hair. Her green eyes sparkled with excitement.

"Hey, she can do it and she's white," Vida whined.

"It must be in her blood," Eva replied.

They headed down Duval Street and over to Blue Heaven for lunch. Blue Heaven was packed but they found a table stuck in back. It was Vida's favorite local dive.

"Sorry about the environs but Vida always insists on this place. I think it has something to do with the chickens," Eva said, pointing to a rooster sauntering by.

"No, it's not the chickens. I like the food. I like that there's no tourist fanfare and hopefully the waitress that looks like my first girlfriend is still working here," Vida said, scanning the crowded room.

"Why you would want to be reminded of your first girlfriend is beyond me. I get them out of my head as soon as the good parts are over." Eva sniffed.

"The way you go through girlfriends, it's a good thing. You'd overload your memory. I'm surprised you remember names," Vida replied.

"Sometimes I don't," Eva said. She turned to Mercedes. "You've got a girlfriend?"

"Yes and no."

Eva cocked an eyebrow. Vida nodded sympathetically.

"She's not real keen on this modeling thing," Mercedes said.

"Vida's got the same problem. I just don't get it. Your girlfriend digs your looks until she realizes she's not the only one looking. But looking isn't touching, the money's good. It's not porn and shit, where you're dried up at thirty. So what's the big deal?" Eva said.

"Maybe you should talk to our girlfriends," Mercedes replied.

Vida's favorite waitress was a tall woman with a mane of dark hair that hung past her waist. She came to take their order.

"Welcome to town, Vida," she said. "Back for another shoot?"

Vida nodded.

"Couldn't have picked a better weekend with the Women's Festival in town," the waitress said.

"I think that was an added incentive on management's part," Vida said, falling into the waitress's dark eyes and remembering happier times.

They ordered the daily specials and between bites Eva made Vida tell the story of her first love.

"So she dumped you and that's why you're so hung up on her?" Eva asked.

"She didn't dump me. It was a mutual parting," Vida said.

Eva took a sip of ice tea. "Honey, was it your idea to leave or was it hers?"

"Hers," Vida replied.

"You were dumped."

"All right, I was dumped."

"What's makes her so special?" Mercedes asked.

"I don't know, maybe it's just that first-time-around glow you get when you fall in love," Vida replied.

"What, you can't do that now?" Eva said.

"It's not the same," Vida said, savagely poking her eggplant taco with her fork.

"What about Kirsten?" Eva asked. "No fuzzy warm feelings there."

"I think I got talked into that one," Vida said.

"It wasn't love at first sight," Eva said.

"More like dinner and incredible sex," Vida said.

Mercedes smiled. "Nothing wrong with that."

"Unless your relationship goes downhill from there," Vida said.

"What, another fight before you got on the plane?" Eva asked.

"Exactly," Vida replied.

Kirsten was convinced that Vida's career as a model was detrimental and that she did herself a disservice by wasting her time baring her body for the pages of an extremely popular women's catalogue. It didn't matter that it paid twice as much as Kirsten's job teaching art history at the university. When the modeling was through she'd devote herself to some other career that took her fancy. It was Vida's laissez-faire attitude toward future employment goals that drove Kirsten nuts. Opportunity, Vida knew, would present something at the right time. Kirsten didn't see it that way. She saw Vida's modeling as an affront to her authority and found it personally repugnant that her girlfriend's scantily clothed body could be viewed by anyone. What was once a point of contention between them had quickly turned into a rift neither of them was capable of repairing.

They finished lunch and Vida took a few longing gazes at the waitress before tipping her extravagantly.

"Well, ladies, I'm on at one-thirty. Thanks for lunch," Eva said, making her way toward the hotel. "Now, you two, don't do anything I wouldn't do," she said over her shoulder.

"We wouldn't even know how," Vida called back.

"What have you got planned?" Mercedes asked.

"Nothing really," Vida said, wishing she felt more cheerful in paradise.

"I have an idea," Mercedes said brightly. "But you've probably already seen it."

Vida put her arm around Mercedes' shoulders. "It doesn't matter. If I have seen it, let's do it again."

"You mean it?"

"Yes. Now lead on."

They started off by renting mopeds and riding to Whitehead Street to see Ernest Hemingway's house. Vida had never been there, and she'd never ridden around Key West on a moped. They toured the house, and soon Mercedes' enthusiasm rubbed off on Vida. They sat on the lush grounds of the house and played with the six-toed cats. It wasn't the famous writer's digs that Mercedes had wanted to see but rather the cats. Mercedes loved cats. She had four of her own and she told Vida about the various ways they had come together.

Vida could tell she loved them dearly. Vida's mother had been a firm believer in the higher nature of animal-lovers, that they were better people. Kirsten disliked dogs and swore she was allergic to cats. As Mercedes rolled about kissing, hugging and playing with the cats, Vida wondered if perhaps her mother had been right.

They ended up having cocktails and dinner at Sloppy Joe's Bar and Restaurant, feeding each other fried shrimp and telling stories, Vida of her college days and the dark-haired girlfriend and Mercedes about escaping small-town life in Arkansas for the lights of L.A. and her current glamour.

"You were lucky you didn't get eaten alive," Vida said.

"It must have been just as hard for you to get in," Mercedes said.

"Not really. I posed for a college calendar because I was short on rent, that's hardly the same as packing up an old car and going to a strange city," Vida said, feeling suddenly much older than her twenty-eight years and kind of sad at her loss of innocence.

Mercedes must have sensed this. "What's wrong?" she asked.

"I just feel so jaded. I'm not excited about things anymore . . . except for today. I had fun today, the old-fashioned kind, the looking for the kicks and finding them anywhere. I liked it. Thank you," Vida said.

"Anytime," Mercedes said.

It was that one drunken confession that led to so many more that by the end of the week Vida and Mercedes were fast friends, soon to become something more. Vida sat on the plane after leaving a teary Mercedes in the able hands of Eva as they waited for their flight to L.A. and Vida flew to Phoenix. Vida put headphones on, plugged in

9

a CD and thought about how wonderful it was to feel Mercedes between her legs, her tongue making Vida quiver.

They hadn't necessarily meant for that to happen. Rather, Mercedes had packed a picnic basket and a small ice chest filled with local seafood. They cooked it in a big cast-iron pan that Vida, protesting all the way, lugged from the car. Mercedes coaxed her on until she found them the perfect secluded spot. Then, like the good backwoods girl that she was, she lit a beach fire and cooked her way right into Vida's heart.

Neither of them talked about going home. Instead they lived entirely in the satisfaction of the present moment.

"It's very Zen, you know," Vida said, looking up at the stars and wiping her buttery fingers on the cloth napkin she had neatly spread across her lap.

"What do you mean?" Mercedes said, handing her another crab leg.

"Living in the present moment, the here and now, not thinking about tomorrow or next year," Vida replied. "Enjoying right now without anticipating your next move, plan, sentence or thought. That's what I've enjoyed so much about being around you. Everything is about what's happening right now."

"Well, right now I'd like another glass of wine," Mercedes said, holding her glass out.

Vida poured them both another glass of hearty red burgundy.

"Cheers, my darling, and damn, you can cook. You know, I'm a sucker for a woman who can cook," Vida said.

Mercedes blushed and started to clean up the camp. They rinsed dishes in the ocean, listening to the even pounding of the waves against the shore. They lay on the Pendleton blanket Vida insisted on buying for the excursion, telling Mercedes she wanted something that reminded her of her comely hind end and having sat on the beach together was the best souvenir Vida could think of. Prior to their beach excursion, they had resorted to completely uncensored flirting. Since they each figured they couldn't sleep together because they were both involved with other people, everything else was fair game. Eva was completely disgusted with their reserve. As far as she was concerned why bother flirting if you were going to keep on acting like sisters at the convent.

"Girlfriend, just go for it. You know you want to," Eva told her.

"I can't do that to Kirsten. We may be fighting at the moment but we still live together," Vida had staunchly replied, but lying there next to Mercedes and listening to the ocean, looking up at the perfect star-filled night, Vida was having second thoughts.

"You know that present moment thing you were just talking about?"

"Yes," Vida replied.

"Do you ever wish that sometimes you could live in the present and forget the rules that govern the future?"

"Meaning?" Vida said, rolling up on one elbow and looking inquiringly at Mercedes.

"Meaning all I want to do is kiss you right now and not think about tomorrow."

Vida leaned over and kissed her.

Now, as Vida sat on the plane and reran the scene through her head, the here and now of Zen no longer applied. Kirsten would be horrified. Not so much about them making love but that it was totally unplanned, rudimentary by her standards, meaning it involved no toys, and a beach was highly unsanitary and public. Vida was amazed at herself for experiencing such a complete act of abandon.

It hadn't been until the next morning when she awoke to find Mercedes gazing at her with the look of complete infatuation that Vida felt the first pang of remorse. And it wasn't guilt about cheating on Kirsten, but the knowledge that she would disappoint yet another woman in her life. She was beginning to think that perhaps she was the emotionally barren one, not her lovers. She kept hoping one day someone would break through.

11

I want someone to walk into my life and make me gasp for air, make me hunger for their touch, make me crave them. Take all this passion I have bottled up inside, welcome it, breathe it, seek it, take it inside them and want more. Vida closed her eyes and tried to find the path, the message, the moment when her perfect lover would arrive. She floated into a daydream, hoping this woman would take form. Instead, she got a color, an intense splash of cerulean blue. Vida laughed at herself, twenty-eight years old and still naïve enough to dream of perfect lovers. Maybe she'll be a scuba diver, Vida thought wryly. Why a color? Why cerulean blue?

She got off the plane expecting to meet Sonja because Kirsten had had previous engagements. Kirsten has an endless stream of previous engagements, Vida thought as she walked into the waiting area at Sky Harbor, watching the loved ones, the faraway friends, the parents, the children, all cooing in the delight of being reunited. Vida felt like the businessmen scurrying past them on to the next deal, not thinking of when they would arrive home.

She met Kirsten holding a half a dozen red roses. They both blushed. Kirsten reached out eagerly to touch her and Vida kissed her deeply, suddenly wishing Kirsten could be the one to make her feel all those things. Kirsten pulled her close.

"I'm sorry. I missed you so much," Kirsten whispered in her ear.

"I thought Sonja was coming to get me," Vida said, as they headed toward the baggage carousel.

"I rearranged things so I could be here. Vida, I am sorry. I don't mean to neglect you, and I'm frightfully embarrassed about that little scene I put you through before you left. I didn't *mean* anything by it. It's just hard sometimes, the way everyone looks at you, and it's not just the men, the way they have, 'I want to fuck her' in their eyes. Sometimes, I just can't deal with it. Call me stodgy. I did miss you."

Vida squeezed her hand and tried not to let guilt and remorse march righteously into her thoughts. "I missed you too," Vida said.

Kirsten smiled and grabbed Vida's bag.

They drove across town in silence, and Vida watched the concrete of downtown turn into the lush palm-tree-lined streets of Scottsdale. At the large, brown adobe house they called home, Vida could tell the gardeners had come by. The shrubs had been trimmed and a bed of white petunias had been replanted. The sun would fry them to a crisp in a few days' time, but Kirsten had always insisted on having a garden that was not conducive to the desert climate. Vida smiled at her dedication to a lost cause.

"What?" Kirsten asked, getting Vida's bag out of the trunk.

"The flowers, they look nice."

"I thought so."

When they got inside, Vida picked up an envelope on the kitchen counter. "What's this?" Vida said. It was fat like it was full of something.

"It's yours . . . if you want it," Kirsten said.

Vida opened the envelope to find a card out of which slid a beautiful gold ring. She cupped it in her hand. Vida studied the ring, counting the rapid beats of her heart with precision. *One, she loves you, two, she loves you not.* It seemed an eternity before Vida could make herself look up from the card to meet her lover's eyes.

Kirsten waited.

"You mean it?" Vida said, handing her the ring.

"I want us to be together. I want you to be my wife, or I'm your wife, or however we do it. I love you."

Vida held out her hand and Kirsten slipped the ring on Vida's finger, looking more intense, more passionate than Vida had ever seen her. Maybe this could work, Vida thought as she led Kirsten upstairs to the bedroom.

Chapter Two

Edie Farnsworth was standing at the water cooler at the *Phoenician* magazine swallowing two aspirins and cursing the fact that women have cramps. It didn't help matters that Jules had taken her out the night before, got her drunk during dinner and then took her home and ardently seduced her the way only a fuck buddy can, which meant with complete disregard for the physical limits and mental toll that staying up half the night would take. Edie was beginning to think that turning thirty was definitely taking its toll. She didn't bounce back like she used to. A wave of nausea crept through her. Edie rested her head on the top of the water cooler and tried to calculate exactly how much work she absolutely had to get done before she could go home and sleep the whole thing off.

She heard Laura and Susan coming down the hall. Oswald was following close behind. Susan rolled her eyes when she saw Edie. "Living too fast again, I see," she chirped at Edie.

"Leave me alone," Edie moaned.

"Edie, darling, we must talk," Oswald said.

"Oswald, please tell me it's not another crisis. I'm not up to it today," Edie said.

"No, darling. It's good news. It's about your piece on New River. It's stunning. The board loves it. They think you're absolutely brilliant!" Oswald was glowing with success, adjusting his big, black glasses and looking the perfect, fat fag.

"You'd think a genius would know better than to go out and drink and prowl her nights away," Susan lectured.

"Go fuck yourself," Edie said, still hugging the water cooler and refusing to face them.

"Are you going to let her talk to me like that?" Susan said, looking sharply at Oswald.

"Yes, she's the resident genius. Edie, come with me. I'll fix you proper," Oswald said, putting a fatherly arm around her and leading her off.

Laura saw a flash of blue eyes and a very pretty face that didn't acknowledge her presence.

"Who was that?" Laura asked, feeling herself already intrigued.

"Edie Farnsworth, commonly referred to as the resident asshole," Susan snarled.

"Hmm," Laura said, refraining from asking if the asshole was married.

"The higher-ups love her, but the advertising department thinks she needs a serious attitude adjustment," Susan said.

Laura watched as she regained her composure as the official tour director for her new boss, the head of advertising. All Laura had heard was that Edie Farnsworth was considered brilliant, daring, overworked, and up to every deadline she was ever assigned. She was famous at the magazine and Laura didn't particularly care for Susan's opinion of her. For the first time in months Laura was intrigued with the brain and body of someone new.

They were in a staff meeting the following week and trying to decide who was going to go upstairs and tell Edie that some reformatting was necessary before going to press.

"It's not going to be pretty," said Susan.

"I'll go. I think it's time we repair the rift between the advertising department and the editor. Perhaps I could be the emissary," Laura said.

"More like sacrificial lamb," Joel said.

"It'll be fine. Give me the stuff," Laura said.

"You don't have to do this," Susan said.

"I'll be fine," Laura said.

"Don't say we didn't warn you," Susan said, eyeing her suspiciously.

A few minutes later, Laura stood in the doorway of Edie's office. She straightened her shoulders, did a perfunctory knock on the already opened door and put on her most stunning smile. Edie was nowhere to be found. She heard a string of obscenities from beneath the desk.

"Motherfucking, cocksucking piece of shit," Edie said as she attempted to pry a stuck drawer loose.

"You have a foul mouth," Laura said before she could stop herself.

"Who asked your fucking opinion anyway?" Edie said.

"Excuse me?"

"You heard me, or would you like me to continue my litany of offense."

"No, I'd rather you didn't," Laura said.

"Fuck me up the butt!" Edie said, pulling on the drawer.

"Does your mother know that you talk like this?"

"Look, I don't know who you are, but why don't you go away."

"I will not go away."

"Suit yourself," Edie said. "But don't expect me to clean up my mouth."

"Do you think you could get up from under that desk and talk to me?"

"Fuck!" Edie said, giving the drawer one last push.

Laura leapt back as the giant old desk toppled over and everything on it came sailing across the room.

"Yes!" Edie said.

"You're pleased about this?" Laura asked, surveying the office floor that was littered with pencils, papers and other sundry items.

"I got the drawer unstuck," Edie said.

"And demolished your office in the process," Laura said, putting her hands on her hips.

"Destruction is the official brethren of creation," Edie said.

Laura watched as Edie attempted to right her desk. When it became obvious that she couldn't do it herself she looked at Laura. "I don't suppose you could help me?"

"That depends on whether you're going to apologize for your rude behavior," Laura said.

"All right, I admit I was perhaps a bit abrupt."

"A bit," Laura said, starting to tease. She was finding it difficult to be rude with this darling little woman with short dark hair and beautiful blue eyes. She was once again tastefully dressed, and she was brilliant, Laura knew. Laura had a thing for smart women. She'd read Edie's stuff. Her reputation withstood the scrutiny.

"All right, I was rude and I'm sorry," Edie said, looking at her. "Now, are you going to help me?"

"Yes," Laura said, grabbing the other side of the desk and helping to right it.

"Thank you," Edie said as she started to pick up the papers and other items strewn across the floor.

Laura helped her.

"Who are you anyway?" Edie asked.

"Laura Barnes."

"You're from advertising," Edie said, snatching back the pen jar Laura was holding.

"Does that make me a leper?" Laura said, still thinking it possible to charm herself into Edie's good graces.

"As good as. Give me the fucking changes." Edie held out her hand.

"You know, I think it's possible we could repair some of the animosity between our departments. I'm willing to try," Laura said, knowing it was completely fruitless.

"Well, I'm not. Why can't you people get organized? This is ridiculous. Now, if you don't mind, I've really got some work to do," Edie said, glancing over the changes then glaring at Laura. She slammed the pen jar down on her desk and picked up the phone.

"Edie, come on, let's be adult about this. How about I take you to lunch tomorrow to make up for this?" Laura said, trying to placate her.

"I don't think so," Edie said. "Hello. Hey, Gerald, look we've got to hold for a bit. Yes, changes, from advertising as usual," Edie said, turning her back on Laura.

"I'm sorry," Laura said.

"Forget it," Edie said, putting the phone down.

"Lunch?"

Edie shook her head. "Thanks but no thanks."

"Can't say I didn't warn you. The woman's a pariah," Susan said, pouring them both another cup of coffee when Laura returned from upstairs.

"It was fine until she found out I was from advertising. She had an instant mood shift. You would have thought I told her I killed small animals and children for a pastime," Laura said, thinking about Edie's eyes. They were incredible. Part of it had to do with her coloring. She had dark hair and olive skin so her eyes were already contrasted, but it was their color. They were an intense, startling blue.

Laura got up.

"Where are you going?" Susan asked.

"To see if she'll go to lunch with me."

When Edie looked up from her desk to find Laura standing in her doorway, Laura smiled.

"Lunch?" she inquired.

"Go away," Edie said.

Laura nodded. "Maybe some other time."

"Like fucking never," Edie screamed as Laura walked back down the hall.

"I told you so," Susan said.

Laura rolled her eyes.

"Why do you care?"

"I don't know," Laura lied.

Laura lay in bed that night and tried to figure out how she was going to get Edie to go to lunch. She was still trying to convince herself that moving back to Phoenix was a good idea, but at least this thing with Edie was taking her mind off it. Leaving Seattle and her friends was difficult, but not running into Sharon anymore was a relief. She'd been through the gamut of emotions concerning a broken love affair and had grown tired of always turning around to find Sharon, or one of their mutual friends, exhuming the dead horse for yet another go-around.

Laura wanted a chance to start fresh. But her new start was taking an entirely different form. Here she was, practically stalking a woman who wanted nothing to do with her, and she had no intentions of stopping herself either. This was totally new behavior for her. She was reckless, consumed and totally focused on getting Edie's attention.

If she could just get her alone for half an hour, Laura thought. *I've got it. If she won't come to lunch, we'll bring lunch to her.* She got up and figured out what she'd wear. It had to be something stunning. She laughed at herself. She hadn't been this excited since . . . she didn't know when. *I don't who you are, Ms. Farnsworth, but you're already doing amazing things for my sorry little life.*

Edie was on the phone when a waiter rolled in a cart filled with silver-lidded plates.

Puzzled, Edie looked at him. "I didn't know we had room service here."

The waiter smiled and handed her one yellow rose, per his customer's instructions. Then he went out and came back with a card table and two chairs. He set down a white linen tablecloth and silverware and then proceeded to set the table.

"Are you still there?" the caller inquired.

"Yes, I'm sorry. It is just there's something odd going on. I'll get back to you after I've sorted this whole thing out."

"Don't make it three days, Edie."

"I won't. I promise."

Edie was still holding the yellow rose and looking thoroughly confused when Laura walked in.

"You!"

"I figured if you wouldn't go out to lunch with me then maybe if I brought lunch to you . . ."

Edie looked at her intently. "Why are you doing this?"

"Because I want us to be friends," Laura responded, her gaze never leaving Edie's.

"Why?"

"Because you have the most incredible blue eyes, and I'd like to gaze into them occasionally and I can't do that if you hate me," Laura blurted.

Edie laughed. "I'm impressed with your honesty. Maybe you're not so bad after all."

"Will you at least have lunch with me and find out for certain?" Laura pulled out a chair.

Edie sat down. "But you have to promise me something."

"What?"

"That you won't tell anyone."

"Why not?"

"It'll ruin my reputation," Edie said, lifting up one topper and inhaling deeply. "It's from Lucci's. I absolutely adore sirloin tips on penne pasta."

"I know. I asked. I won't tell anyone, especially not Susan."

Edie bared her teeth and growled.

"She is a bit difficult at times," Laura said.

Edie smiled. "Perhaps we can be friends."

And after a wonderful meal of Caesar salad, garlic bread and pasta, Edie decided that Laura was attractive, witty and fun, Edie's three prerequisites for a playmate.

This was the beginning of many lunches, clandestine lunches. And they did become friends of sorts, meaning Laura was falling in love and Edie was simply continuing to live as she had always had. Laura was trying to play slow and safe, feeling Edie out for signs of affection. From what she could tell, they were readily given.

One evening after work, Laura let Susan talk her into going to the theater. She didn't understand why Susan was so adamant about her going, but Laura knew that Edie did the theater reviews—theirs was a city magazine that covered all the Phoenix happenings—and she was hoping, despite being seen with Susan, that she might run into Edie. In the lobby Susan and Laura sipped Champagne and checked out the crowd. Susan spotted Edie and Jules.

"Well, hello, hello," Susan said, cornering them against the bar.

"Hi, Laura," Edie said.

"Just you two for a night out on the town tonight?" Susan asked.

Jules smiled facetiously.

"Where's Selena? Or is this Edie's night out?" Susan asked.

"Why don't you mind own business, Susan," Jules said, taking the glass of Champagne Edie handed her.

"Just asking," Susan said.

"Since when are you working for the paparazzi?" Jules said.

"Since when did you become famous?" Susan quipped.

"I must be, to have piqued your interest so," Jules said.

"Just call me the guardian of the lesbian hearth. When the cat's away . . ."

Jules moved closer to Susan. Edie intervened. "C'mon, Jules. We'll miss the show. See you later," Edie said, looking at Laura.

"I positively despise that woman," Jules said, looking over her shoulder at Susan, who waved coyly.

"Does Selena know you're out?" Edie asked.

"She does now."

"Great!" Edie said.

"Don't worry. She's not into handguns."

"Oh, gee, that makes me feel tons better," Edie said as they settled into their seats.

"Well, if you'd just marry me, we wouldn't have all this drama," Jules replied.

"I can't *afford* you," Edie said.

"Unfortunately, darling, you're right," Jules said, twisting her new diamond tennis bracelet and letting it catch the light.

"Who's that?" Laura asked as she and Susan took their seats several rows behind Edie and Jules.

"One of the femme fatales of the lesbian world," Susan said. "Her name is Jules."

"Is she Edie's girlfriend?"

"More like one of her liaisons. Technically speaking she's Selena Shelby's girlfriend."

"Who's she?" Laura said, watching Edie and Jules.

"Selena owns The Grill, and suffice it to say she's Jules' financial backer, if you get my meaning," Susan said.

"Do Jules and Edie sleep together?"

"Not according to Selena, but you tell me," Susan said, nodding in their direction. Jules had just put her head on Edie's shoulder.

Still, Laura thought, Jules did have a girlfriend, so Edie wasn't exactly attached but she couldn't bring herself to ask if Edie had a girlfriend. Edie didn't act like she had a girlfriend. She made no mention of living with anyone, but then, they hadn't talked in those terms. Laura had told Edie why she moved back to Phoenix, about the mess with Sharon. Edie had been sympathetic.

The following day when Laura and Edie snuck off to lunch, Edie made no reference to the night before except to say that the next time Laura wanted to go to the theater Edie would be more than glad to take her. "I go all the time. It's nice to have someone to go with," Edie said congenially.

But that wasn't quite like asking her to go out on a date. Laura was starting to wonder. Maybe Edie was waiting for her to make the first move. She was, after all, the one who had initiated their friendship, or perhaps Edie thought she was still mending her broken heart. She went upstairs that afternoon to see if maybe they might go to dinner. She got out of the elevator and tried to summon her courage, telling herself *I can do this, I can do this*. Someone had to take the plunge, she told herself as she knocked on Edie's office door.

She should have known something was up. Edie's door was never closed.

"Come in," Edie called out.

An attractive Hispanic woman was sitting on Edie's desk. She turned to look at Laura, with her long dark lashes fluttering slightly as she sized Laura up.

"Hi," Edie said. "Laura, this is Concepcion."

"Nice to meet you," Laura said, knowing she was blushing and could do nothing to stop it.

"Charmed," Concepcion said, getting up off the desk and remov-

23

ing her foot from between Edie's legs. She slipped on her red leather pumps. She touched Edie's cheek. "She has beautiful eyes, don't you think?" she said, looking at Laura.

"Yes," Laura said before she could stop herself.

"So I'll see you tonight. Father is looking forward to it. I'm sending my driver Ramon to pick you up. You can relax on the way out but no side trips. I know how you are. And bring clothes," Concepcion said.

Edie smiled. "I'll be there."

Concepcion gave Laura a look that could only be construed as territorial.

"What's up?" Edie asked after Concepcion had left.

"Oh, it was nothing. Have a good weekend," Laura said, leaving too quickly.

Edie looked puzzled, but Laura didn't care at that point. There was no denying that Edie was a player and Laura was perfectly mortified.

Laura turned the corner and ran smack into Sandi.

"Hey, stranger, when are we doing lunch, or better yet cocktails," Sandi said.

Distraught, Laura looked at Sandi. Sandi was a friend of Edie's and worked as a graphic designer at the magazine. Laura had considered telling Sandi about her crush on Edie and about seeing Edie with Concepcion but she changed her mind.

"What's wrong?"

"It's nothing," Laura lied. "I'll see you later."

Sandi walked into Edie's office, and Laura headed to the elevator.

"Hello, perfect timing. Ramon should be here shortly. We can hit a couple bars and then I'm off," Edie said, organizing her papers in preparation for Monday's onslaught. When Sandi didn't reply, Edie looked up. Sandi was glaring at her. "What?"

"What did you do to her?" Sandi asked.

24

"Who?"

"Laura."

"I didn't do anything. Why? What's wrong?"

"She's upset."

Edie shrugged. "She came in here to ask me something and Concepcion was here."

"No wonder," Sandi said, shaking her head.

"What?" Edie said, putting her jacket on.

"Can't you see it?"

"See what?"

"She's in love with you, you moron."

"Oh," Edie said, grimacing. Just what she needed, an ad sales rep in love with her. She headed toward the door.

"That's all you have to say."

"It hadn't really occurred to me. We go to lunch, that's all."

"In other words, you probably would have slept with her by now if she was one of your *usual* women friends," Sandi said.

"Well . . . yes. I guess that's true."

"Edie, do you love any of these people you go out with?" Sandi asked as they waited for the elevator.

"I love you," Edie said, dodging the question and pressing the already lit elevator button. She was feeling cornered.

"No, I mean it. Do you love Jules, or Concepcion, or who's this latest one?"

"Sarah." She'd met Sarah at the gym, but really she was just a fling.

"Well?"

The elevator came and they stepped inside.

Sandi stared at her, waiting for an answer.

"Jules already has someone, and Concepcion is the kind of woman who makes a great lover but a terrible partner and Sarah, well, Sarah is a dancer and she has a great body," Edie said, fondly remembering making love in the dance studio, Sarah pinned up against the bars, her legs wrapped around Edie's waist.

"That wasn't the question. Do you love any of them?"

Edie looked up at the numbers, two more floors to the street. "Well?"

"No, I don't. I like them, but I'm not in love. I've tried. I just haven't met the kind of woman I'd like to commit to. Maybe I'm not capable of loving anyone," Edie said, wondering if she had some sort of emotional detachment syndrome.

"What are you afraid of?" Sandi asked.

"All right, if you must know, I'm afraid of failure. If I keep love and sex separated nobody gets hurt. I don't make any promises and nothing gets broken."

Sandi put her arm around Edie's shoulder and whispered, "Laura is a nice woman and she really likes you. Think about it."

Ramon was out front holding the door open to Concepcion's vintage Rolls. It was parked in the fire lane. His face lit up when he saw Edie.

"My man," Edie said, slapping his hand. "How are you?"

"Fine, Ms. Edie, just fine."

"Sandi's coming with us to tip a few before we head to the ranch. So take that cap off and let's go party," Edie said, snatching his chauffeur's cap.

Ramon laughed and hopped in the front seat.

When Laura came out of the front of the building, she saw the three of them standing there. She tried to turn around but there were too many people flowing out of the building, eager to start their weekend. It was like trying to swim upstream. She relented to the current. Then Edie saw her.

"Laura!" she called out.

Determined not to show her disappointment, Laura put on her best face and straightened her shoulders.

"Hey, come have a drink with us," Edie said, taking both her hands. "Come on. It'll be fun." Edie pulled her toward the car.

Laura tried to smile. "No, Edie, I can't." She waved at Sandi who was already in the car.

"Are you sure?"

"Some other time," Laura said.

"Okay. Have a nice weekend."

"You too," Laura said, trying not to imagine Concepcion seducing Edie in a big bed under a huge fan in some grotesquely large hacienda in the desert.

"Lunch on Monday then?" Edie said, getting in the car.

"Yes, lunch," Laura said. She went back to her office and gathered up everything she had planned to do on Monday. She was going to be sick for a couple of days next week. By Wednesday she would have herself composed enough to face Edie and have cured herself of her new, extremely unhealthy pastime.

In the car Edie looked over at Sandi. "I don't think she really likes me," Edie said.

"You're spending the weekend at your lover's house. How's that supposed to make her feel?"

"Like I knew she was coming into my life. It's not my fault I have a lover," Edie said, perplexed at Laura's behavior and wondering if some of the things she'd been feeling were somehow related to Laura.

"*Lovers*," Sandi said, "as in plural. That's the problem. When are you going to figure out that most lesbians don't approve of multiple partners?"

"Jules, Sarah and Concepcion don't seem to mind," Edie said matter-of-factly. And it was true. They all suspected Edie's non-monogamy.

"Do they really know about one another?"

Edie screwed up her face, hoping to make Sandi laugh with her best imitation of a Keebler elf. "Not exactly."

"I didn't think so," Sandi said.

"They don't ask. I don't tell."

Ramon pulled up in front of Pookies, a local men's bar on Indian School, their first watering hole of the evening. Edie liked the black and white tile floors and neon lights and the lack of female patrons, meaning she wouldn't run into any of her former liaisons.

"I have to have you to dinner by seven," Ramon warned.

Edie gave him a tap on the shoulder and a nod. "No problem."

On Tuesday evening there was a knock at the door. Laura looked up from her work, puzzled. She got up from her desk and checked the peephole. It was Edie. She felt her heart start to pound, and she experienced an instant hot flash. Oh, my God, she thought. What's she doing here? She took a deep breath and opened the door.

"Hi," Edie said.

"Hi."

"You must be really sick. Two days in a row. I brought you some chicken soup from Segal's. It's a Jewish deli on the central corridor. It's the best," Edie said, holding up the container.

"I thought that was an old wives' tale," Laura said.

"No, Segal's chicken soup is a well-known cure for almost any malady," Edie assured her.

"Why don't you come in?" Laura said.

"If it's all right. I can just drop off the soup and go," Edie said.

"Please come in."

Edie touched her face. "You're flushed. Do you have a fever?"

"I don't know," Laura said, feeling herself grow warmer as she stood in such close proximity to Edie.

"I like your house," Edie said, looking around. "It's very tasteful. Are you dating an interior designer?"

Laura laughed. "No, why?"

"Because your place has definite signs of an interior designer."

"Actually, I studied interior design before I switched to advertising," Laura said, getting out two bowls, some bread and a bottle of Merlot, thinking she was suddenly in dire need of a drink.

28

"Should you be drinking if you're sick?" Edie said, taking the proffered glass of wine.

"It's a well-known cure for any malady," Laura said, tapping her glass with Edie's. "Cheers."

"To your health," Edie said, staring a little too long. "Can I see the rest of the house? I'm most interested to see how you did the rest. I'm rather fond of interior designers myself."

"Are you dating one?"

"No, but I'd like to. Right now I have a loft with next to nothing in it. I need some expertise," Edie said.

Laura blushed and Edie smiled. It was an obvious flirtation and Laura was thrilled.

"Come, I'll show you the rest," Laura said.

"Please."

Edie thoughtfully took in the rest of the house. When they got to the bedroom, Edie wandered in leisurely. She sat on the bed and bounced on it. It was a four-poster bed with dark ornate posts and an immense white down comforter. She pointed at the neat, little fireplace in the corner. "Very romantic," she said.

"Yes," Laura said, wishing she had the balls to walk over and take Edie in her arms, the perfect seduction scene. *She's already on the bed*, temptation told her.

"Some woman will be very lucky," Edie said, getting up.

"I wish," Laura said, knowing she'd lost her chance.

Edie smiled and took her hand. "You just haven't met the right one. But she's coming. I can feel it."

"So you're a psychic as well as a homeopath," Laura replied.

"I have many hidden talents."

"I'm sure you do," Laura said.

"Come, let's go have soup."

"And more wine."

"Yes," Edie said, still holding her hand and leading her downstairs.

❧

Laura experienced an immediate recovery and was at the office the next day. Edie had a beautiful bouquet of white lilies on her desk with a thank-you card. She beamed when Laura walked in. "I love them. Thank you."

Laura smiled. "Can I take you to lunch?"

"I have a better idea. Are you game?"

"Sure."

"Okay, great. Hold on a minute." Edie picked up the phone. "Oswald, I need you to do me a favor. Laura needs to take the rest of the afternoon off. Will you call downstairs and tell them?" Edie rang off, then said to Laura, "All set. I hope you didn't have any truly pressing engagements this afternoon."

Laura smiled. "And if I did?"

"I'd make you cancel them," Edie said.

"Where are we going?" Laura asked a few minutes later as they left the building.

"You'll see," Edie said, heading toward her car.

"Nice car," Laura said, admiring the Porsche.

"Thank you."

"What is it?"

"It's a nineteen fifty-six Porsche one-sixty sport, commonly referred to as the bathtub edition. Do you like it?"

"It's beautiful," Laura said, running her hand down the smooth, black surface.

"Top up or down?" Edie asked.

"Let's have it down," Laura said, looking at the perfect blue sky. "October in Phoenix is considered fair weather to me. My blood is still working on Seattle climate control. To me it seems warm."

Edie pulled out a leather bomber jacket from the back seat. "You might want this later," she said, handing it over.

"Thanks," Laura said.

When they hit the city limits Laura was confused. "Where are we going to lunch?"

"Sedona."

"We can't go to Sedona for lunch," Laura said.

"Sure we can."

"But it's so far."

"That's all right. It's a good long drive and we'll talk. You can tell me your life story and I'll tell you mine."

"This is more than lunch," Laura said.

"Yes, it's a date. Is that all right?" Edie looked over and Laura could see her swallow hard as if this was a big move for her.

Laura melted into her eyes. "Yes."

"Good. You start."

"What do you want to know?"

"Everything," Edie said, taking her hand gently.

"Where do I start?"

"At the beginning."

Chapter Three

Vida was sitting on the kitchen floor at a party she was attending with Kirsten. Her whole life was falling apart. She was turning the ring on her finger that Kirsten had given her. She wished she had the courage to swallow the thing and have it done. Their relationship was past working and all she wanted was out.

Instead, she was at another endless social function pretending to have fun. She had just gotten back from a shoot in San Diego where she had once again spent another incredible week of sleeping with Mercedes and wondering what kind of a partner she was that she'd permit herself to have a lover and feel no guilt, no remorse and no intention of behaving herself.

And now Kirsten had been hit once again with another of her peers' jutting remarks about her girlfriend's job. After an appropriate amount of ridicule Vida had left. She exited not as she would have wanted to, with a snarl and growl or with witticism and a smart retort.

Rather she had slinked away embarrassed that she made a ridiculous amount of money for looking good. More money than most of those chiding women would ever see. But she was the loser, the almost porn star, who bared her body for money. A body that Kirsten reveled in and now found too polluted for her own sophisticated tastes.

Sonja walked in. She read Vida's crisis immediately. "Are you okay?"

"No, actually I need another drink and then a river and some bricks to put in my pockets," Vida said, looking up at Sonja, wondering how she had managed to be Kirsten's best friend for all these years. She was the only one of Kirsten's friends that Vida liked.

Sonja poured her another glass of wine. She sat down beside her. "So what's up?" Sonja said, lighting a cigarette and handing it to Vida, who took a long drag.

"It's such a mess by now I wouldn't even know where to start," Vida said sadly, taking another drag.

Sonja lit another cigarette for herself.

"Do you ever wonder where love goes? Is there someplace in the universe where all those incredible feelings go after we manage to shove them out of a relationship?"

"Honey, if you find that place, send me a ticket."

Vida laughed.

"I mean it," Sonja said.

"Sometimes when Kirsten is sleeping I look over at her and I remember the times when we used to get along, used to enjoy each other's company. Now we just live in the same house and arrive together for social gatherings. But the feeling's gone and, needless to say, ugliness has taken its place."

Sonja looked at her watch.

"Do you have time for this?" Vida said, trying not to take offense.

"No, it's not that. I'm trying to calculate how much time we have together before she finds you and whether we have time for another smoke," Sonja said.

"I left her with Cassandra Hollander. We've got time." Vida took another cigarette and reached up on the counter for the wine bottle. She refilled their glasses.

"I like Cassandra," Sonja said.

"So does Kirsten. I think she wishes I was Cassandra, only with my particular accoutrements," Vida said.

"It's your *accoutrements* that get you in trouble."

"I just wish I could have a girlfriend that liked them, that didn't find me offensive, that wasn't threatened . . . someone with cerulean blue eyes."

"Cerulean blue?"

"I know it sounds funny, but whenever I think of my soul mate, I see a color, cerulean blue, and eyes are the only thing I can think of. So now I hope she has blue eyes. It's silly."

"You never know."

The kitchen door swung open. Vida's heart practically stopped. Sonja grabbed her cigarette.

"You're smoking," Kirsten said.

"She was holding my cigarette," Sonja said.

"No, I was smoking," Vida said.

"What are you doing?" Kirsten asked.

"Avoiding you," Vida replied.

"Why?"

"Because you're a bitch," Vida said.

"At least I'm not a bitch in heat," Kirsten said.

"And why don't you tell me how you really feel," Vida chided.

"Don't go there," Kirsten warned.

"That's what your friends think, and you're starting to feel the same way. Is that what this is about? If you think I'm sleeping around why don't you just ask?"

"Get up!" Kirsten said, grabbing Vida's hand.

"No, I'm staying here until you're done with this soiree, and then I want to go home where I'm going to pack and walk out of your life with the same lack of pomp and circumstance as when I walked in. You probably won't even know I'm gone."

34

Kirsten glared at her. Sonja was attempting to ease her way out of the kitchen.

"I want you to get up and I don't want a scene. You will go with me into the living room where you will be cordial for at least thirty minutes. Then I will take you home where I think it will be in your best interests to apologize and sleep off all this wine. We'll talk when you feel better."

"I want to go home now!" Vida said.

Kirsten squeezed her wrist hard. "Get up."

Vida winced slightly but didn't move.

Sonja moved forward. "Kirsten, let her go," she said softly.

Kirsten ignored her. She was digging her nails into Vida's wrist. Vida set her jaw but she could feel one tear forming at the corner of her eye.

"Vida, do as I say," Kirsten instructed.

"You're hurting her. Let her go," Sonja said.

"This isn't your concern," Kirsten said, her gaze never leaving Vida's.

"Vida's my friend. It is my concern."

"When she gets up, I'll let her go," Kirsten said.

Sonja calmly came over to Kirsten and said in a low voice, "You're hurting her and if you don't let go I will be forced to go and get our social worker friend Sally, who just happens to be in the next room, and report a case of domestic abuse. That is not going to sit well with the rest of your friends. I'll take Vida home and you two can talk later."

Kirsten glared at Sonja and left the room without further incident. Vida held her wrist gently and started to cry.

"Shhh . . ." Sonja said. "I'll get some ice."

When they were in the car, Vida said, "Thank you."

"Nothing like the threat of public disgrace."

"That always works," Vida said, smiling coyly.

"Are you okay?" Sonja said, looking over, concern etched in her face.

"Yes."

"Does she do that often?"

"It's not what you think. We've had the occasional tussle. Nothing really bad."

"I'm just a little confused. I didn't think women did that to other women," Sonja said.

Vida smiled and cocked her head apologetically.

"Am I being the naïve straight woman again?"

"No, I hate to burst your balloon, but violence isn't necessarily strictly a male trait. And lesbians don't have the same kind of boundaries that keep a lot of men from hitting women. Men aren't supposed to hit women, but no one says women can't hit other women."

"Has she ever hit you?"

"No."

"Good. Are you sleeping with someone else?"

Vida nodded. "One of the other models."

"So Kirsten's behavior isn't totally uncalled for."

"No."

"Do you want to go home?"

"I want to get some clothes. I need to think."

"Come stay with me. I'm suffering empty nest syndrome since Miranda moved out. You can have her room," Sonja said.

"I don't want to impose," Vida said, looking out the car window. It had started to rain and the streetlights had gone all blurry, or maybe it was her eyes.

At the stoplight, Sonja gently turned Vida's head to face her. "I want you to come to stay with me, for a few days, months . . . years, whatever. Otherwise I'll be forced to worry about you. I won't get any sleep and I'll have bags under my eyes and then I'll never get a man."

"Well, since you put it that way." Vida smiled.

They pulled up in front of Kirsten's large house. Vida looked up at it and thought of the thousands of times she'd sat just like this looking at the house and dreading going inside. Now she felt like a fugitive about to skip town.

"I'll be quick," she said, getting out of the car.

"Take your time. I'll stand lookout. Three honks means grab what you can and let's go. I don't think she'll show, though."

"I hope not."

Vida sprinted for the front door. She'd be quick, pack like all those people you see in the movies shoving things in bags and making a hasty exit. She didn't think. She just grabbed clothes, bank books, address book and her one addition to the household, a picture of her mother and father.

Within ten minutes she was back in the car. "Done."

"Are you okay?" Sonja said, handing her a cigarette.

"Actually, I feel an overwhelming sense of relief."

Sonja nodded and started the car.

"Is that bad?" Vida asked.

"No, I think that's normal and healthy."

"You're an incredible woman."

"Tell that to the next man I meet," Sonja said.

"I will."

After Vida got settled in Sonja's guest room, the phone rang downstairs. Vida heard Sonja pick up and she wondered if it was Kirsten chasing her down. She went downstairs to see what was going on. Vida could feel her heart pounding as she listened to Sonja's phone conversation.

"Vida's here," Sonja said. "She's going to stay here for a few days. She just wants some time to chill."

Vida went over to the sink.

"She's gone to bed," Sonja said, looking at Vida as she got herself a glass of water. "I won't let anything happen to her."

Vida looked at Sonja as she set down the phone. "Thank you."

"She didn't buy it," Sonja replied, lighting another cigarette.

"That's on her," Vida said. "This isn't going to do wonders for your friendship."

"Probably not, but right now you're my concern," Sonja said. "Let's get your bed made."

"You don't mind being a guardian angel?"

"No, not at all, so I don't want you to worry about it, okay?"

"All right," Vida said.

In the morning Vida got up early and made coffee. She had dressed in her running gear and was feeling more than chipper.

"I didn't know you ran," Sonja said as she came into the kitchen and took the cup of coffee Vida handed her.

"On a regular basis, best way to keep trim but not bulky. The folks at Vanessa's are kind of picky about that."

"And here I thought you must have an incredible metabolism. You eat like a horse," Sonja teased.

"I hate to burst your bubble but I do have an incredible metabolism. I run to keep everything upright. Running actually makes me thinner than I'm supposed to be," Vida said, smiling apologetically.

"You're disgusting," Sonja said.

"Sorry."

"Well, you're certainly going to give the old geezers in the neighborhood a charge. In fact, if I were not undeniably straight you'd give me a charge. I'm not so certain you're not," Sonja said, blushing. "You're beautiful."

"Well, if you ever decide to switch sides of the fence . . ."

"I can count on you?"

"In a heartbeat," Vida said, lightly kissing Sonja's cheek.

It took Kirsten three days to arrive at the porch of Sonja's house. Both Sonja and Vida had been waiting for this moment.

Vida had been out for a run and was returning to Sonja's when she saw Kirsten's red Alfa Romeo parked out front. She slowed to a walk and tried to catch her breath. Sonja and Kirsten were sitting on the porch and drinking what looked to be gin and tonics.

"Hi there," Vida said.

Sonja got up. "I'll leave you two alone."

Kirsten stood up. "How are you?"

"Truth?"

"Please," Kirsten said.

"Sad, I feel sad. Let me go get a clean shirt and drink. I'll be right back."

"Promise?"

"Promise. I know we need to talk."

Vida ran cold water over her face and tried to collect herself. It was now or never. She grabbed a shirt and glass of Gatorade. Sonja had disappeared. She has the uncanny ability to do that, Vida thought. But I'm a big girl and I know what I have to do.

Vida sat down next to Kirsten.

"Are you all right?"

"Truth?"

"Yes," Vida said, meeting her gaze.

"I miss you dreadfully," Kirsten said, starting to cry. "I'm sorry things have gone off so badly."

"Shh," Vida said, holding her. "It's all right. Please don't cry. I still love you."

"But you just can't live with me," Kirsten said, sobbing harder.

Vida pulled her tight. "Just not right now."

Chapter Four

Laura lay on the couch and tried not to think about Edie, tried not to think about the night she had been faced with seeing Edie with yet another woman. Seeing her with Concepcion had been difficult enough, although Edie didn't appear to be overly attached to her. At their lunch in Sedona they hadn't necessarily talked about Concepcion but around her, about the difficulty of finding a true love in today's world and how it would be nice to find someone, that special someone to spend your life with. Laura had taken it as an act of faith that Concepcion was a playmate, not a soul mate.

But she couldn't deny the night, about a week after Sedona, she sat having cocktails at The Grill and saw Edie across the courtyard, meeting a woman and kissing her ardently, and the look on the woman's face, of complete glee and anticipation. Susan was with her and had seen the exchange as well. She then proceeded to fill Laura in on Edie's rather prodigious love life. It was more than Laura could bear.

The next day she had gone up to Edie's office and told her she couldn't see her anymore. Edie stood there while Laura tried to explain how she felt.

"I know about your other women and I can't do it. I can't feel that way about you. I can't be just another one of your girlfriends. I'm not like that. I'm sorry," Laura had blurted.

Edie looked at her and said nothing. Laura had rushed from the room.

The next day, feeling remorseful at not giving Edie a chance to explain herself, Laura had gone back.

And the second travesty had occurred. She was standing in the hallway when Concepcion came rushing out of Edie's office. She looked distraught and then instantly furious when she saw Laura, who was trying to do an about-face as quickly as she could manage.

"It's you! This is all your fault!" Concepcion said. "She won't see me anymore because she's in love with you. Do you know how long I have loved her . . . tried to make her love me back . . . until you!"

"Concepcion, stop it right now!" Edie said from the doorway. "That's enough."

Edie's power over this woman was terrifying. Concepcion had fairly crumbled as Laura looked on, horrified.

That night she'd tried to process the whole thing and decided she needed to talk to Edie, find out what was really going on.

The next morning she summoned up all her courage and she went back, but Edie's office was dark. And the next day the same thing and the next until Oswald's secretary told her that Edie was taking some time off. Laura was distraught. By Friday she was in Oswald's office trying to find out what was going on.

Oswald offered her a chair and explained, "She's gone underground."

"What do you mean?"

"She's trying to collect herself, put some distance between things," Oswald said.

"You mean women," Laura replied.

Oswald met her gaze and hesitated before speaking. "Yes."

"Why?"

"It's necessary sometimes. As I'm sure you've noticed she's a little too popular."

"Oswald, I need to talk to her. Where is she?"

"I honestly don't know."

"Where does she live? Where's the loft?" Laura said.

"I don't know. It's always been a secret. She doesn't take people there. No one knows where it is. I swear," Oswald said.

"I think I'm in love with her. But I need to know if it's crazy. I mean, she's got these women that she sleeps with, and then we go out and she won't touch me but I know there's something there. I wasn't imagining it. I know I wasn't."

"You weren't," Oswald assured her.

"But she didn't try to seduce me."

"Because she was *courting* you. She only courts the woman she loves. The rest are playmates. The rest are women that chase her, that she succumbs to, but they are not the ones she loves."

"I don't understand."

"Are you Catholic?"

"No, why do you ask?" Laura said, totally puzzled at the change of topic.

"Edie is. Do you know anything about Catholic girls?"

"I hadn't really given it much thought."

"Catholic girls are an odd mixture of sanctity and perversion. They thrive on prolonged desire and ambiguous courtship."

"I'm not following you."

"She doesn't *want* you for a lover."

Laura's face fell.

"That is to say, as just a lover. You are something more. Someone to spend time with, develop a relationship with, and who knows?

Perhaps marry, or however you girls do it. That's why she has not tried to seduce you."

"How do you know all this?" Laura said, secretly thrilled yet instantly suspicious.

"I have *known* Edie for ten years. We talk. I know how she works better than she knows how she works."

"For real?"

"Trust me. Go home, get some rest and don't worry. Edie will reappear when she's cleaned everything up, and she will be praying that you will still be there."

"All right. Thank you, Oswald."

Oswald touched her shoulder. "You're a nice woman and it's time Edie settled down. You'd be good for her."

Laura put a couch pillow over her face and tried to fall asleep. She knew she had to be patient, but every minute of every day that Edie was gone seemed an eternity and she knew then that she was hopelessly in love with Edie.

It was late Monday evening, nearly nine. Laura had stayed on to finish a project. Throwing herself into her work was the only way she could keep herself from going mad. Her shoulders ached, her eyes were tired from staring at numbers and images on the computer, and she thought perhaps tonight she could finally sleep. Like a sleepwalker she got in the elevator to go down to the parking lot. She didn't notice the elevator was going up. It opened on the fourth floor and Edie stepped in. She was carrying a stack of papers and was dressed in a black sweatshirt and jeans. Laura almost didn't recognize her.

"Edie?"

"Yes?" Edie said, looking as tired and worn out as Laura felt. She pressed the button to go down.

"Oh, Edie," Laura said, falling into her arms. Edie dropped the stack of papers and held her. "I can't stand it anymore," Laura whispered into her neck, pulling her close.

"It'll be okay," Edie murmured. "I've missed you."

Laura pulled away and looked at her. Her eyes filled with tears.

"Don't. Please don't," Edie said, wiping Laura's tears.

The elevator stopped and the door opened. Laura felt like an adolescent fool. Edie bent down to collect her papers. Laura knelt down to help.

"Like when we first met," Edie said, smiling. She touched Laura's cheek.

"When are you coming back?"

"Soon," Edie said, taking her hand and kissing the palm gently.

"Will you be here?"

"Yes," Laura said, watching Edie disappear again.

The following Friday morning Laura walked into her office to find a bouquet of red roses and a card that read, "Thank you for being patient." Laura rushed out of her office, almost toppling Susan.

"Hey, who's the secret admirer?" Susan said.

Laura was long gone before she'd finished her sentence.

Edie was standing at her office window, wondering, hoping and wishing for things and praying they'd all come true. There was a knock on her door and she slowly turned around. If you could dive into someone's eyes and lie basking on the beach of the waters of her soul, that was what Laura did. They stood in silence looking at each other. Edie walked over and took Laura gently, slowly, in her arms.

"How are you, beautiful lady?"

"Wonderful," Laura whispered, her lips slightly touching Edie's ear.

"Dinner?"

"Yes," Laura said.

"I'll come get you."

"Or I could come get you," Laura said, pulling away and studying Edie.

"All right," Edie said, knowing this was the moment of trust Laura had been waiting for. She scribbled the address of the loft on a Post-it.

Laura took it. "I'm not pushing . . ." Laura said, seeming uncertain.

"I know."

"Seven?"

"Perfect," Edie said, never taking her eyes off Laura.

"Restaurant of choice?"

"Surprise me."

"I will," Laura said.

When the buzzer rang Edie tried not to jump. She was dressed in a classic Giorgio Armani suit and she had kept herself to two drinks. She had spent days trying to fathom this moment and still couldn't quite pinpoint what moved her about this woman, what was different from all the others. There were more women than Edie cared to recollect. They'd all chased her. She didn't know how to chase. She only knew how be charming, how to be seduced, and how to leave. She knew nothing of how to conduct a relationship, and she was frightened.

"I'll be right down," Edie said.

Laura waited nervously by her car, a gold Acura. She'd dressed carefully in black slacks and a tight red shirt. When Edie appeared, Laura could see her choice was having the desired effect. Edie was blushing.

"You make me feel new," Edie said.

Laura smiled. "Good." She was trying hard not to think of how many other dates Edie had been on in her life. It doesn't matter, she told herself. Tonight she would make everything new.

When they pulled up in front of Lucci's Italian Restaurant Edie smiled. "You are a true romantic."

"I hope so," Laura said. She stopped herself from saying, *I want to be everything for you. I want to make you feel me, know me, love me, desire me, in ways different from all the rest.*

Laura refrained from interrogation until they got to the main course. She'd let Edie be attentive, charming, witty and vague long enough. The salad was lengthy, the soup took even longer and now she was done waiting.

"Edie?"

"Hmm . . ." Edie said, looking up from her lasagna, her mouth full.

"Remember when we went to Sedona and I told you about my failed love affair and how I had moved here to start over, and then somehow between here and there, I never heard yours. I'm inclined to think that it was a willful omission on your part."

Edie smiled and said, "This is a prime example of why dating smart women is dangerous."

"Who are you really?"

"I'm a serial killer."

"Edie . . ."

"There's not much to tell. I'm a Catholic school girl from an upper-class family with long list of girlfriends but no partners."

"Why is that?" Laura asked.

"Never met the right one."

"What really happened?"

Edie studied her for a moment. "Cassandra Hollander happened, and I've never been the same. She was eighteen, a senior at Xavier, and I was seventeen. We fell in love and she broke my heart," Edie said flatly.

"Pretty skimpy details. How'd she break your heart? Fell for a man?"

"No, she went to college first and that seemed to change a few things."

"Like what?" Laura said.

"I don't rightly know. I loved her and would have spent the rest of my life with her. She turned down Berkeley so she could wait a year for me. Then she went to the University of Arizona in Tucson. She was going to transfer wherever I ended up. I know what people say about first loves and young lovers, but it was different, like when you find that one person in the universe that you know you're supposed to meet, and you're supposed to fall in love and be together forever. It was weird, like everything was right, like we would be the exceptions, make first love work. Only it didn't."

Laura took her hand and kissed it softly. "You never cease to amaze me."

"Why? Because you thought I was a slut and now I'm a tragic figure," Edie said, looking as if she was going to get slapped or put a quick end to the date.

Instead, Laura laughed. "It is something like that."

"I'm glad to put your mind at ease. Now eat. Your food is getting cold."

On the way back from the restaurant, Laura asked Edie about the loft.

"I spent my vacation fixing it up. I've been meaning to do it for a long time and then I finally had a reason to."

"And what was the reason?" Laura asked, glancing at Edie as the light changed.

"That I might show it to you," Edie said shyly.

"I'd like to see it."

When they pulled up out front, Laura waited for Edie to make the next move.

"Would it be forward to ask you up for a nightcap and a tour?" Edie asked.

"No, I'd love to see it."

"Great."

Laura parked the car in front of the loft. They got in the lift that was an old freight elevator. Edie gave the door a good swing, then she unlocked the button for the fourth floor with a key. Laura wondered if she had the whole floor or if it was partitioned off.

"You've got to take your vitamins to do this on a daily basis," Laura said as the elevator creaked upward.

"I take them every day," Edie said. "I hope you don't think this is one of my seduction scenes. It's not like that."

"And why not?" Laura said, coming toward her. She pressed the stop button and cornered Edie, taking her ardently in her arms and kissing her. Edie melted into her kiss. Laura felt her face get hot and then she got lost in Edie, not stopping to think, just wanting to feel her. She ran her hands under Edie's shirt and up her stomach, almost to her breast, before Edie started to pull away.

"This is kind of sudden," Edie said.

Laura buried her face in Edie's neck. "Edie, I've been courted," she said, kissing Edie's neck and taking her breast in the palm of her hand. "Do you want me to stop?" she whispered in Edie's ear. She traced the outline of it with her tongue.

"No," Edie said, moving closer. Laura moved her thigh between Edie's legs.

Feeling Laura's thigh between her legs gave Edie a jolt. She slammed up against the wall, hitting the start button. She barely noticed until the door opened on the fourth floor and Edie's neighbors Kate and Shannon stood watching. Edie tapped Laura on the shoulder, interrupting her pursuit of Edie's nipple. She looked over and tried to smile.

"Good evening, ladies," Edie said, trying to straighten out her disheveled clothes.

"I'll say," Kate said.

"Don't do anything I wouldn't do," Shannon called out after them.

Edie took Laura's hand and led her down the corridor to the loft. Laura kissed the back of her neck and ran her hands up Edie's thighs as Edie tried to get the key in the lock. If Laura had given her the chance, Edie might have been overwhelmed but Laura had her undressed and was teasing her before she really knew what hit her. Laura slid her tongue across Edie's nipples, covering her body with her own, letting their bodies rest against each other. Their heat and wetness grew as Laura kept touching her and then moving away until Edie couldn't stand it anymore. She pulled Laura's hand between her legs.

"Please . . ." Edie pleaded.

Laura pushed her fingers inside, spreading Edie's legs farther apart. Edie melted into her, her hips grinding against her, wanting more, taking more, until she arched her back and let out a low moan, pulling Laura in tight, her body quivering.

Edie opened her eyes and looked at Laura. "Sweet Jesus," she said, smiling. She pulled Laura on top of her.

"You *are* a Catholic girl," Laura said.

"Who told you that?"

"You did. Oswald did too," Laura said.

Edie gently stroked Laura's thigh and between her legs.

"What else did he tell you?"

"That you slept with the ones you didn't love and courted the ones that you did," Laura said, as Edie pushed her fingers inside her. Her breath grew more rapid as she watched Edie.

"He's right, you know."

"So right," Laura said, closing her eyes.

Edie watched her as the light from the street lamp flooded across her body. "You're lovely," she murmured as she ran her hand up Laura's stomach to her breast.

Laura opened her eyes for a moment, smiled and eased down onto Edie who pulled her closer. She softly moaned in Edie's ear and

Edie felt her heart leap gladly at this chance for love, thinking, *I can love you. I want to love you*, Edie told herself as she felt Laura come in her arms.

It was nearly dawn when Laura tried to take her again.

"No, no, no, we're not going to be able to walk as it is," Edie said, pulling her up toward her. "We don't need to make all the love we're going to make all in one night. Come here, I want to hold you, talk to you."

Laura fell into her dazzling blue eyes. She lay on Edie's chest, looking up her.

"This isn't just for tonight, is it?" Laura asked.

"No," Edie said passionately. "No, no, no," she said, kissing Laura's forehead. She looked deeply in Laura's eyes. "I love you."

"That's good," Laura said, resting her head on Edie's chest, tracing her nipple with her finger.

Edie ran her hand through Laura's hair. "Would you believe me if I told you that you're wonderful?"

"Yes," Laura said, reaching for her again. "Just once more?"

Edie pulled her close. "Once more," she murmured.

When Laura awoke it was mid morning and Edie was gone. She sat up in an instant panic.

"Edie," she called out, trying to quell her first thought that Edie had done another disappearing act. Then she remembered she was in Edie's bed.

At that moment Edie came walking in carrying breakfast on a dark mahogany tray, complete with a rose, just like in the movies, Laura thought.

"Good morning, pretty lady. Did you sleep well?" Edie put the tray down and sidled in next to her.

Laura smiled. "Yes, and I'm starving. Just when did you have time to concoct all of this?"

Edie smiled. "I had it sent. There are perks to being the ex food editor."

"You and your connections."

"They say the way to a woman's heart is through her stomach. Do I still have your heart?" Edie asked shyly.

"Are you asking if I'm going to throw you out of bed for eating crackers?" Laura replied.

"Something like that," Edie said.

"I love you, Ms. Farnsworth, and nothing will change that."

Edie snuggled in next to her and closed her eyes.

"What are you thinking?" Laura asked, taking a bite of a bagel.

"I'm not thinking, I'm praying," Edie said, opening her eyes and taking the strawberry Laura offered her.

"Are you really religious?" Laura asked, becoming slightly concerned that she might end up in church every Sunday and in Bible study on Tuesday nights.

"I am when it comes to love. Well, perhaps it's more like I'm superstitious. You know, too-good-to-be-true stuff."

"No more relationships gone awry and no more multiple girl-friends," Laura said.

"Agreed," Edie said, removing the tray and taking Laura in her arms.

"Any plans for the day?" Laura asked, glad it was Saturday.

"Uh-huh," Edie said. "Getting you in the tub and then spending the rest of the day in bed." She arched an eyebrow.

"Hmm . . . sounds wonderful. Is that what the nutrients were for?"

"You read me like a book already," Edie said.

Chapter Five

The mechanic drove her old Saab off to the lot and Vida took one last long look at it. The salesman handed her the keys to her new car.

"It's you," he said.

Vida smiled. "Yes, it is," she said, getting in her new yellow Land Cruiser.

"Okay, well, if you need anything, here's my card."

"Thanks," Vida said.

Just then the mechanic came running back out. "Hey, wait, you forgot this," he said, giving her the gold ring hanging on a chain. "It was on the rear-view mirror."

"Oh, yeah," Vida said, holding out her hand. It fell in her palm. "Wouldn't want to forget that." She hung it on the rear- view mirror.

"Most people wear those on their finger," the salesman said.

"Most people," Vida said, starting the Land Cruiser.

As she drove off the lot she thought, *new life, new car, new place. I can do this.* She had stayed with Sonja for two months and decided it was time to step out on her own. She bought a condo, bought some furniture and moved in. She thought this would help her resolve some issues, but she was discovering it was harder than she had imagined. She couldn't stop thinking about Kirsten, about the night she had moved out, about the last time they made love, about holding Kirsten while she cried. *God, I really am a bitch.*

She drove up to Squaw Peak and parked. One long hike up a tall mountain would hopefully take her mind off it. She should call Mercedes, she should call her dad, she should go out to dinner with her new friend Miranda, but she wanted to be alone.

I need to think, I need to buy some new music, and I need to get a pet. I'll go to the Humane Society and find something furry. I need a dog and a cat. The three of us will weather this together.

When Vida got home she had an English bulldog named Bertrand and a kitten named True Love, True for short, and she felt better. Bertrand wasn't sold on the kitten but by morning she found them both sleeping together at the foot of her bed. Miranda was on the phone asking her how her first week in her new pad had gone. Miranda was Sonja's daughter and they had become fast friends while Vida had been staying with Sonja. They were close in age and had a lot in common.

"Why don't you come over for breakfast and see?" Vida said, trying to shake the morning cobwebs from her head.

"Be right there. Do I need to bring anything?"

"Yes, everything you need for breakfast. I don't have any food."

"I'll shop, you shower and we'll cook," Miranda said, laughing into the phone.

"I don't know what I'd do without you," Vida said.

"You'd find a good woman and settle down," Miranda replied.

"Are you offering?"

"I wish, but you know I have a fascination with dick," Miranda said.

"Yeah, when are you going to settle down?"

"When I find the right dick."

"Oh, God, hurry, I'm starving and I can't wait for you to meet my new roommates."

"Roommates . . . already? Are they cute?"

"Adorable."

"Oooh, I'll be right there."

As Bertrand was slobbering all over her ankle, Miranda said, "You call this a roommate?"

"Best kind," Vida said, pulling True off the curtain, "This is True Love, True for short."

"Are you sure you shouldn't be going to therapy?"

"Positive," Vida said, unloading the groceries.

Miranda raised an eyebrow. "I have a list of good shrinks."

"I don't need a shrink. I have you."

"And my mother," Miranda said, scooting Vida aside.

"Thank God for Sonja. You two are my guardian angels."

Miranda moved her to a stool.

"What are you doing? I'm supposed to be fixing you breakfast."

"Darling, I've seen you in the kitchen and you're a perfect hazard. I'm hungry and I'd like to eat something *edible*."

"Well, thanks a lot. You could teach me."

"Okay, cooking show begins. Are you going to pay attention?"

"I'm all eyes," Vida said.

"All right then, let's start by having a Bloody Mary." Miranda opened a cupboard looking for glasses. There were four. "Boy, going minimal, are we?"

"I haven't done much household shopping," Vida said, watching Miranda mix the drinks.

"Perhaps we should go shopping after breakfast. Do you have a pan?" Miranda handed her the tall Bloody Mary garnished with a leafy celery stalk.

"Yes, I bought a set of dishes, a pan set and some utensils."

"Cheers. Welcome to your new home," Miranda said.

"Thanks."

"Are you really doing okay?" Miranda asked.

"Better than I thought I would be."

"Have you talked to her?"

"Not for a couple of days. I wish I had the balls to just disappear," Vida said, taking another sip of her drink.

"You could you know."

"No, I can't. I feel rotten enough having walked out but leaving altogether seems a worse crime," Vida said, clinking the ice cubes in her now half-empty glass.

"Why?"

"Because I think it's easier if you know that the person is still around, you can still talk to them if you have to."

"I don't understand. When it's over it should be over. Why prolong it?"

"You just don't understand lesbians. It's never over. I still love Kirsten . . ."

"You just can't stand living with her," Miranda said, furiously beating the raw eggs with a fork.

"You really don't like her."

"Truthfully?"

Vida nodded, and Miranda mixed them both another drink.

"I think she's a bitch and I think she was mean to you."

"I'm not exactly a saint."

"I know that, but you're secure enough to know who you are and what you want out of life, and for the most part you're realistic and pretty upbeat and for some reason Kirsten couldn't handle that. I don't think she could handle you."

"Wow!" Vida said, "You've got some strong feelings about this."

"I'm sorry," Miranda said. "Hash browns?"

"Please."

"I just had to get that off my chest."

"You're probably right. I don't like making someone, especially someone you love, feel bad or nervous . . ."

"Anxious, uptight, possessive and jealous," Miranda said.

"Yes."

"So now that you're done with that scene, what are you looking for in a good woman?"

"I don't think I understand you straight people. Is that what you do? Walk in and out of each other's lives with a 'hey this didn't work out move on' attitude."

"What's left? Mourn the death of a love affair. It's over, let it die gracefully," Miranda said, chopping up an onion.

"I guess you're right. So why do I think about her all the time?"

"Because you're a lesbian and lesbians do that. Oh, that reminds me. I bought you a little present," Miranda said, going over to her purse and pulling out a small book.

"*Robert's Rules of Lesbian Break-Ups*?"

"Precisely. If you won't go to a therapist, then at least read this. It's supposed to be hysterical."

Vida thumbed through the first couple of pages. She smiled. "I think this just might work."

Vida turned on some music while Miranda fried the potatoes and started the eggs. Then she set the table.

"Good, now come eat."

"And then can we take Bertrand for a walk?" Vida said, scratching his ears. He looked up appreciatively.

"Yes, but can we get the kitty off the table first?" Miranda was holding both plates and looking with consternation at True who was rolling around on the place mat looking the picture of cuteness.

Vida scooped her up and kissed her little face. "I don't know what I'd do without these guys."

"They sleep with you, right?"

"Of course. And it's a great comfort," Vida said, remembering reading in bed the night before having herbal tea instead of a Scotch and surrounded by creatures that loved her unconditionally. Her life was a mess but she found herself with a single-minded determination to fix it.

"It'll get better," Miranda said, seemingly reading her thoughts.

"I know." Vida just wished she could convince her extremely depressed girlfriend that this was all going to work out for the best. She couldn't decide which end was worse now that she had experienced being both the dumped and the dumper.

She felt guilty for leaving, knowing it was impossible to stay, and yet she missed Kirsten and at the same time avoided her as much as she could. She couldn't go back, not now that she had gotten away, this far away. What was it about that woman? It wasn't like Vida hadn't left and come back before.

Vida studied her phone messages. One of them was from Kirsten reminding her of the annual snooty gala dinner where all those who were or wanted to be something got together at Taliesen, a posh country club built by Frank Lloyd Wright, to network, et cetera. Vida hated it with a passion, but it was an important event for Kirsten's work, a good place to get funding for women's art. Sonja and Miranda were going and Vida ought to be going but the thought of everyone wondering about her relationship with Kirsten wasn't something she relished and if she went without Kirsten, or worse, if Kirsten went without her there would be talk.

She picked up the phone and called the university.

"Hi there," she said when she got Kirsten.

"Hi. Anything wrong?" Kirsten asked tentatively.

"No, does something have to be wrong to call?" Vida said, feeling instantly defensive.

"No, I'm glad to hear from you. I miss you."

"How are you?" Vida asked.

"Okay, I guess."

"Really?"

"No," Kirsten replied quietly.

"Will you go with me to the gala?"

"As your date?"

Vida swallowed hard. "Yes. Believe it or not I miss you too."

"Then I'd be delighted."

"I'll pick you up at six."

"Be there with bells on."

Vida hung up the phone, wondering why she couldn't get over her. She couldn't even casually sleep with Mercedes anymore because she could only think of Kirsten.

A week later, when she pulled up in front of the house, Vida realized her mistake. Kirsten had made all the reservations and paid in advance. Vida should have told her about the car before.

"New car?" Kirsten said, getting in. She was wearing a long black gown with a set of white pearls. Vida had decided on a black suit with a teal blouse and boots. She had pulled her hair back.

"Oh, yeah. I needed a change," Vida said, trying to act nonchalant. It didn't work.

"Why? Did the old one smell of me?" Kirsten said snidely.

Vida sighed.

"I'm sorry," Kirsten said.

They drove in silence.

"Music?"

"Please," Kirsten said.

The Vivaldi CD got them to the edge of Scottsdale. The stately palm trees of Phoenix gave way to the saguaro cactus and creosote bushes of the native desert. The brittle bush was in yellow bloom and the prickly pear cactus had purple fruit hanging from its multitude of branches.

"Do you remember the first time we came here?" Vida said.

Kirsten nodded and stared out the window.

Vida saw her shoulders quiver and she knew she was crying. She turned off on the road toward Taliesen and then suddenly veered into a patch of dirt off the side of the road.

Kirsten looked up, her eyes frantic, her face tear-stained. "Where are you going?"

"Frank won't mind," Vida said, driving the car in between two juniper trees so they couldn't be seen from the road.

"Frank?"

"Frank Lloyd Wright," Vida replied.

"Is this why you got a four-wheel drive?" Kirsten said.

Vida laughed. "Yes." She took Kirsten's hand. "Let's try and make the best of tonight."

"I can't!" Kirsten said, beginning to sob again. "I miss you and I can't pretend I don't."

Vida looked down at their hands, wrapped gently in their own harmless embrace. She took Kirsten in her arms. "Please don't cry," she said, wiping her tears away. Kirsten looked so sad. "I'm sorry I hurt you. I don't mean to hurt you. I just can't stand what we do to each other."

Kirsten nodded and kept crying while Vida kept wiping the tears away.

Vida softly kissed her eyelids and her cheeks, whispering, "Shh . . . it'll be all right."

It would have been all right if Vida hadn't kissed her, softly at first, then harder, their tongues finding each other. Remembering other, better days, Vida reached for Kirsten's breast, rubbing her finger around her nipple, remembering how soft her nipples were, and then wanting to taste them. She unbuttoned Kirsten's dress and took a nipple in her mouth, feeling Kirsten kiss her neck. She reached up under Kirsten's dress spreading Kirsten's legs, going inside deeper, feeling Kirsten just as eagerly reach for her until they were both holding each other tight and coming within seconds of each other.

"I'm sorry. I shouldn't have done that," Vida said, suddenly frightened.

"Please, don't say you're sorry," Kirsten said, still holding her.

Vida got teary-eyed. "It's just so hard."

"Don't you start," Kirsten said, pulling her closer. "I miss you. I miss us and I miss doing *that*."

Vida laughed. "Me too."

A car drove past them on the nearby road and the lights shone on the back window as the car rounded the turn.

"We better get going before we get arrested," Kirsten said, trying to smile.

Vida touched her cheek and started the car.

They sat next to Sonja and Miranda and tried to put on their best faces. It didn't work. Sonja read through them.

"Are you okay?" Sonja murmured between courses of the dinner. Kirsten had gone to the restroom.

Vida looked at her and thought about lying. "No. I don't think this was a good idea and then we had a little relapse on the way up here, which was nice but not smart."

"I see," Sonja said.

"I can't go back and she's miserable and I feel bad for making her miserable. It's so hopeless. I wish sometimes I could just walk out of my life for a while until we both felt better," Vida said.

"Do you want me to tell you that someday this will all seem funny?" Sonja said.

"Please."

After dinner, Vida got herself cornered near the bar by Effie Myers, a petite gadabout on the Phoenix scene. Effie must have heard and she was being less than subtle about her advances. She'd always had a thing for Vida and was making no bones about the fact that now that Vida was unattached, the impediment removed, she was going to take full advantage of it. Vida saw Kirsten watching them. She had that old look in her eyes, a mixture of anger, possession and jealousy. Vida extricated herself with that same old feeling of anxiety and remorse for not being what her lover wanted.

Kirsten was watching the dance floor when Vida found her. She came up behind her and whispered, "May I have this dance?" Vida tried to put on her best face.

Kirsten looked up and smiled. "I'd love to."

Effie was watching them and turned away, clearly disgusted. When they returned to the table, Kirsten's face was flushed, and Vida felt slightly aroused. It felt good being close to Kirsten again.

Sonja and Vida tried to keep Kirsten's spirits up but Effie made it a point to loom in the background. Kirsten drank a lot and Vida tried not to mind until the suitable hour for leaving finally arrived, meaning an end to the tedious festivities. Effie followed them to the parking lot. Vida felt her adrenaline start to flow. She knew Effie wasn't part of the farewell committee.

"So, Vida, now that you dumped your wife, when are you going to take on someone with some real oomph," Effie called out.

Vida watched Kirsten's shoulders sink. She took her hand and gently squeezed it.

Vida turned around and Sonja moved closer. Miranda was behind her with a slightly bemused look on her face.

"First off, Effie, what goes on between Kirsten and me is none of your business, and secondly, if you were the last lesbian on the planet and I had to choose between you and these five fingers, you'd lose."

Sonja blanched while Miranda laughed outright.

"You're just saying that because you don't want to hurt your wife's ego. I'll call you later and then we'll talk. I've got what a woman like you wants, trust me," Effie said, turning her back slowly.

Before anyone really knew what happened, Vida had flown across the parking lot and slammed Effie hard in the back.

She almost fell. Effie caught herself and turned around, ready for a fight, but Vida already had her hand around her throat.

"Don't fucking ever talk to me like that again. Don't insult my wife or my intelligence, you got it?" Vida said.

Sonja and Miranda were trying to pull Effie from Vida's grasp.

"Vida, honey, let go. That's enough, okay," Sonja soothed.

Vida squeezed hard and let go. Effie started to come toward her but Sonja got between them. She glared at Effie.

Effie shrugged her shoulders and straightened her suit jacket. "Yeah, well, you can just fuck off," Effie said.

Vida tried to lunge at her but Miranda got ahold of her. "Vida, come on, let's go home," she said. "She's not worth your time."

"All right," Vida said, watching Effie stalk off.

"Come on, take Kirsten home and then go home and have a stiff drink, okay, honey?" Sonja put her arm around Vida.

Vida looked at her. "Is this going to be funny someday too?"

Sonja chuckled. "Yes. In fact, I think you'll have the secret admiration of the Pink Mafia for years to come."

Vida smiled. "If you say so."

"She had it coming," Miranda said.

Kirsten was leaning up against the car. She looked pitiful.

"Come on, sweet lady, let me take you home," Vida said, opening the car door.

Kirsten tried to smile. "Thank you."

"Anytime," Vida said.

They didn't talk on the way home. When they pulled up in front of Kirsten's big brick house with its neatly trimmed shrubs, Vida looked over at Kirsten.

"Are you going to be all right?"

Kirsten nodded. Vida couldn't help thinking that communication was not one of their strong points.

"It's going to get better. We just need to give it some time," Vida coached.

"It's not going to get any better for me. I love you," Kirsten said, looking at her intently.

Vida touched her cheek. "I know you do. I never doubted it."

"Can't you come up? I miss you so much."

Vida shook her head. "Not yet, okay?"

Kirsten nodded and got out of the car.

Vida watched her go. She got this queer feeling in her stomach. She got out of the car and called out, "Kirsten!"

She turned around.

"I love you too."

A few days later day when Kirsten called her at the photo studio, Vida knew the night at Taliesen had been a complete mistake.

"I wanted to thank you for the other night, for defending me against Effie," Kirsten said.

"It's a good thing her office is in the political science building or life would be really complex. Sometimes I don't miss college," Vida said.

"Because of the politics?" Kirsten queried.

"No, not that. It's all the dyke professors," Vida said, instantly regretting the statement.

"Does that include me?"

"No. Art history was always my favorite subject," Vida lied, thinking they would both have been better off had Vida never walked into Kirsten's classroom.

"Speaking of art, there's this exhibit of post-modern masters at the Heard Museum. I thought we could do dinner and then go one evening after work," Kirsten said.

"I can't. Eva is in town for a shoot. She came in last night. She's going to stay at my place for the week. She's cooking Creole. Why don't you come over?" Vida asked, knowing Kirsten would decline. She didn't like Eva.

"Some other time," Kirsten said curtly.

"Kirsten, come on." Vida wished Kirsten would get over her dislike of her friends.

"It's fine really. Have fun. We'll do it some other time," Kirsten said, ringing off.

❧

"Vida, come on," Sid said, pointing his camera at Vida.

"No dinner date with the ex-babe," Eva said.

"No," Vida replied, taking off her robe to do the shoot.

"Mercedes says hi and she misses you," Sid said, putting his tongue between his fingers held up in a peace sign.

"Stop that!" Vida said, disgusted.

"Just telling it like it is," Sid replied, taking a photo of Vida scowling.

"What's that, a blackmail picture?" Vida asked.

"Exactly."

"You're just jealous because she gets more action than you do," Eva said, putting her arm around Vida while Sid took the shot.

"So when are you two moving in together," Eva asked.

"I'm not ready for that. We're great in bed but I'm not so sure about life partners. The problem is that she thinks we're perfect. Maybe I'm jaded."

"Do you remember the real reason you moved in with Kirsten?" Eva asked as they changed into women's executive suits and Sid screamed at them to hurry up.

"Fuck off, you stupid prick," Eva screamed back.

"Where's the love?" Vida chided.

"Do you remember?"

"I'm sure I had good reasons," Vida replied.

"You told me it was because you wanted the stability and I asked you about passion and you said there was enough."

"I wanted to settle down. I was in a nesting mode."

"And now?" Eva asked, straightening out her white silk shirt in the mirror.

"And now, I'm bed-hopping again. What are you getting at?"

"Mercedes is not a bad choice. She's young and exciting."

"You forgot malleable."

"Exactly."

"Maybe that's the problem. I don't want to be someone's mother. I want to fall head over heels in love for life."

"Well, in that case, it's a good thing Mercedes is doing the Country Collection for a while. It'll buy you some time and perhaps quench some of her desires," Eva said diplomatically.

"Do you two think you could pay attention long enough for me to get some good shots?" Sid said.

Eva put her hands on her hips and looked straight at him. "Did it ever occur to you that we might be bored, that standing around in hideous lingerie is not our life's calling? We may make a lot of money but we don't get a lot of respect. Do you know what it's like standing around at a party and someone asks you what you do for a living and I've got to say I model fucking underwear. And look at Vida, that girl has brains. What do people think of her standing around in her underwear all damn day long?"

Sid laughed. "What does that make me?"

"A stupid prick with a camera standing around taking pictures of fucking underwear," Eva replied.

They all started laughing.

"Let's pack it up for today and go have some fun," Sid said.

Chapter Six

Edie was having a small get-together at the loft. Laura was out of town on business and Edie was taking advantage of some downtime. Being a committed woman was more labor-intensive and time-consuming than she had remembered. When she had lived with her only other long-term lover, Cassandra, they had been so busy with college and night jobs that most of their time together had been squeezed in between. Laura, on the other hand, expected her for dinner, to play on the weekends and to attend various social functions. Edie still worked ten hours a day as the magazine's senior editor as well as the theater critic, so she was forced to fulfill her duties as monogamous lover in whatever time was left. She was finding this incredibly difficult.

"I'm telling you, Sandi, this is not easy," Edie said, pouring them both another glass of Merlot.

"Edie, how can this be harder than juggling two or three lovers?" Sandi replied.

"It is. All I had to do with them was have logically spaced amorous evenings."

"In other words, you just had to fuck them."

"It was a little more complicated than that," Edie said, indignant. She suddenly pined for her single days. It wasn't that she didn't love Laura, rather it was the fear of failure. She missed the chase and the highs of infatuation without the ultimate end of domesticated, monogamous life. She was in for the long haul now and it made her understandably nervous.

"Oh, do tell. You're the only woman I know that was able to pull all that crap off and not get found out and shot by one of your jealous lovers. You're lucky to have gotten out of the Pink Mafia gauntlet alive," Sandi said.

"You are completely over-dramatizing."

"Edie, no one gets that much action and not get roped into a relationship."

"One has to be very careful and plan well," Edie said, pushing the buzzer for her friends Bear and Linden to get into the building.

"So when are you and Laura moving in?" Sandi asked as she kissed her girlfriend, Linden, on the cheek as they entered.

"Who's moving in?" Bear asked. She was Edie's oldest friend. She was a career bouncer at the women's bars in town. She was a large Native American woman with long, black hair neatly pulled back in a ponytail. She and Edie had a long history of cruising women, and Bear, of all people, understood the pitfalls of marriage.

"Edie will be moving in with Laura shortly," Sandi said.

"Let's not rush things," Edie said, getting Bear a beer and Linden a glass of red wine.

"So this is the bachelor party," Bear said.

"You know there's a lot involved in a lifelong partnership," Edie said, pouring herself a Scotch on the rocks.

"Are you suffering a case of nerves?" Linden asked.

"Not everyone is as lucky as you two." Edie pulled a tray of black bean spinach roll-ups out of the fridge and set them on the counter.

Bear popped one in her mouth. "I love these things," she said.

"Edie, you can't still be scarred from Cassandra. My God, that was eons ago, and you two were mere babies when you started out. You can't have expected that to last," Linden said.

Edie smiled at Linden. Sandi was indeed a fortunate woman. Linden was a petite woman with short blonde hair and pretty green eyes. She was sweet, treated Sandi well and let each of them have their own space. To Edie it appeared the perfect relationship.

"There are three things I fear in life," Edie said.

"Which are?" Sandi prodded.

"Rodents, children under the age of five, and commitment."

"Those are good fears," Bear said, chuckling.

"I don't get what rodents have to do with small children and marriage," Sandi said.

"They all gnaw at your body parts, rodents at your ankles, small children at your mind and wives at your heart," Edie replied.

"Good lines. You should have been a writer," Linden said.

"I only like plays," Edie replied.

"Then write plays," Sandi chided.

"Someday maybe," Edie said, knowing Sandi was referring to Edie's long-time dream of becoming a playwright. This commitment thing was only going to further hamper that, she thought ruefully.

"In the meantime, we need to cure you of your fears. Fear is a bad thing. It cripples your life. Do you want to be a cripple for the rest of your life?" Linden asked.

Edie squirmed. She felt like she was on a teetertotter at the park with her present self on one side and future self on the other side. Her present self felt like jumping off and resuming her former life, sending her future self sailing off into the wild blue yonder. Unfortunately, she was a forward-looking person, and the thought of completely derailing a prominent future bothered her.

"What do I have to do?" Edie asked.

"Touch a rat, play with a two-year-old, and resolve your relationship with Cassandra," Linden replied.

"Gee, is that all?" Edie replied.

"Yes," Linden said.

"I can't."

"You can," Linden said.

At the pet store the next day, Edie was screaming, much to the alarm of the patrons and the shopkeeper. Bear was holding her tightly while Linden stuck her hand in the cage of a white rat.

"I don't think this is such a good idea," Edie said, petrified and sweating profusely.

"No, look. It's sweet," Linden said, cradling the rat in her hand. The rat's nose and whiskers quivered as it stared at Edie. "Now give me your hand."

"I can't do it," Edie said.

"You can," Linden said, calmly taking Edie's hand and unfurling it.

"Just touch it like this." Linden stroked the rat's back.

Sandi winced. Edie took a deep breath and touched the rat with her forefinger, hoping this would do.

"Okay, now cup your hands like this and hold it," Linden said.

"No way," Edie said, backing up into Bear, who resumed her hold on Edie.

"Edie, look how small it is compared to you. You could step on it and break its neck before it ever did you any harm. It trusts you. Can't you do the same?" Bear said.

"I never thought of it that way," Edie said. She cupped her hands and let the rat crawl onto them. The rat's nails poked against her palms. The rat itself was soft and warm. It looked at Edie tentatively.

"I won't hurt you," Edie told the rat.

"See, you did it," Linden said.

❦

The following day they went to Linden's sister's house to meet her little girls aged one and a half and three years old. They were nothing compared to the rat.

When Laura returned home Edie spent an amorous evening with her but went back to the loft afterwards, telling Laura she had work to do. Laura was disappointed, but Edie told her everything would be all right.

Now she sat in the hallway waiting for Cassandra to get out of a staff meeting. Being back on the campus of Arizona State University was giving her an anxiety attack. She was reliving the last days of the relationship with Cassandra. With a wet paper towel pressed against her nose, she sat back in the old wooden chairs lined up in the hall. It would be another fifteen minutes before Cassandra appeared, and Edie prayed the attack would stop by then. Her anxiety attacks and subsequent nosebleeds had begun at college. The pressure of school, work and her relationship with Cassandra that had been slowly withering put Edie in the psych ward for a brief spell. She got dumped by Cassandra and barely finished college with the help of some compassionate professors. It was not a good period in her life. These were secrets she kept from her friends, and she preferred to keep it that way. The shrinks at the hospital told her she would have to take medication and learn to relax.

Edie had explained all this to her old-time college buddy Oswald. At the time, Oswald was using his trust fund to start up a small magazine that explored the odd side of life in Phoenix. Edie went to work for him. Together they learned the magazine business and it kept Edie so busy she had learned to put her past behind her.

She didn't know exactly what she wanted to ask Cassandra. She just knew that they needed to talk about what had happened between them and somehow set the whole thing right. She focused on what Linden had said concerning facing her fears and she knew that seeing Cassandra was one of them. She closed her eyes and took some deep breaths.

"Are you all right?" a woman's voice asked.

Edie opened her eyes to stare in the face of a concerned pretty, blonde woman.

"I'm fine."

"You're bleeding."

"I'm having an anxiety attack, which manifests itself in nose-bleeds."

"Let me get you some more tissue. By the way, I'm Vida," she said, digging around in her purse.

"Thank you," Edie said, getting upright and studying the woman more closely.

"Are you a student here?" Vida asked.

"No. I used to be," Edie said, hoping she didn't recognize the woman from one of her unfortunate encounters in the psych ward.

"Me too. It still gives me the heebie-jeebies just being on campus but my girlfriend, or rather ex-girlfriend, is a professor of art history here."

"Are you waiting for her?" Edie asked, realizing that talking to Vida was calming her down and her nosebleed had stopped.

"Yes. Look, you've stopped bleeding."

"Talking to you must have relaxed me. I'm waiting for my ex-girlfriend too. I haven't seen her for eight hundred and seventy-eight days, ten hours and three minutes," Edie said, looking at her watch.

"You've been keeping track," Vida said.

"I'd like to stop."

"That's why you're here."

"Yes."

"Can I ask you a personal question?" Vida said.

"Sure." Edie stared at Vida, trying to place her face. She had definitely seen her before.

"Are those real?"

"Are what real?" Edie asked.

"Your eyes. I mean, are they contacts or is that their real color?"

71

"No, they're real. I know they're kind of a freaky color."

"They're beautiful. Cerulean blue. It's my favorite color."

"You must be a painter."

"No, but my mother was."

"Tell me your name again," Edie said.

"Vida, Vida Sumner."

"Edie Farnsworth. It's nice to meet you."

"The feeling is mutual."

Cassandra came out of the office first and immediately saw Edie. "Edie? What are you doing here?"

"I came to see you."

"Is everything all right?" Cassandra said.

"Yes, I just needed to talk to you for a minute."

"Okay, let's go to my office. You look good," Cassandra said, stroking her cheek and looking at her intently.

As they walked down the hall together, Edie turned and looked at Vida, who smiled.

"She's single," Cassandra said.

"Unfortunately, I'm not," Edie said.

Vida watched her go and then spotted Kirsten.

"What's up?" Kirsten asked.

"I came to see if you had had lunch yet," Vida said.

"Not yet. I was planning on going with Cassandra but it appears she's busy," Kirsten said.

"Does that mean you'll have lunch with me?"

"Yes. I should know better, but I'd still like to," Kirsten said.

"We won't fight and I won't disappoint you," Vida said.

Later after lunch and a couple glasses of wine, Kirsten was sitting on Vida's bed after taking a tour of Vida's new condo.

"You need some stuff on the walls but the furniture is very tasteful," Kirsten said.

Vida sat down next to her on the bed. "How are you doing, really?" Vida asked, wondering if Kirsten was having as hard a time as she was living alone.

"Better than I thought I'd be doing. I went to the art exhibit with Cassandra. It was nice."

"That's good."

"I've got that conference coming up so I've been working on my paper on Mary Cassatt," Kirsten said.

Vida took her hand. "I miss you," she said before she could stop herself. Being without Kirsten was harder than she had envisioned.

Kirsten smiled sadly. "I don't know if that's good."

Vida began to slowly suck her fingers, watching as the color rose in Kirsten's face. Vida drew her down on the bed and slowly unbuttoned her shirt. She ran her tongue around Kirsten's nipple.

"Vida, what are doing?"

"Seducing you," Vida said, kissing her stomach. Kirsten had lost weight. "You need to eat more." Vida traced the outline of a rib with her tongue.

"I don't think this is a good idea."

"It's a great idea," Vida said, undoing Kirsten's slacks and praying she was wet. She was, and Vida reached inside. Kirsten moaned softly. Vida pulled her slacks off and Kirsten wrapped her legs around her, letting Vida in deep.

Vida held her tight while she came. Then Kirsten pulled Vida up and took her in her mouth. Vida held the bedpost while Kirsten's tongue softly flicked against her. Vida slid down and felt Kirsten enter her. Vida came instantaneously. She opened her eyes and smiled at Kirsten.

"I love you," Vida said.

Kirsten kissed her ardently and put her hand between her legs. "Show me."

❧

Later as Vida lay across Kirsten's back, her fingers still inside Kirsten, the woman with the cerulean blue eyes came to mind. Vida wondered if she had been silly in thinking of a dream lover. Maybe this was as good as it gets, she thought, that falling in love, getting laid in the afternoon and learning to talk nicely to each other was all there was. She was far more compatible with Kirsten than she was with Mercedes. Perhaps the dream of finding one's soul mate, that perfect companion, was just that, a whimsical fancy that a grown woman should know better than to believe in.

"I should go," Kirsten said.

"No, don't. I want you to stay. I want to wake up next to you."

"Vida, what are we doing? I don't know if my heart can take this."

"Falling back in love."

"I don't know."

"Come here," Vida said, pulling her back down on the bed.

Kirsten curled back up in her arms.

"I've decided I'm going to go back to school. I haven't got much more left of the modeling thing. I've got one more shoot for the spring catalogue and we're off for a while. Maybe we could go somewhere."

Kirsten leaned up on her elbow and looked at Vida. "You are a beautiful woman with brains and the most sensual manner that I have ever known but the longer we're apart the more I think it might be better. I don't hurt you and you don't hurt me."

"That's fair," Vida said, fighting back tears.

Kirsten stroked her face. "Go to San Diego and we'll talk when you get back in November."

Vida got out of the shower in her San Diego hotel room and put on one of the complimentary white robes. She was waiting for Eva and then Mercedes to fly in. Her flight had been first and she was glad for the downtime before they arrived. She had to suppress the urge to call Kirsten and find out how she doing even though her new lover was probably coming across town at this very moment. What was it about love? When Kirsten was still madly in love with her, Vida wanted out, and now that Kirsten was seemingly over her, Vida was obsessed with getting her back. Life and love, it seemed, never made much sense in her opinion. Just then Eva and Mercedes came bursting in the room. Both of them were talking a mile a minute.

"Vida, we absolutely have to go surfing. We met this guy on the plane and he'll give us lessons," Mercedes said, bubbling over with excitement.

"Yeah, he'll give you lessons all right," Eva said, placing her hand on her hip.

"I can handle him," Mercedes said, pouring a glass of Champagne.

Eva gave Vida a hug and whispered, "Is everything all right?"

"A little too all right," Vida replied.

"I told you not to go there," Eva said.

"I couldn't help myself."

"Couldn't help what?" Mercedes asked.

"Nothing, darling," Vida said, stroking Mercedes' cheek and pulling her close.

"I missed you so much," Mercedes said. "Can we go surfing?"

"Of course," Vida replied.

"You two can go but I am not setting foot in those shark-infested waters," Eva said, gulping down a glass of Champagne.

"Eva, come on. It'll be fun," Vida chided.

"No way. All right, I'm off. I know you two got some business to attend to," Eva said, winking at them.

Mercedes blushed.

"See you all tomorrow. Remember the shoot is at eight sharp," Eva said.

"I need a shower," Mercedes said before Vida could protest.

Vida lay on the bed and listened to the shower. She picked up the room service menu. "I think we shall have seafood tonight," she said.

Mercedes got out of the shower and sat on the bed toweling dry her long hair.

"Are you hungry?" Vida asked, sitting down behind her and brushing out Mercedes' hair. "You have gorgeous hair," she said, kissing her neck.

"I'm hungry for you."

It was two in the morning when Mercedes' cell phone rang. Groggy from Champagne and sex she answered it and then handed the phone to Vida.

"It's for you," she said, touching Vida's shoulder.

"Hello?"

"I don't ever want to see you again," Kirsten said.

"Kirsten, how did you get this number?"

"The mailman."

"What?"

"He inadvertently delivered your cell phone bill to the house."

"Kirsten, let me explain."

"What could you possibly explain?" Kirsten replied. "You're in bed with another woman that you call at least twice a day. I think the facts explain themselves."

The line clicked dead.

"Are you all right?" Mercedes asked.

"What a mess."

"I thought you two were through."

"We are."

"So when are you moving in?"

"We'll talk later. Let's get some sleep," Vida said, fighting back tears.

Part Two

Two years later

Chapter Seven

Edie had been up since four-thirty going over her proposal. She quietly slipped into the walk-in closet and clicked on the light, peering through the crack to see if Laura had woken up. She rummaged around for her "lucky" suit, a dark teal blazer, black shirt and trousers. She debated over the tie and decided it was too butch; today she needed to be hard femme, not soft butch. Somehow the men with the money seemed to prefer that look. She grabbed shoes and slunk out of the closet.

"Edie?" Laura called from the darkness.

Edie crawled on the bed. "Good morning, sweetheart," she said, kissing her forehead.

"What time is it?" Laura asked.

"Six," Edie answered, snuggling in next to her, contemplating for half a second if she had time for a quick seduction.

"What are you doing?" Laura asked.

"Gym, work, power lunch, board meeting at the Marriott."

"Today's the big day," Laura said.

"*The* big day, wish me luck," Edie said, feeling suddenly extremely nervous and highly vulnerable.

"You'll do fine," Laura assured her.

"I hope so."

"You're incredible. They'll love you."

"I wish I felt incredible," Edie said, pulling her close.

Laura ran her hand up Edie's shirt and across her nipple. Edie closed her eyes and smiled.

"We probably don't have time," Laura said.

"We could make time," Edie said.

"Later, when I'll have your full attention."

"I can hardly wait," Edie said. She kissed her deeply then leapt off the bed. "Okay I'm off."

Laura tried to grab her.

Edie laughed. "You'll have to be faster than that."

Laura slowly took off her nightgown, smiling seductively at Edie. Edie felt her face flush with desire. She leapt back on the bed.

"Fuck the gym," Edie said, mentally rescheduling the rest of her day.

"I'll give you a workout," Laura said.

"Hmm . . ." Edie lay on her back while Laura kissed her stomach and moved lower. "What about my full attention?" she murmured.

"Oh, I think I have that now," Laura said, spreading her legs and taking her in her mouth.

Edie ran her fingers through Laura's hair. "You do."

Laura looked up at her and smiled.

Later, showered and dressed, Edie kissed Laura on the cheek, grabbed a bagel and was flying toward the door.

"Edie, wait!" Laura said.

"I've got to go," Edie said.

"Dinner tonight, remember?"

Edie looked at her and registered a total blank.

Laura coached. "Bia and Julie . . ."

"Oh, yeah, how are they doing?" Edie asked, remembering that they were Laura's friends from Seattle. Julie had gotten a promotion at the computer software company she worked for and they had just relocated to Phoenix.

"They're fine."

"All settled in?"

"Yes." Laura said, "And . . ."

"And what? I give."

"Dinner tonight at Giorgio's, and then I thought we'd take them dancing. Show them the sights, you know."

"What time?"

"Six."

"Can I be slightly late?"

"By second round?"

"Yes," Edie said, kissing her and racing out the door.

"Don't forget!"

"I won't. I promise," Edie yelled over her shoulder.

That evening, Laura, Bia and Julie sat sipping cocktails in a corner booth near the front window in Giorgio's when Edie arrived.

"You said you'd be here by the second round," Laura said, looking fondly at Edie. "I was getting worried."

"And here I am," Edie said, patting Laura's hand. "I'm sorry I'm late. Traffic was hell."

"You nearly got yourself killed," Bia reprimanded. "I saw you come flying across the street almost getting run over on the way."

"And you must be?" Edie said, intentionally disregarding the comment.

"This is Bia and this is Julie. This is the infamous Edie," Laura said as the waiter handed Edie her much-needed drink.

"It's nice to meet you," Edie said, sitting back in the booth, running her hand through her hair. She took a deep breath.

"Busy day?" Bia inquired. She was a petite woman with brown hair and brown eyes and a slender pretty face. She was wearing a white linen dress and sandals.

"Every day is a busy day for Edie. If a day had twenty- eight hours in it, she'd figure out a way to fill them all," Laura said.

Edie smiled and said, "Luckily she puts up with me," looking kindly at Laura.

"So how did it go?" Laura asked.

"Mildly horrified, skeptical, patronizing, noncommittal—and that's the good news. They are, however, in need of a, quote, 'women's play' so if I took out the, quote, 'homosexual aspect,' which of course is basically the entire play, they might consider it." Edie rolled her eyes.

"So what did you say?" Laura asked in an innocent voice.

"I told them to go fuck themselves," Edie said matter-of-factly.

"Edie!" Laura said, clearly mortified.

Bia laughed hysterically. "That's good. I certainly admire your candor."

"Why thank you," Edie said appreciatively.

"I don't think telling the emissary from the NEA to go fuck himself is a good idea. You just cut your own throat," Laura said.

"They weren't going to give us the money anyway, and the whole idea behind their funding is for new art, not the same old shit repackaged. We'll figure something out but I'm not going to change it. Why bother doing it in the first place then?"

"What's the play about?" Julie asked. She seemed a mousy type with plain brown hair and glasses, but Edie appreciated her asking.

"It's called *Daughteronomy*. Imagine Moses as a lesbian diva and go from there," Edie said.

"I can see where getting funding might be a problem," Bia said.

"Who wrote it?" Julie asked.

"Oh, you know, a group of us tossed the idea around," Edie said.

"And Edie wrote it all down, painstakingly went over every line, edited it to perfection and then showed it to her friends. Thank God her friend Sandi is doing the production or Edie would have gone stark raving mad by now," Laura said.

"Yeah, it's true." Edie took a last sip of her drink and thought about having at least three more. Maybe then she'd feel human again. She was really beginning to understand why the playwrights she reviewed took it all so personally. Today as she stood in that boardroom she felt like she was experiencing artistic gang rape. And now she was tired, and disappointed, and in need of sleep.

"I think it sounds incredible. How did it all get started?" Julie said.

"Theater critics don't usually write plays," Bia said.

"My friend Sandi was tired of listening to me complain about the lack of plays about women and she dared me to write one. I told her I had to have a good wager to inspire me. So the deal was, if I could pull this off she'd go with me to the Galapagos Islands, and she had to promise to be an enthusiastic traveler."

"Quite the wager. Why the Galapagos Islands?" Bia asked.

"I've always wanted to go there but it's hard to find a fellow traveler," Edie said, remembering that she and Cassandra had been going to go the summer after graduation. Ever since then it was a pilgrimage for Edie that she knew she had to make one day.

Giorgio, a large man wearing a white outfit and chef's hat, came up to the table. "Oh, my darling Edie, it is you. I did not believe Ray. I come to see with my own eyes. We have missed you."

"Giorgio, I've been neglectful. We haven't been out much but when we come it's here," Edie said.

His face lit up. "Tonight then we make something special for you in honor of your reappearance. We do not like that little man that comes here. His words do not do us justice. But you, you use words like I do about food, words with flare and pizzazz," Giorgio said, bringing his fingers to his lips. "When you come back?"

"I'll tell you what, I'll make a guest appearance just for you," Edie said.

He smiled and leaned down to whisper in her ear. She nodded.

"Ladies," Giorgio said, "we'll take good care of you tonight." He snapped his fingers at the waiter who came promptly.

"One of the perks of being the food editor. The food is incredible and McNeil does tend to be less than thrilled with his present job assignment. I used to love doing the food route," Edie told them.

"But you gave it up?" Bia asked.

"I only did food to schmooze my way up the corporate ladder. I wanted to know everything about the magazine business, so I've basically covered it all. I'm the senior editor now but I still write some of the theater articles in my spare time."

"Not everyone has your energy for things," Laura said.

Edie eased back into her wine and hoped the conversation spotlight was going to turn to someone else. She'd been "on" all day and was fast losing her wind.

Dinner was full of culinary surprises and Giorgio's constant fluttering attentions. Edie was gracious and appreciative, witty and delightful, but what she really wanted to do was have a glass of wine, sit in the tub and look over the play again. She knew that after today there would be things she'd need to fix, not as the art committee had recommended but other things. Laura's friends were nice and Bia was perfectly darling, but Edie wasn't in the mood to play.

When she eased back in the seat of the Porsche with Bia at her side, after Laura insisted that they ride separately so no one would get lost on the way to the Crowbar, she looked over at Bia and said, "This is all bullshit, isn't it?"

Bia laughed. "I wondered when you were going to come clean."

"This play thing is about coming clean but I didn't think it was going to be so difficult," Edie said, taking a good look at her.

"It's difficult because it's honest and it's art. Those are the requirements," Bia said.

"You know the magazine is about schmoozing and politics and sardonic writing aimed at snooty intellectuals, but it doesn't have substance. I want substance. I don't want to spend the rest of my life stroking people like Giorgio."

"You want to be the one to make things and have people stroke you," Bia chided.

"I want to make things. We can skip the stroking part."

"I think it comes with the territory."

Edie nodded and started the car; the stereo was still on and came blasting out.

"Whoops, sorry about that," Edie said, flipping the CD out.

"Quite all right," Bia said, putting her seat belt on.

Edie pulled a joint out of the visor. "Got a perk from a friend today. I thought I might need a little cheering up after the corporate debacle. Interested?" Edie asked.

Bia smiled. "Love to. You're not as domesticated as Laura thinks."

Edie handed Bia the joint and lit a match. "And as I see it, neither are you."

"No," Bia said, taking a long drag, leaning back in her seat. She clicked the CD back in.

Edie pulled out quickly and barely made the yellow light. "I like you already," she said, taking the joint from Bia.

"Ditto," Bia replied. "Do you always drive like a maniac?"

"Yes."

Bia laughed.

They sat at a table, ordered drinks and watched the dance floor. Edie drummed her fingers to the techno music.

Laura rolled her eyes. "Go dance, take Bia with you."

Edie looked over at Bia with a gleam in her eye. "You like to dance?"

85

"Love to, but unfortunately . . ." She glanced over at Julie.

"I have no rhythm," Julie said. "Please take her dancing so Laura and I can tell tales about you two."

Edie jumped up. "Let's go." She grabbed Bia's hand and they headed for the dance floor.

"She's a definite keeper," Julie said.

"You think so?" Laura said.

"Come on. She's cute, driven, devoted. What more could you want?" Julie said.

"I get worried sometimes. I wonder if I can keep up," Laura said, watching Edie and Bia dancing together.

"She is a ball of fire."

"It's crazy, though. She runs like this until she drops, sleeps for a day and then starts all over again. I worry about her," Laura said, looking at Julie and feeling like a novice seeking advice.

"Are you asking me if I know what that might be like?"

"Yes," Laura said, chuckling.

"You let them run because if you try to pen her it won't work. People like Bia and Edie need all that stimulation or else they wilt. I know that it's difficult living with someone who needs to be involved in a million projects, but it's what attracted us to them in the first place. It's not fair to expect them to give it up to make us happy. People run at different speeds."

"You're right. I'm glad they hit it off. Edie needs a friend like Bia, someone to run with. She used to have a lot of girlfriends—at the same time—and sometimes it makes me wonder . . . you know, I'd like her to have someone to play with."

"Someone safe?" Julie inquired.

"Well, yes."

"Bia's safe."

"I know."

ᙙᙖ

On Sunday morning Edie was typing up one of her articles for the upcoming week when she looked up to see Bia standing in the doorway of the study. The study had been Laura's enticement for getting her to move in. Moving in was more a matter of bringing her clothes over and spending every night there. Laura wanted them to live together and Edie was anxious about it, but the time had come to settle in or flee. Laura had offered to sell her house and get one together but Edie loved the house.

She did not, however, sell off the loft, much to Laura's chagrin. Laura saw it as a lack of faith. Edie viewed it as a sound business decision. She had gotten the loft for a song and was hard put to let it go. Laura accepted her explanation that the loft was close to downtown and could serve as an office and a workspace for the play. Laura was slowly coming to terms that there would always be parts of Edie she would not understand.

"Haven't you ever heard of weekends?" Bia asked.

"No, explain them to me," Edie shot back.

"Well, you see, they're these things that come in between work, a time you go and have fun," Bia replied.

"Do I have to?"

"It's good for you."

"Perhaps you could teach me."

"Has anyone ever told you that you have the most incredible blue eyes?" Bia said, coming to sit on the corner of the desk.

"Has anyone ever told you that you're beautiful?"

"Are you flirting with me?" Bia asked, her face a mixture of surprise and delight.

"I would never," Edie said.

"Good, because you know I'm a married woman."

"Ditto."

"Are you coming golfing?"

"Not likely. I'm a hazard with a golf club, but I might be enticed to come have a drink if I could flirt with you again," Edie said, knowing she was crossing the line and not caring.

"Then you must."

"I'll see you around the thirteenth hole," Edie said.

"I'll be waiting," Bia said.

That afternoon Edie came romping across the golf course carrying a gym bag and dressed in gym apparel. She jumped up on the cart, startling Bia.

"What hole are we on?"

"The ninth," Bia said. "You're early."

"How come you're not playing?"

"I'm like you, a hazard with a golf club."

"Why are you here?"

"I like the scenery. I like to drive golf carts and I like to drink beer."

"I brought more," Edie said, pulling a six-pack of Hornsby Hard Cider out of her gym bag. "It's contraband at the country club. Do you like it?"

"I do. It's a good sipping beverage."

"I needed to come sip."

"Did you get your stuff done?"

"Yes, finally. It's the play. It cuts into work at the magazine."

"Work does suck, it cuts into fun time but of course you don't have any concept of fun." Bia grinned.

"I do," Edie said indignantly.

"Could've fooled me," Bia said, opening them both a bottle of cider. "Tell me how you play."

"What do you mean?"

"What do you do for fun?"

"Go to the gym, take long walks, read, fix the car, socialize," Edie said.

"Gym and walks are exercise, reading is probably masquerading as research, and socializing usually has a business edge to it."

"I play. I know how to play. Right now I'm playing with you," Edie said. Her cell phone rang.

Bia rolled her eyes.

"It's a pleasure call," Edie whispered, glancing at the caller ID.

"You're lying."

"I am," Edie said.

"So we can finally see the theater and talk to the guy, but it has to be, like, now," Sandi said, her voice crackling across the line.

"Sandi, I'm on the golf course in my gym outfit. I'll never make it. No, I don't have clothes at the loft. Laura made me move them all to the house or otherwise I wasn't truly moving in. Shit, I hate not being centrally located."

"Edie, you've got to be here in twenty minutes," Sandi said. "You can do it."

Edie had her gym bag out on the green and was rooting through it. "Okay, but run me through the details while I figure this out."

Bia sat chuckling as Edie held up remnants of outfits she had stuffed in her bag. She ended up with a pair of black jeans and a flannel shirt that was wrinkled and had a hole in the sleeve.

"What does this guy dress like?" Edie asked.

"In a suit and tie," Sandi replied.

"Fuck," Edie said, holding up a smelly T-shirt.

Bia shook her head.

"Edie, what are you doing?" Laura screamed across the green.

"Getting ready for a meeting," Edie called out in reply.

"Sandi, I've got to go. I'll be there."

Bia took off her polo shirt.

"What are you doing?"

"Giving you my shirt. It's the best we're going to do."

Edie gave her the bad flannel. "It's not going to go over big at the clubhouse."

"Fuck them," Bia said.

"You're incredible," Edie said, putting her gym bag back together. "You and Julie are still coming for dinner, right?"

"Yes. Edie, one day I want to teach you to play."

"Okay."

She took off running toward Laura and pecked her on the cheek. "Where are you going?" Laura asked.

"I'll explain later. See you at dinner," Edie said, taking off at a quick sprint for the car.

Bia made it her summer project to teach Edie to play. They took up racquetball together, for the fun of it. They went to lunch everyday someplace entirely different, foraging the distant and obscure corners of the city, for the adventure of it. Bia bought Edie *Cosmic Ray's Hiking Book* and they tried to get themselves killed on eco-challenge psycho-hikes. They'd come home scraped up and bloody but smiling and happy.

They had gone hiking on a beautiful but crisp Arizona winter morning, meaning it was in the fifties and you got to wear a sweater. Bia was standing on a boulder in a wash doing a masterful impression of her boss in the process of pontificating on her poor copyediting skills. Edie was laughing hysterically. Bia put her hand on her hip and smiled at Edie. Edie realized at that moment that she was in love with her best friend. Part of her was elated, but a strange terror seized the rest of her. So she buried her revelation and only took it out carefully when she was alone to examine how deeply and utterly she loved Bia. Looking for clues to how she felt, she went over moments they had together and everything they did. It was frightening.

Then it happened, the confession of all confessions. They had finished playing racquetball. They were showering in separate stalls—the height of eroticism, Edie thought, knowing Bia was so near and naked, trying to picture what she looked like as she soaped away sweat.

"You let me win again," Edie said.

"I didn't let you win. It was fair and square. You're a better racquetball player."

"The universe is not fair and I am not better," Edie said, meeting her outside the shower and snapping her with a towel.

90

Bia snapped her back with precision aim.

"Ouch! You are, however, better with a towel," Edie said, grabbing her from behind and winding her towel around Bia's waist so Bia's towel would no longer be a weapon, and then they were hugging each other in that clumsy, first-lover kind of way. They were both clearly surprised. Bia touched Edie's face, softly, with a strange, sad look in her eyes.

"What's wrong?" Edie asked, alarmed.

"Would you be angry with me if I told you that I had fallen in love with you?" Bia said, her face etched in seriousness.

Edie pulled away.

"I'm sorry. I shouldn't have said that," Bia said.

"No, it's not that," Edie said, scooping her back up in her arms. "I'm so scared. You make me feel things I know I shouldn't feel. I love you and I know I'm not supposed to, but I can't help it. But I know you love Julie, and Laura's your best friend." Edie started to cry.

"Don't cry, please don't cry," Bia said, wiping the tears away.

"But I want to hold you, touch you, feel you," Edie said.

Right then the volleyball team came streaming in the locker room. Edie backed away.

"We'll talk later, okay?" Bia said.

"Laura's picking me up for her office party tonight," Edie said.

"I know. Soon?"

"I'll make you dinner tomorrow night at the loft," Edie said.

"Perfect. Make it a late night?"

"Please."

Bia held her tight and whispered, "It's not bad, Edie. It's not. Love is never bad."

"I know," Edie said, taking her hand.

"There you are," Laura called out, strolling into the locker room.

"Hi, Laura," Bia said.

"Are you all right?" Laura asked Edie.

"She's fine, just being her usual stress monkey self," Bia answered for her.

"Are you ready?" Laura asked.

"Let me grab my stuff," Edie said.

"I'll meet you out front," Laura said, kissing Bia's cheek. "Tell Julie hi and we'll see you guys this weekend for the barbecue?"

"Yes."

"I'll be right there," Edie said.

"Edie," Bia said, catching her arm.

Edie turned to look at her. "I don't care what happens. I love you and I'm glad you love me." She pulled her close and then grabbed her bag and walked away.

"Edie," Bia said.

Edie turned.

"Ditto."

"See you tomorrow," Edie said.

"I can't wait," Bia said, touching her fingers to her lips and sending Edie a kiss.

Edie blushed and had to tear herself away.

Later that night, Edie fell asleep dreaming of Bia and for the first time she wasn't frightened. The universe wasn't fair but it believed in true love.

In the morning watching Laura sleep, Edie freaked. She'd made herself swear that she wasn't going to cheat, that when she entered this relationship that she would not stray, and now she was straying. She called Bia.

"Hi," Bia said.

"I need to think. I'm going to take a few days off and go somewhere."

"Okay," Bia said.

"I'm sorry," Edie blurted.

"Don't be sorry, just go think," Bia said.

"I'll call you when I get back."

"All right."

"Bia?"

"Yes?"

"I love you."

"I know," Bia said.

"You're going where?" Laura asked.

"I need to go to Sedona for a few days. I'll be back Monday," Edie said, rapidly shoving clothes in a duffle bag.

"But what about the barbecue?" Laura asked, clearly alarmed.

"I'm sorry," Edie said, avoiding her eyes.

"Edie, what is this about?"

"Nothing. I just need to go," Edie said.

"You're running."

"I'm not running," Edie said.

When Edie got back, she could see that Laura was attempting to be sympathetic, at least initially.

"I know the play and work are taking a lot out of you but leaving like that worries me," Laura said.

"I'm fine. I just needed to get a grip on things, and I didn't think it was a good thing to put you through it," Edie said, setting her bag down.

"Edie, what's going on?"

"Nothing," Edie said, avoiding Laura's gaze.

"I can't help you if you won't talk to me."

"I don't have anything to say."

"I can't handle your guest appearances and I can't handle you walking out of our lives," Laura said. "I feel like I don't even know you anymore."

"I'm fine, we're fine."

"No, we're not fine. I have to try to explain to our friends why you took off and I don't know why. I'm not going live like this. You have to talk to me. And this thing with the play . . . you're so distracted. I need you, damn it, and you're not there. This isn't good," Laura said, her face red with anger.

Edie stood mute.

"Talk to me!"

"There is nothing to say."

"Tell me how you feel. This isn't fair, Edie."

"Life isn't fair."

"That's lame," Laura said.

Edie shrugged her shoulders.

"Tell me what is going on in your head."

"I can't," Edie said.

"Are you even listening to me?"

"I am listening."

"But are you hearing me? What am I saying?"

"That you're unhappy."

"You are a rocket scientist after all," Laura taunted.

Edie felt herself losing it.

"Well, what do you have to say for yourself?"

"If you continue to talk to me in this fashion, you can go fuck yourself," Edie said.

Laura slapped her. The blow stung. They stood staring at each other.

"There are a lot of things I will tolerate. *That* is not one of them," Edie said, picking up her bag and turning to leave.

"Edie, wait."

"No," Edie said, closing the door behind her.

Laura called Bia.

"Slow down, I can't understand you."

Laura was sobbing into the phone.

"Tell me what happened," Bia said.

"We got in a fight. She's so distant. I can't stand it. I just wanted her to talk to me and she wouldn't, and then she told me if I continued to act in this fashion I could go fuck myself."

Bia restrained herself from laughing. She started to say that everything would be all right.

"And then I hit her," Laura blurted.

"You *hit* her?" Bia said, instantly appalled.

"I didn't mean to, it just sort of happened."

"Where is she?"

"I don't know. She left."

"Oh, Laura."

"I know it's bad. I didn't mean to . . ."

"I know you didn't," Bia said.

"What should I do?"

"Let her chill and go see her tomorrow . . . preferably with flowers," Bia advised.

"I feel so bad."

"It's okay," Bia said. She hung up the phone and looked over at Julie.

"I'm going to see Edie."

Julie nodded. "Does Laura know?"

"No, she doesn't. She thinks Edie is just behaving badly."

"I see."

"I might not come home tonight," Bia said.

"I figured as much."

"I know you know what this is about, so if you want to leave me you are perfectly within your rights to do so," Bia said.

"Do you want me to?"

"No, I love you and I can't imagine my life without you but I need to do this too."

"All right," Julie said.

Bia turned to leave. "Julie?"

"Yes."

"If circumstances were different would you still let me have my cake and eat it too?"

"I don't know. I think it's hard to expect one person to fulfill all of their partner's needs, for one person to belong exclusively to another, but I do not promote nonmonogamy for its own end. I know you care deeply for Edie, and whatever shape it gives your relationship is up to you, but I don't want to know about it and I don't want to ever talk about it again."

"I understand."

Bia went to the loft and Edie answered the door with a large Scotch in hand. "Hi," she said.

"Are you okay?" Bia asked hesitantly.

"Were you sent on a reconnaissance mission?" Edie took a sip of Scotch.

"No, Laura doesn't know I'm here."

"But she called you."

"Yes," Bia said.

"Want a drink?"

"Please," Bia said.

Edie poured her a drink, handed it to her and leaned up against the kitchen bar.

"I didn't mean for this to happen," Bia said.

"I know," Edie said, taking another sip.

"We could forget about it," Bia said. "I don't want to fuck up your life."

"You make my life," Edie said.

"Edie . . ."

"If I can't be your wife I want to be your lover," Edie said.

Bia walked toward her. She took Edie's face in hands, looked at her hard and then kissed her deeply. "I love you, I want you, and I need you."

Edie took her hand and led her to the bed. She kissed her neck and unbuttoned her shirt, taking her breasts softly in her mouth, slipping her shirt from her shoulders, kissing her stomach. Kneeling, she undid her shorts, sliding her panties down, and took her in her mouth. Bia moved her to the bed, wrapping her legs around her shoulders.

Edie looked up at her. "I have never wanted anyone as much as I want you."

"Oh, Edie . . ."

Later, as they lay in each other's arms, they touched each other with the tenderness of lovers already deep in love.

"You make me feel things that I didn't know I possessed," Edie said, pulling Bia closer, her body wrapped around her.

Bia nestled in Edie's neck, reaching for her again, finding her wet, making her fingers go deep. Murmuring a language that only passion knows, they made love again and then again until night turned to day. With Bia sleeping in her arms, Edie thought, *Now my life is complete.*

In the morning Edie stirred and woke. Bia touched her face.

"It wasn't a dream," Edie said.

"It was better," Bia said, leaning up on one elbow.

Edie rolled into her, nestling her face between Bia's breasts, making happy, murmuring noises.

Bia stroked her hair. "I hate to be the pooper at this party but . . ."

"I know. What time is it?"

"Eight-thirty."

Edie looked up at her. "Don't you wish we could go someplace void of obligations and commitments and just enjoy ourselves?"

"I think I went there last night," Bia said, getting up.

After they'd washed up and gotten dressed, Edie sat on the edge of the bed and put on her shoes. Bia put on her coat and came over to kiss her good-bye, then headed for the door.

"Bia?" Edie said.

"Yes, darling," Bia said, turning.

"This wasn't a one-time thing?" Edie asked.

Bia laughed. She came over, sat on the edge of the bed and took Edie's hand. "No, I hardly think making love to you one night even begins to appease my appetite."

Edie smiled. "And that's okay?"

"Yes, very much okay," Bia said.

"You're not in trouble?"

"Only if I'm late for work," Bia replied.

Edie knew then that making arrangements about the time they spent together was something they would do but not discuss.

Laura waited until after lunch to go see Edie. Times like these she was glad they no longer worked in the same building. The *Phoenician* magazine had outgrown their current office space so they had rented an additional space down the block. She went to the florist and picked up half a dozen bright yellow sunflowers, Edie's favorite. When she got to her office, though, Verna, Edie's new secretary, told her she'd gone home for the day.

"She was completely fagged out," Verna said, sliding her overly large cat's-eye frames up her slender nose.

Laura had never gotten used to Verna's strange, British slang, and only Edie would have hired such an eccentric woman for a secretary. She looked like something out of a bad Sixties film.

"Nice flowers. Pity she's not here," Verna said.

Laura looked down at the flowers and suddenly felt stupid.

Verna smiled sweetly and leaned her head to one side and waited for Laura to make her next move.

"I guess I'll see her at home then," Laura said.

"Guess you will," Verna replied.

Laura left feeling angry for not knowing where Edie was and for holding those stupid flowers and having no one to give them to. She was half tempted to hand them to the first downcast stranger she met on the street and be done with the whole thing. Instead, she dialed

Cynthia, her secretary, from her cell phone and told her she wouldn't be back to the office. She requested her day's assignments to be faxed to her at home.

"Not feeling well?" Cynthia chirped into the phone.

"No, I'm not. I'll finish it up later. Just fax the stuff, will you," Laura muttered.

"Consider it there," Cynthia replied in her best singsong voice.

Secretaries and significant others . . . the bane of an urban woman's existence, Laura thought as she cut across town and made for home. Her heart leapt when she saw Edie's Porsche in the driveway. Then she suffered a swift adrenal rush when she realized Edie might be home to get her things and get out. Laura crept inside the house. It was quiet, no sound of someone packing, and no evidence of Edie working in the study or out on the veranda having a cocktail. Puzzled, she went upstairs to the bedroom.

Edie was face down on the bed, fully dressed and fast asleep. Laura sat down on the bed next to her and stroked her hair, pushing it off her face. Edie opened her eyes and smiled.

"I'm so sorry," Laura said.

"Hold me," Edie said.

Laura held her and started to cry softly.

"Don't cry. This was my fault. I promise to be a better partner. It was just all the pressure from the play. I should have told you," Edie said.

Laura didn't know whether or not to believe her. "Maybe you should take some time off work. Oswald will cover for you," she suggested, giving Edie the benefit of the doubt.

"I think you're right. Come on, let's go have a drink and talk," Edie said.

It wasn't as difficult as Edie had anticipated. Laura and Julie were used to her and Bia spending time together. Now, instead of going out to breakfast and reading the paper on Sunday morning while the girls went golfing, they spent it in bed. Their friendship now included making love and being in love, but it didn't threaten their primary relationships, and in that Edie began to enjoy the freedom of being Bia's lover but not her partner.

"It's like Candide's best of all possible worlds. You can love me but you're not obligated to me," Bia had told her. And she was right. Edie felt a lot less pressure. She was a better partner with Laura because she wanted to make their time together special, she guessed in part to assuage her own guilty conscience for straying. Laura thought Bia was a miracle worker for turning Edie into the most wonderful and thoughtful partner. And sometimes Edie marveled at Bia's amazing ability to be a wife, a mistress and Laura's best friend all with the same incredible amoral grace and finesse. She felt guilty, yet Bia never looked better. Edie was hard put not to think that it would be better if they came clean, but Bia wouldn't have it.

"You're amazing," Edie said, as they stood in the aisle at Petsmart picking up dog food, balls and bones for Lance, Bia and Julie's little dog.

"You're just saying that because I devoted my lunch hour to your sexual fulfillment," Bia said.

"That might be influencing my judgment," Edie said, as she hoisted their purchases up on the checkout counter.

"I daresay it is," Bia said, digging in her wallet.

Edie came up behind her and whispered in her ear, "You missed some whipped cream." She ran her finger behind Bia's earlobe.

Bia turned. "You said I was all clean."

"You are. I'm teasing. Of course, I don't think I'll ever look at fruit in quite the same way," Edie said, thinking of the marvels of their afternoon liaison. Edie had convinced Oswald that she needed longer lunch breaks, and Bia only worked part-time. They met every afternoon and had dinner together when Laura was busy.

"Let's go buy some new sheets while we're at it," Bia said.

"So we can initiate them later?"

"Yes," Bia said, picking up the dog food.

Edie took it from her and tucked it under her arm. Bia looked at her quizzically.

"I never got to carry your books at school," Edie explained, taking her hand as they headed across the parking lot.

Edie opened the car door for Bia and threw the dog food in the back. Going around to her side of the car, she looked over to see a pretty, blonde woman struggling to get a fifty-pound bag of food out of the shopping cart and into the back of her Land Cruiser.

"Here, let me help," Edie said, grabbing one end of the dog food. Together they hoisted it into the back of the SUV. Edie's sunglasses had slid down her nose.

"Aren't you Cassandra Hollander's friend?" the blonde woman asked, staring at her.

"Yes, we met that day at the university. You were waiting for Kirsten. Vida, right?" Edie said.

"Yes. You're Edie."

Bertrand licked Edie's shoe.

"He likes leather," Vida explained.

"Well, hi there," Edie said, leaning down to pet him. "He's beautiful. What's his name?"

"Bertrand," Vida said, never taking her eyes off Edie.

"Like Bertrand Russell?"

"His namesake."

"Good name," Edie said. They stood quietly looking at each other until Bertand pulled on his leash.

"Thanks for helping," Vida said.

"No problem," Edie said, turning to walk off and then, catching Vida's gaze one more time, she stopped for a moment.

"Pretty lady," Bia said, as they pulled out of the parking lot.

"Yes," Edie said, distracted.

"What are you thinking?" Bia asked, obviously intrigued.

"It was strange looking at her, like I was traveling somewhere."

"Mild euphoria, mild fatigue, mild depression from cocktails at lunch, and your alpha waves could be at ten cycles per second, which produces telepathy in some people," Bia replied.

"What do you mean?"

"You were reading her mind."

"It was like we were going to get to know each other, not now but later."

"Maybe she's your next girlfriend," Bia said.

"I've got more than I can handle right now," Edie said.

"Right now isn't forever, Edie," Bia said.

Puzzled, Edie looked over at her. "Are we calling it quits?"

"Not so long as I have breath in me," Bia said.

Edie breathed a sigh of relief. "I couldn't live without you," she said, taking her hand and kissing it.

Bia touched her cheek and smiled. "I know, me either."

"I still wish we could live together," Edie said, tentatively looking in Bia's direction as she pulled on to the Squaw Peak Parkway.

"Edie, who do you spend more time with, Laura or me?"

"You."

"And who do you make love with more often?"

"You."

"And who do you piss off on a more consistent basis?"

"Laura."

"And who do you fight with more often?"

"Laura."

"So why would you want to live with me?"

"I miss you when I'm not with you," Edie whined.

"I know. I miss you too."

"Someday, maybe, when we're old and gray and it wouldn't matter anymore," Edie said.

"Okay," Bia said.

"I wish it could be before then."

"Someday, Edie, you'll understand why I won't let our love ruin your life, and you'll thank me," Bia said.

"Oh, you and your mysteries," Edie said.

"Somebody has to keep you jumping."

"And you do."

Bia smiled. "Where are we going?" They'd passed Bethany Home and were approaching Northern.

"To car-fuck in the reserve and see if we can get arrested by the park police. I'm taking the afternoon off, remember?"

"I'm game for the first part, but let's try and avoid the second." Bia ran her hand up Edie's thigh.

"Are we ever going to get tired of each other?" Edie asked.

"Are we full of questions today or what? No, I still crave you on an hourly basis and I doubt that will ever change."

"Why is that?"

"Because we're lovers and not partners. I'm convinced domesticity kills lust."

Edie nodded, parked the car and pulled Bia close to her.

"I'll give you that," Edie said.

"You'll give me more than that," Bia said, reaching for her.

Chapter Eight

The following Monday afternoon, Edie came running up the stairs to the loft. A business meeting had kept her late. Luckily, Bia was taking some time off, so she arranged her schedule around Edie's odd hours.

"Are you sore?" Bia asked, taking off Edie's clothes.

"Sore?"

"From fucking Laura all weekend."

Edie was shocked. "How did you know about that?"

"Laura told me. She said it was wonderful," Bia replied, easing Edie back on the bed.

"What else do you two talk about?"

"You. She loves to talk about you and so do I. We have a lot in common that way," Bia said.

"I feel guilty about sleeping with her," Edie said.

"Edie, she's your wife."

"I know, but I feel like I'm cheating on you." Edie took off Bia's shirt and kissed her shoulder.

"You and Laura are supposed to make love. It's a part of a good relationship."

"You're not jealous?"

"No, I want you to make Laura happy," Bia said, running her hands across Edie's breasts.

"What about you?" Edie asked.

"You make me happy. Are you ever jealous of Julie?" Bia smiled.

"You two don't make love anymore."

"We do sometimes," Bia said, taking one of Edie's wrists and tying it to the bedpost.

"Then I am jealous," Edie said, watching Bia tie her other wrist to the bed, thinking for a moment that this was a strange topic to be discussing prior to soft bondage sex.

"I knew you would be."

"Is that why you said it?" Edie asked.

"Yes and no. I wanted to see if you cared enough to be jealous," Bia said.

"I do. I love you more than anything or anyone."

"That's good."

"What's making love to Julie like?"

"Is this okay?"

"Oh, yes," Edie said. "Feeling a little wild today?"

"Uh-huh. I don't want you to think that marital sex is all there is."

"Never. But you didn't answer my question."

"Making love to Julie is gentle, more about talking and connection than sex. Lots of foreplay and then coming."

"Not like this?" Edie asked.

"No, not like this." Bia smiled.

"Was it ever like this?"

"No, we're older. Remember?"

"But you and Julie were younger once."

"Oh, you. That's enough talk," Bia said, taking Edie in her mouth and slowly inserting her finger up Edie's butt.

"When did we get these?" Edie said, indicating the rope cords.

"Today. They're a present. Like them?" Bia said, looking up.

"Yes, very much."

"If this doesn't give you twelve-second multiple orgasms nothing will."

Edie did have twelve-second multiple orgasms. She pulled at the ropes, begging for Bia to stop, which of course she didn't. When the deed was done, Bia crawled up and lay on Edie's stomach. Edie opened her eyes and smiled.

"Oh, my," Edie said.

Bia straddled her and began gently thrusting against her.

"I want to touch you," Edie said, pulling at the cords.

Bia teased her. She stuck her finger inside herself and pulled it out, placing it slowly in Edie's mouth. She did it again and again with Edie pleading with her to let her go. Instead, Bia set herself down on Edie's face. Edie dove inside her while Bia moaned softly and finally collapsed on Edie's chest.

Later as they lay in each other's arms, Edie whispered a litany of *how I love you* and neither of them doubted she did.

"I don't care who you slept with as long as you always come back to me," Edie said.

"And I will . . . always," Bia said, dragging Edie off to the bath.

When Laura came home from work that evening she found Edie fast asleep on the bed. She sat down next to her and thought about the wonderful weekend they'd spent together and how incredible her wife was. She went downstairs and made dinner, waiting for Edie to rise from the dead and be her ever-charming dinner companion. When Edie rose she was subdued at dinner.

"I'm sorry," Edie said, slumping down at the kitchen bar.

"It's okay, sweetheart. I know you have a lot going on."

106

"And that's all right?"

"Yes, I love you and I really am trying to understand," Laura said, wrapping her arms around her.

"You're a good woman," Edie said.

"You *are* incredible," Laura said, smiling.

Edie touched her face. "So are you."

A couple days later Sandi stood at the door of the loft. She needed to talk to Edie about the play and Verna, her secretary, told her she'd gone home for the day. Sandi called from her car phone to discover no one was home at Laura's. She was taking a chance on the loft. When she pulled in the garage at the loft and saw the Porsche she knew. The elevator had an out of order sign on it so she climbed up the four flights of stairs.

Rather than buzz, Sandi used the key Edie had given her as a backup. She heard music playing. Edie went home for the day all right, Sandi thought smugly: her home away from home and the office. She stuck her head in door and called out but didn't hear any response until she crept inside. She looked over and saw Edie in the bed. She thought for a second it was Edie and Laura making love, sitting up wrapped around each other, the sheets covering their lower halves, thrusting toward each other, making lovers' noises. Sandi was feeling the acute sensation of being a voyeur. Then she saw the woman she assumed was Laura. She wasn't a blonde. She wasn't Laura. She heard them coming together. Sandi tried to back out of the room but it was too late. She knocked against a table. Edie turned around and saw her.

Sandi stood paralyzed for a moment. The woman looked over Edie's shoulder. It was Bia.

"Oh, fuck," Edie said, as Sandi tried to leave. Edie grabbed the sheet, wrapped it around her and flew out the door after her. "Sandi, wait!" Edie cried out.

She caught Sandi on the stairs.

"Edie, what are you doing?"

"I think *that* was fairly obvious," Edie said.

"This isn't funny, Edie," Sandi said, appalled. "I thought you loved Laura. I thought you weren't going to do things like this anymore."

"I do love Laura."

"Then why are you sleeping with Bia?"

"It's complicated. I love her too."

"Too?"

"Well, yes. Sandi, I can't really explain it. I don't want to hurt Laura but this thing is something neither of us can get around."

Just then the art dykes, who lived next door to Edie, came up the stairs. One of them grabbed the corner of Edie's sheet and threatened to pull. Edie snatched it back.

Bia came out on the landing. "Edie, is everything okay?"

"Yes," Edie said.

"Hi, Sandi," Bia said.

The art dykes rolled their eyes at each other. "She gets more traffic," one said.

"Hey, Edie, when you're done there come over and give us a try."

"Don't tempt me."

"Edie, this isn't good. You're supposed to be a committed woman and you're still playing around," Sandi lectured.

"It's not like that," Edie said.

"What's it like then?"

"I don't know. I am madly in love with Bia and would marry her in a second if she'd let me but I still have feelings for Laura and would hate to let her down. Bia is my soul mate and Laura is my wife. How's that?" Edie said.

Sandi looked at Edie and then Bia. "Look, as far as I'm concerned I didn't see anything and I don't know anything. And I don't want to know anything."

Edie nodded and so did Bia.

∞

"Do you think the universe conspires to create deception?" Edie asked Bia as they lay together after Sandi left.

"I think the universe believes in love, sees it as its best creation and does everything in its power to make it grow," Bia said, kissing Edie's eyes closed.

"Love is beyond rules," Edie murmured.

"Yes, I think so. Look, my favorite place on the planet is between your legs. Unfortunately we have other partners who I don't think we should give up, for reasons I absolutely refuse to reveal."

"This isn't good, you know. I don't want to hurt Laura but I don't want to be without you. These rules are yours and I don't think I can abide by them forever."

"You'll have to," Bia said.

"I know. But I stand in protest."

"Protest noted," Bia said, getting up and starting to dress.

Edie lay on the bed and watched her.

"Edie, there's something I need to tell you."

"Yes."

"I went to the doctor the other day and . . ."

"And you're fit as a fiddle," Edie said, feeling her heart start to race.

"Not exactly. Three years ago I was diagnosed with leukemia."

"What?" Edie said, jumping up.

"It was in remission, but now it's back," Bia said, coming to sit next to her.

"I see," Edie said. Her chest got tight.

"This doesn't mean with treatment something can't be done."

"You could still get better," Edie said, putting her hand to her nose. It had started to bleed.

She got up and went to the bathroom to get a towel. Her heart was racing and she felt like she was going to puke.

"Edie, are you all right?" Bia called out.

"I'm fine," Edie said, shoving the towel in her face to drown out the sobs.

They'd circled the campus grounds for the third time to no avail. It reminded Edie of going to school and never finding parking and then paying a lot of parking tickets. Some things never change.

"Fuck!" Edie said. "This is ridiculous."

"Once you have it where to park it," Bia said, quoting a line from their favorite lesbian movie.

"*Costa Brava*," Edie replied.

"Very good," Bia said, smiling and squeezing Edie's hand.

Edie smiled back.

"You know, everything is going to be fine," Bia said.

Edie nodded, thinking back to the afternoon. For Bia's sake she would pretend to be all right, but later, when she was alone she knew she'd break. She could feel herself standing on the edge, with a sense of sheer panic eating away her insides. Edie didn't believe in Bia's optimism. She knew Bia would not have mentioned the leukemia if something was not afoot. Everything could work out, but that same sense of losing Edie had felt before when she knew she was losing Cassandra was coming up fast behind her. She could feel its breath on her neck and she knew it would happen again: That which she had loved too deeply would be taken.

"Are you sure you're okay?"

"Positive," Edie responded with false bravado, thinking this was the first time she'd lied to Bia.

"I don't want *this* to come between us," Bia said, looking at Edie with an uncertainty Edie hadn't seen before.

"Nothing will ever come between us. You're my soul mate."

Bia kissed her hand.

"I have an idea," she said. She flipped a quick u-turn and headed down the central corridor of the university toward the theater building.

"I sense a parking violation," Bia said.

"It won't be."

She pulled up in front of the theater building.

"Edie, they'll tow it if you park here."

"We're not parking here. I'm letting you out to go open the doors."

"Both of them?" Bia said, getting out.

"Uh-huh."

"Are you going to do what I think you're going to?"

"I swear you're the only one who understands me," Edie said. She swung the car wide, pulled in the side mirrors and slowly drove the Porsche up the eight concrete steps and into the lobby. She backed it around so it faced the front doors, in case they had to make a rapid departure. Bia clapped as Edie got out of the car.

"You *are* simply amazing," Bia said.

"I think this calls for a bit of the bubbly," Edie said, taking Bia's arm and leading her to the concession stand where she bought them both a glass of Champagne.

"Cheers," Edie said.

"Cheers," Bia said.

"I'm not going to think about you dying," Edie blurted.

"I'm not going to let you," Bia said.

They stood watching as people arrived for the class play and looked at the car parked in the lobby. Julie and Laura arrived. Edie got them Champagne and Bia and herself another.

"God made drink so that we could be jubilant," Edie said.

"And the devil created the hangover so we'd know suffering," Bia said.

"Sometimes I wonder if the two of you aren't becoming the same person," Julie chided.

"It's known as TLB syndrome. It happens to people who spend a lot of time together," Edie said.

"TLB?" Julie asked.

"Typical Lesbian Behavior," Bia answered.

Julie laughed. "Only you two would come up with that."

Laura got a strange look on her face and looked quizzically at Edie. "Edie, isn't that *your car* parked in the lobby?"

"As a matter of fact it is," Edie said.

"What is it doing there?" Laura inquired.

"I couldn't find a parking space."

"You can't park it there," Laura said.

"Sure I can. It's parked, isn't it?"

"Oh, no, there's the Dean of the College," Laura said. "How are you going to explain this?"

"Watch," Edie said. The dean was a friend of Edie's father's. And Edie spent her four years of college on the dean's honor list.

"Edie Farnsworth, my goodness. I haven't seen you in ages. How is your father?" the dean asked.

"Good. Very good."

"How's that play of yours coming along? I'm looking forward to my favorite student resting on her own laurels for once."

"I'm getting there."

"I say, isn't that your little bathtub Porsche?" he said, pointing to the car.

Laura looked at Edie with raised eyebrows and a sense of vindication written across her face.

"Yes, it is."

"Couldn't find a place to park, eh?"

"Parking hasn't improved since I was a student."

"You always were ingenious. Don't run anyone over on your way out," he advised.

"I won't."

"Well, let's go see this latest montage of underdeveloped talent." He looked over at security and waved his okay; they walked off.

"I can't believe it," Laura said. "Are you accountable to no one?"

"God in charge of jubilation," Edie replied.

"And the devil in charge of suffering," Bia finished.

They both laughed.

Julie shrugged. She took Laura's hand. On the way into the theater she told Laura, "They'll pay for their jubilation and suffering in price beyond measure."

Edie grinned.

"What do you mean?"

"I'll tell you later."

"Do they know that?"

"Yes."

After the play, Edie opened the car door for Laura.

"I'm not going to be part of this prank."

"I'll take her home," Julie said. "I just need to talk to Bia for a minute."

"Okay," Laura said, staring stonily at Edie.

"I'm going to tell Laura you're sick because I know you haven't and someone should," Julie told her.

Bia nodded.

Edie shut the car door behind Bia and they drove out the front doors.

It took forever to get the car through the droves of people as they drove down the central corridor. When they turned out onto the street they ended up a couple cars ahead of Julie and Laura. Laura saw Bia put her head on Edie's shoulder and remembered that same gesture from a long time ago when she had seen Edie and Jules at the theater that night. She looked over at Julie.

"What's going on?" Laura asked, feeling the creep of panic as it washed across her.

"Nothing," Julie said, her knuckles constricting on the steering wheel.

"Are they having an affair?"

"No."

"How can you be sure?"

"Bia is dying."

"What?"

"She has cancer. Edie makes her happy. Let them be," Julie said.

"What are you talking about?"

"Bia had leukemia three years ago. She was in remission but it's back and it's spread. The prognosis isn't good."

Laura sat quiet, letting the news sink in. "How are you doing?" she asked finally.

"I went through it the first time. I don't have a lot left. I've divested most of my emotions. What I can't give her, Edie does."

"Does Edie know?"

"I hope so."

Laura sat in the library having a Scotch when Edie got home.

"Sorry if I made you angry. I didn't mean to," Edie said, being her usual apologetic self.

Laura burst into tears.

"What's wrong?" Edie said, coming over to hold her.

"Bia." Laura sobbed.

"It's going to be all right," Edie said, knowing this was her second lie of the day.

Six weeks later, Edie sat in the waiting room at Good Samaritan Hospital. Julie had gone to get them coffee. She had her eyes pressed into the palms of the hands as she sat hunched over. She did this to stop herself from crying. She thought back to the first lunch hour that she had waited for Bia and she hadn't showed up. Edie knew it had started. Bia had collapsed at home and gone to the hospital. Edie had put on her best face, bought flowers and gone to see her lover attached to a slew of tubes. That was the beginning of treatment, of holding Bia's hand while she puked from the medication, of reading her books, making up funny stories, of trying to keep both their spirits up. It was like they were bumping down a dark hallway together with no end in sight, except this, morphine and waiting.

Sandi touched her shoulder. Edie sat up.

"Are you okay?" Sandi asked, sitting down next to her.

"No, I feel horrible," Edie said.

"You look horrible."

"I can always count on you to tell me like it is. How is the baby?" Edie asked, referring to the play, which they called "the baby," something they doted on and fussed over.

"The baby is fine."

"I'm not doing well," Edie said.

"I know, but you've got to keep it together for everyone's sake."

"I don't usually have regrets. I don't believe in them, but this time I do. I never should have gone there. How can I let my lover die, and no one knows she was my lover, and I get to walk around pretending this isn't that big of a deal when my whole life is crumbling around me. I am not going to be able to pull this off," Edie said, getting up and going over to the big picture window that looked out over the city. The lights of Phoenix twinkled below.

"You have to," Sandi said, glancing up. Julie was coming down the hall with two coffees.

"How are you holding up?" Sandi asked, getting up and giving Julie a hug.

"I feel hopeful and helpless at the same time. I want her suffering to end but I don't want to let her go either."

The nurse came out of Bia's room.

"She's awake and she would like to see you," the nurse said to Julie.

Edie stared out the window, tears streaming down her face.

"It's time, isn't it?" Edie said to Sandi who came to stand beside her.

Sandi held her while they waited.

Julie came out after a short while. "Edie, she wants to see you."

Edie got up and straightened her shoulders. If ever she needed courage it was this moment. She went in the room and sat next to the bed and took Bia's hand.

"Hey, girl, I'm going to miss you," Bia said.

Edie burst into tears.

"That's enough now. You've got to be good so we can meet up later," Bia said.

"In another life," Edie said, contemplating the afterworld for the first time since this started. She had never found comfort in those theories until now.

"We will always be together in here and in here," Bia said, pointing to her head and her heart.

"Oh, Bia," Edie said.

"Kiss me now so I can rest," Bia said.

Edie kissed her and tried to remember all the good times they had had together, but all she could envision was beeping hospital machines and the smell of sterile hospital rooms. Edie watched Bia's eyes close. She listened to her shallow breathing, took one last look and quietly left the room. She knew Bia would die soon, and she couldn't bear to be there.

Edie came out of the room to face the inquisitive looks of Julie and Sandi. Laura would be there soon and Edie knew she had to get away.

"She's resting now," Edie told them.

They nodded.

"I need to get some air," Edie said.

"We'll wait here for Laura," Sandi said.

"Edie?" Julie said.

"Yes?" Edie replied, looking at Julie and suddenly wondering how she had managed to put up with all their antics and still love them both. At that moment Edie felt more shame than she had ever known.

"Are you all right?"

"I am so sorry," Edie said, knowing Julie would understand what she meant.

"You made her happy when I couldn't. I wanted her to be happy."

"What about you?"

"I have the rest of my life to pursue my passions. She doesn't."

"You are too good," Edie said. She left.

Laura sat by Bia's bedside and watched her sleep. Julie came in and touched her shoulder.

Laura looked up. "It's so sad."

"I know."

"Is Edie back?" Laura asked, wondering where Edie had gone to get some air. Most people went to the hospital courtyard, wandered around a bit and came back in. But Edie wasn't most people. Laura had called her cell phone and gotten no answer. She had called the loft to find the same.

"She'll be back," Julie said.

Edie took a cab to the airport and now stood at the monitors looking for a departing flight and trying to decide where to go. She went up to one of the counters where a young woman sat waiting. She cheerfully asked for her ticket.

"I don't have one. I was hoping to get one."

"Where would you like to go?"

"I don't rightly know. Maybe you could help me."

The woman looked puzzled.

"Where have you always wanted to go?" Edie inquired.

"Oh, that's easy. I love Belize. The beaches, the locals, the tropical drinks, and the men in tight swim suits. It's marvelous."

"Okay, I'll go there. Is there a flight?"

"As a matter of fact, there's one in two hours and one seat left. I can probably get you a good price."

"Perfect," Edie said.

"Which credit card will you be using?"

"I'll pay cash," Edie said, getting a wad of bills out of her pocket.

"And luggage?"

"I don't have any," Edie said, beginning to think this wasn't looking good.

"Okay," the woman said.

"I thought I'd just get a suit and a sarong when I got there."

"Sure. Great idea. Here's your ticket and you'll be leaving out of gate B four."

"Thank you," Edie said, taking her ticket.

Edie knew she'd be stopped by security. Sure enough, they scanned her laptop and then escorted her to a separate room where a large woman dressed in black security garb sat waiting.

"Hi there," Edie said.

"Hello, I need you to empty your pockets," she said.

Edie pulled out her wallet, passport, house keys, computer discs and five thousand dollars.

"And your laptop."

Edie pulled her laptop out of the case and her manuscript of the play that was wedged in behind it.

"Any particular reason you don't have any luggage?"

"I didn't know where I was going so I didn't know what to pack," Edie said.

"And the cash?"

"I don't have time to get traveler's checks."

"This is not how most people travel," the woman stated.

"Look, this is not what you're thinking."

"What am I thinking?"

"That I'm a terrorist. I know I fit the profile except for the penis part and the nationality but it's not like that."

"What's it like then?" the woman said, taking a seat behind the table and indicating that Edie do the same.

"I'm running away."

"Running away from what?"

"I'd rather not say."

"That is your choice but you won't be getting on the plane."

Edie took a deep breath. "I was having an affair with my wife's best friend who is dying at this moment in the hospital of cancer. I can't face my wife any longer because I swore to my lover that I wouldn't tell, and I can't live with the guilt any longer. I thought if I left for a while my wife could move on and forget about me."

"And you won't ever have to confess what a prig you've been," the woman said.

"Exactly. So it doesn't make me a terrorist. It makes me a horrible human being but that is something I'll have to deal with. It shouldn't affect my air travel."

"I don't think your plan is going to work."

"It's all I've got," Edie said, lamely.

"All right then," the woman said, getting up.

"I can go?"

"Yes," the woman said.

Edie got on the plane for Belize, took two Valium and had four martinis and then slept her way to paradise.

A week later, Sandi confessed to having a set of keys to the loft. She and Laura discovered that nothing was missing. The car was still parked in the garage and no luggage was taken. It appeared she had disappeared off the face of the planet. Laura was forced to call Edie's parents. Her sister Corinne answered the phone.

"I see," Corinne said, after Laura had related all the facts.

"I've filed a missing persons report but they haven't found anything. Her credit cards and cell phone show no activity," Laura said, wishing she had been able to speak to Edie's father, Adrian, but he was out having lunch with his wife. Adrian was good at dealing with Edie.

"I guess we'll just have to wait and see," Corinne said.

"I'm sure she's all right," Laura said, without much conviction.

"I'll tell my parents when they get home. Keep in touch, Laura," Corinne said rather coldly.

Laura hung up the phone thinking that Edie's family would probably blame her for losing their capricious daughter.

❧

Corinne relayed the news when her parents got home. "What do you mean gone missing?" Adrian asked.

"More like ran away. You know, for having lived with her for so long, Laura really doesn't know Edie that well," Corinne said.

"A week ago Edie's friend Bia died. They had a memorial service for her here and then the funeral was in Seattle, near Bia's family," Edie's mother, Rocelyn, explained.

"So? I mean that is sad but why would that make Edie leave?" Adrian asked innocently.

"They were lovers, Dad," Corinne said.

"Bia and Edie? What about Laura?" Adrian said.

"Exactly," Corinne said. "Don't worry, she'll be back when everything blows over. Her wife may not know her but I do. Edie will stay away just long enough for Laura to move on and then she will miraculously reappear."

"You think so?" Adrian said.

"Yes, dear, Corinne is right. We just have to wait."

"How did she get like that?" Adrian asked.

"I think it's your family's good looks," Rocelyn replied.

"I'm going to kill her when she gets back," Laura said as she sat with Sandi at the loft later that evening.

"You may not have to," Sandi said, pouring them both a Scotch on the rocks.

"What is that supposed to mean?"

"Did Edie ever tell you what really happened after Cassandra dumped her?" Sandi said.

"Just that it broke her heart and tainted her view of relationships."

"It's a little more complicated than that."

"What are you talking about?"

"She ended up in the university loony bin for a couple of months. It wasn't pretty."

"But the police have checked all the hospitals, rehabs and all that. She would have shown up."

"I know."

"You don't think . . ." Laura said, getting scared.

"I hope not."

"She'll show back up," Laura said.

"Sure she will," Sandi replied.

It was the mail that finally tipped Laura off. Edie's mail came to the house but nothing important like a mortgage statement or credit cards bill, just junk mail. Laura called Edie's solicitors, who informed her that Ms. Farnsworth had expressly instructed them that under no circumstances were her whereabouts to be revealed. Together with her accountants they were dealing with her financial affairs, they told her. At least she was alive, Laura thought, but she'd strangle her when she returned.

She sat on the couch and cried, wondering how Edie could do this to her. What kind of a woman does this to her lover? Laura was beginning to understand that the person she thought Edie was could have been some sort of romantic mirage. She knew she would spend however long Edie was gone going over their relationship and trying to figure out what went wrong. *And then I'm going to throw her ass out,* Laura thought. She wiped away her tears and said aloud, "If only I could."

Chapter Nine

The problem was, Edie didn't come home for a long time. Almost four months had passed before Edie walked into her mother's kitchen for the Friday night family dinner. She'd brought her mother a bunch of flowers and a bottle of wine for them. Laughing and crying, her mother held her.

"You couldn't send a postcard?" Adrian Farnsworth asked his daughter over dinner.

"I figured that when my decomposed body didn't show, you'd know I was alive. It was a journey, an adventure of a lifetime away from the other lifetime," Edie told him.

He nodded.

"Meaning you didn't want us to know because then Laura would find out and that was the last thing you wanted. Her punishment wouldn't be nearly as horrid if she knew you were simply out having a good time bumming around the tropics," her sister Sal said.

"Yeah, you're right," Edie said.

"Lip service, Sal. She's messing with you again," Corinne said. "No, I think you were running."

"I did bring my sneakers," Edie teased.

"I take it you're not going to tell us why you felt the need to go underground," Adrian said.

"It's kind of complicated, Dad," Edie said. "But I feel better."

He took her hand. "We're just glad you're back."

After dinner, while Edie helped her mother clean up, they had a talk.

"You can't blame Laura for Bia's death," her mother said.

"I know."

"You have to tell her why you left. You have to tell her that you loved Bia."

"She knows," Edie said, drying the dinner plates and stacking them neatly in the cupboards.

"No, you have to tell her you and Bia were lovers."

"You knew?"

"It was hard not to know. You brought Bia to Friday dinners a lot more than Laura," Mom said. "One night I saw you in the kitchen and you and Bia were kissing. I was shocked at first and then I put all the pieces together, and I think I understood why that had happened. Laura is a nice woman, and a good influence on you, but she lacks Bia's passion and humor, her sense of fun. I think I also knew why Bia didn't steal you away. Bia knew that she was dying and she didn't want to leave you alone. She had to keep you as her mistress for that very reason. You still should never have done that."

"Bia made me swear I would never tell Laura," Edie said, pouring them both another glass of wine.

"But you have to. Otherwise she'll never understand why you left. You owe her that much."

Edie looked at her mother. "I know. That's why I had to go away. If I left she'd forget about me, chalk it up to a failed relationship and my bad behavior."

"She won't though. She needs to know why you shut her out and that it wasn't her doing, but rather yours."

"I know. It's something I have to deal with."

"You have to, Edie, or it will haunt her," her mother advised.

"I know. But not right now."

"You have to do it soon though."

"Okay."

"Promise me."

"I will."

The next day Edie walked into the theater. Sandi had been carrying on with the play as Edie knew she would. The play was probably better not having her there. Edie slunk down the dark aisle and into a theater seat behind Sandi, who was busy poring over her notes and giving instructions to one of the actors up on stage.

"No, that's not right either," Sandi said.

"Actually, I think that works rather well. I'd keep it just the way it is," Edie said.

"I guess it's your play. You ought to know," Sandi replied. It took her a minute to realize what had happened. She turned back around. "Edie?" She squinted into the darkness.

"Hi," Edie said.

"Where in the hell have you been? We've all been worried sick. Most people do not disappear off the face of the planet for months on end. I can't believe you did that," Sandi said.

Edie slid over the seat's and slipped into the one next to her. She kissed Sandi on the cheek and said, "I missed you too."

"Edie . . ." Sandi said helplessly.

"Look, it was bail out or go straight to the loony bin. Which would you prefer? I took charge this time and did what I thought was best for my own self-preservation. I know that makes me a hardhearted, selfish bitch, but I had to."

"I know," Sandi said, giving her a hug.

"How long was it until my stuff showed up at the loft?"

"About two and a half months," Sandi replied.

"That's pretty good. I would have lasted about a week," Edie replied, watching the actors on stage. They had definitely improved in her absence. It was a good idea to let Sandi take over production. She was more objective and much more practical.

"Laura has more class than you."

"True. Is she seeing anyone?" Edie asked, needing to know the answer but dreading it all the same.

"Yes."

"Have they made love yet?"

"I'm not sure." Sandi shrugged.

"Who is she?"

"She's the next-door neighbor and she has a kid. They moved in shortly after you left."

"I see."

Clearly concerned, Sandi studied her.

"I'm fine. It was my intention that this happen. Where is Julie?"

"She moved back to Seattle. She didn't think there was much point in remaining here."

"All right then, fill me in on the play."

"You're still going to have to face Laura at the magazine."

"I'm not going back to the magazine. You see, I got this grant to write my new play. I met these people with a theater foundation when I was in Belize."

"Edie, we haven't finished this one yet."

"I'm great at multitasking and besides, I think as the playwright I'm a little too involved in the production. I've got enough money from the grant to provide you with a stipend, so maybe you could take a leave of absence from the magazine and finish the production. How does that sound?"

"Oh, Edie, that would be great," Sandi said, hugging Edie again. "You're still an absolute shit."

"I know, but I'm definitely more focused when I'm single."

125

Laura stood in Oswald's office at the *Phoenician* magazine.

"She did what?" Laura asked, her face burning.

"She resigned," Oswald said sadly. "The place will not be the same without her. It will certainly not have the same flair, although I might be able to get her to do some consulting work. I understand that being the senior editor is time-consuming and then there are all those details and production schedules. I know that it would take a lot of time from her play. Mostly, I'm concerned about the artistic flair that she was able to create. I just don't have that. I was wondering if you might be interested in taking over."

"What, do you think that my living with her allowed some of her genius to rub off? No, I don't want the position. I want her back."

"I don't think that will be possible. She was most adamant about being a full-time playwright. It seems she got a grant or some such thing," Oswald lamented.

"Oswald, does this mean she is alive and well and back in town perhaps?"

"Of course, I saw her yesterday."

"Don't you think it might have been pertinent information for me to know?"

"I assumed she had called you, or better yet shown up on your doorstep," Oswald said.

"I'm going to kill her," Laura said, storming out of his office.

"Oh, sweetie, don't do that. Prison is no place for a pretty lady like you."

Laura tried the loft first and then the theater. Edie's Porsche was parked around back. The theater looked like it should have been condemned years ago. How Edie could give up a good job for this pipe dream of a play absolutely baffled her. Laura wished Edie would never have pursued writing plays and she secretly despised Sandi for pushing her in that direction. The play had done nothing but driven a wedge between them. She hated the play and the time it had stolen from her. Even when Edie hadn't been working on the play or at the magazine, Laura had known Edie wasn't living in the present moment with her. Her mind was seemingly always elsewhere. And then when Bia and Julie came to town and Edie started hanging out with Bia she had gotten even less of Edie's precious time. Perhaps their relationship had not been as strong as Laura had imagined. She had more of a relationship with Isabel and she hadn't even kissed her yet. She knew that despite their broken hearts—Isabel's lover had walked out after two years of parenting—they were falling in love.

Laura got out of the car, took a deep breath and walked into the dark theater. She felt her pulse quicken as she looked onstage to see Edie rearranging the set, which was composed of living room furniture. She jumped offstage to survey her work from various angles and then back on again to readjust. The seating section of the theater was dimly lit and Edie clearly did not know she was there until she had gotten onstage.

Edie froze when she saw her.

"Since when have you become the cruelest bitch on the planet?" Laura said.

Edie stuck her hands in her pockets and said nothing.

"Were you ever going to call me, or did you think you could just slink around the valley and I would never figure out you were back?"

"The latter," Edie said.

"You know, when most people go out to get some air they don't disappear for a third of a year."

"I'm not most people."

"So this is it? This is how you end a five-year relationship?" Laura said, feeling her eyes begin to water. "You just exit the scene, come back and forget it ever happened."

"Basically," Edie said, touching her upper lip. Laura could see that her nose had begun to bleed. Edie searched for a Kleenex and, unable to find one, she lifted up her T-shirt and held it to her nose.

Laura looked at her smooth belly, and images of the times she had

127

kissed her way down it danced in her head. Edie must have read her mind because she dropped the hem and used her sleeve instead.

"Edie, I love you. A day doesn't go by that I don't think of you, miss you and want you back. Doesn't that mean anything to you?"

Edie studied the floor.

"I just want to hold you," Laura said, moving toward her. Edie backed away.

"It's not my fault Bia died. It's horrible and sad, but why does it have to change what we had?"

"It changes everything," Edie said. "Look, I know you have someone else, and when she's making you come you won't think about me."

"Edie, it's not like that," Laura said, feeling instantly guilty for betraying Isabel that way.

"It's like that. Now go home . . . please," Edie said.

Laura studied her face. She had seen that stony resolve only once before, when Edie had told Concepcion good-bye.

"I will always love you," Laura said.

"Don't waste your time," Edie said.

Laura gave her one hard, last look and left.

Laura drove home stoically and then broke down. She felt like she was having a heart attack. Her chest felt tight and she sobbed in great, gasping breaths. The phone rang and she automatically picked it up, thinking it was Edie calling to say she was sorry or some such nonsense. Instead, it was Isabel.

"So the little one is all packed off to Grandma's and I've got dinner all prepped. Come over when you're ready and we'll have some wine," Isabel said.

Laura was quiet. She had forgotten they had made dinner plans.

"Laura?"

"I'm sorry. I think I'm going to have to beg off. I'll call you tomorrow."

"Okay."

A few minutes later Isabel was at the door with a bottle of wine and two glasses.

Laura opened the door.

"What's wrong?"

Laura broke down sobbing, her words disconnected. "She's back . . . and she didn't call . . . and she was really mean."

"Who is back?" Isabel asked, clearly confused.

"Edie."

"Oh," Isabel said.

Isabel held her, kissed the tears on her cheeks and then did something that shocked them both. She kissed her, softly at first, and then harder, and Laura kissed her back. Isabel broke away.

"I'm sorry. I'm so sorry," Isabel said, looking mortified. "I shouldn't have done that."

Laura had stopped crying. "Don't be. It was nice, really nice." Laura pulled her close.

"Come for dinner," Isabel whispered in her ear.

"All right. I could use a glass of wine."

"Good," Isabel said, leading her home.

They had wine and barbecued pork tenderloin. The house was full of the soft glow of candles and Isabel rubbed the tension out of Laura's shoulders while they watched a music video.

"You have great hands," Laura said.

"I once entertained the idea of being a massage therapist," Isabel said, gently pulling off Laura's shirt and easing her down onto the rug. Lying face down, Laura did not protest. Slowly, Laura relaxed as Isabel kneaded the tension out of her lower back. Laura thought about how nice it was to be touched. Maybe Edie was right. This was better. Here was this sweet, intelligent, capable woman taking care of her and falling in love. Isabel must have felt it too, because she kissed the back of Laura's neck. Laura felt herself becoming aroused.

Isabel ran her hands down Laura's hips. Laura took her hand and pulled it around front. She was wet and Isabel guided her hand inside. Laura moaned softly and moved so Isabel could go in deeper. Isabel pulled off her own shorts so Laura could reach her. Slowly and then quicker they rocked against each other. It was a sweet, smooth ride. Laura felt Isabel come and then her own quick, hard release.

"I love you," Isabel said as she lay against Laura's back.

Laura rolled over to look at her, saw Isabel instead of Edie and freaked.

"I have to go," Laura said, grabbing her shirt.

"You did what!" Sandi screamed into the telephone.

"It sounds worse than it is. Maybe she'll just think I panicked or that I have intimacy issues," Laura blathered.

"Or she'll just think you're completely fucking out of your mind and never speak to you again."

"Oh, no," Laura groaned.

"You know that you are behaving exactly like the person we shall not name. This is exactly her pattern of behavior. You realize that?"

"What am I going to do?"

"Get up at the crack of dawn, buy flowers, stuff for breakfast, and go over there and prostrate yourself and beg for forgiveness for starters," Sandi said.

"Do you think it will work?"

"It's your only chance."

"All right. I'll call you tomorrow and let you know how it goes."

"You need to forget about Edie."

"I know."

Isabel answered the door still sleepy, her hair messy and dressed in a white robe. It was six a.m. Laura couldn't wait any longer.

"Hi," Isabel said.

130

"I am so sorry about last night," Laura said, handing her the bouquet of white daisies.

Isabel took them. "Was I that bad?"

"No, you were wonderful. It was my fault. Can I make you breakfast?"

"Sure."

Laura set the grocery bags on the kitchen counter. Isabel made coffee and put the flowers in a vase.

"I make a great omelet," Laura said.

"I'm sure you do," Isabel said, pulling her close. "I didn't mean to rush you. I can be patient. I just want your heart when you're ready."

"You have my heart. Can I make this up to you?"

"And how would you do that?" Isabel asked.

"We could put this in the fridge and go back to bed," Laura suggested.

"Now there is an idea."

A month later Edie's play opened. Laura saw the advertisement for it in her complimentary copy of the *Phoenician* magazine. Isabel had suggested they go see it. Laura had adamantly declined and instead suggested they start looking for a house together somewhere out of town. Laura had quit the magazine because it reminded her too much of Edie and was doing some freelance work. Oswald had been distraught at losing his senior editor and the head of advertising in the same week. Laura was contemplating starting her own small advertising agency. She had discovered that once she stopped having to worry about what Edie was doing all the time and trying to be super lover to a woman with more energy than God, she could calm down and start looking at what direction she wanted her own life to go in. Isabel was a nice woman, her daughter Alex adored Laura, and life was only going to get better.

The night the play opened, Sandi ran around checking and rechecking things. Edie stood in the wings and watched the audience file in. Oswald had done a short feature on the play and some advertising for it, so for an obscure, first play there was quite a crowd. To anyone watching, it might seem that Edie was crowd-counting, but she was really looking for people who would not be there. She wished so badly that Bia could be there to see it and that Laura would have forgiven her and come to see the thing she had worked so hard on while they had been together. The play was as much hers as anyone else's because she had been there during those rough times. Edie knew Laura hated the play because she was convinced it marked the demise of their relationship and it was probably best that she believed that. A day didn't go by that Edie didn't think about Laura and hate herself for what she had done. She would never forgive herself or Bia for what they had done to themselves and to their partners. Edie had officially sworn off women and was convinced that living alone was better.

The lights dimmed and Sandi came up behind her. She gave her a big hug.

"Edie, aren't you excited? This is the moment we've lived for," Sandi said.

"I'm fucking ecstatic," Edie said, putting her coat on.

"Where are you going?" Sandi said, panic in her voice.

"I'm going home," Edie said.

"Home? It's opening night. You can't go home. Don't you want to see the play?"

"Sandi, I've seen the play for the last year and a half. Why would I want to see it again? If I never see it again I'll be happy. Now, if you'll excuse me I have to work to do."

"You can't do this."

"I can. Look, I'm done with it. If it goes over well, you do whatever you want with it."

Sandi was crushed. "Why do you always have to wreck everything? This is like the best night of my life and you have to ruin it by being selfish."

Edie smiled sadly. "I wreck everything, remember. Why should you be any different from anyone else I've ever loved?"

Edie turned and left.

"She did what?" Linden asked, as she held Sandi who was crying. Bear, Mattie and Karen huddled around her. The curtain was about to go up and Edie was nowhere to be found.

"She just left and said she never wanted to see the play again. We worked so hard on this and then she had to go and ruin it," Sandi said, drying her eyes and looking over Linden's shoulder to see that the lead character's robe was bunched up in her belt and her socks were showing.

"Shit, hold on," Sandi said. She called the actor over and pointed at her white gym socks.

"She'll be all right," Linden said, smiling. "Now, let's go watch the play that my hard-working, wonderful girlfriend put her heart and soul into."

Sandi smiled.

"Don't let Edie ruin your night. She may have written it but you brought it to life," Bear said, giving Sandi a big hug.

"Thank you. I needed that," Sandi said.

The next morning Edie read the reviews of the play and called Sandi. "Look, I'm sorry about last night."

"Is that an apology for being such an asshole?" Sandi said. "My head's still foggy from all the Champagne I drank at the cast party. You may not have been there but everyone else had a blast."

"Yes, sweetie darling. Now, how did it go?"

"It went well and I think people really liked it."

"Good."

"After the run here maybe we should think about taking it on the road," Sandi suggested.

"You do whatever you think is best."

"I know—because you're done with it," Sandi said.

"Sandi?"

"Yes?"

"Thanks for being such a good friend and putting up with me," Edie said.

"Why don't you come over and have breakfast?"

"I am hungry."

"Good. We'll have our own celebration."

"All right. I think I can handle that."

Part Three

One Year Later

Chapter Ten

Edie sat working on the new play in the old theater she'd rented for the rehearsals. She was still running through the gauntlet of actresses and dancers. Casting was always the worst part. The play was coming together slowly, but she was barely staving off the panic that crept around every corner. Her play, *The Anatomy of a Love Affair*, was a combination of theater, opera and dance, and she wasn't entirely sure she was up to the challenge.

She could see its form, imagine the sound and the dialogue, but translating what the mind envisioned easily into the hard reality of the stage was proving more difficult than she could ever have imagined. But work took away memories, pain and longing. This play was her life now, and she threw everything she had into it.

"I knew we'd find you here," Bear bellowed out across the theater.

Edie looked up to find Sandi, Linden, Karen, Mattie and Bear coming down the center aisle.

"It's time to play. Ever heard of a weekend, Edie?" Sandi said.

"Only for nine-to-fivers, which I am no longer part of," Edie said.

"For your information, it's Friday night and we're taking you out," Bear said, setting down a black duffle bag that looked suspiciously like one of Edie's.

"I think you guys miscalculated. I don't go out anymore," Edie said.

"Tonight you are," Bear said.

"Look, Edie, if we got hauled out of our comfy little love nest to go out dancing, you're coming too," Karen said.

"Oh, my, I forgot how authoritative you can be. It's so sexy," Edie taunted.

"Stop it," Karen said. "We're not buying into your crap this time."

"How have you two love birds been? I haven't seen you in ages," Edie said, completely ignoring Karen's remarks and stalling for time.

"That's because you never come out of this fucking theater. Edie, there is a whole world out there," Karen snapped.

"Sandi, did you have to bring the Master Sergeant with you?" Edie whined.

"I needed reinforcements." Sandi shrugged.

"And Mattie, my little baby dyke, you've cut your hair. You almost look like a lesbian now," Edie said.

Mattie laughed. She was the youngest of the group. Her lover, Karen, was fifteen years older than her, and Edie had incessantly teased them about their age difference when they had first started dating. Karen had been a body builder and Mattie was a pretty little girl complete with dresses and curly brown hair.

Edie was backing away from them but came to a complete stop when she ran into Bear, who was blocking her exit.

"I'm not dressed for it. I'd have to go home and change," Edie said, knowing she would simply drive around to avoid them.

"We brought you clothes," Sandi said, pitching the duffle bag at her, but Edie refused to catch it. The bag fell at her feet.

"Edie, come have a beer with us. It'll do you good," Linden coached. "We're going to the Crowbar. They have a mosh pit."

"Hey, what are you doing?" Edie said as Bear came up behind her and pulled her shirt off.

"Getting you dressed," Bear said, taking the white silk blouse Sandi handed her.

"I'm not going," Edie said.

"Yes, you are. We're kidnapping you. One beer, one dance and then you're free to go," Sandi said.

"Edie, please," Linden said. "For us."

Edie shrugged, taking the black jeans and Doc Martens boots from Sandi.

"Let me go change," Edie said.

"No, you don't. Change here," Sandi said.

"Don't you trust me?"

"No," Sandi said. "You'll disappear."

"All right," Edie said. "One dance, one drink."

Edie pulled off her shirt and put the clean one on.

"You're getting awfully thin," Linden said.

"I believe the term is fashionably lean," Edie said, pulling on her pants, which now fit loose. Sandi gave her a belt.

"We'll grab a pizza at Raimondo's," Bear said.

"You're testing the limits of my patience," Edie said.

"Only because we love you," Linden said.

"All right," Edie said.

Vida sat admonishing herself for her weak moment. How she let her friends talk her into this one was beyond her. But they'd done it and here she was fending off offers for drinks and dances like she knew she would be. That was one curse of being pretty and undeniably single. You were shark bait for whoever came along.

The fluid perimeters of the dance floor came dangerously close, pressing her up against the bar. The crowd weaved to one side like an amoeba groping its way against the wall. One tall, large woman pushed against the center of the mosh pit and sent a small, dark-haired woman smashing against the wall. Vida watched her hit the wall and slide to the floor, the wind knocked right out of her. She fell down on her side, her head hitting the floor as the music blared.

"Are you all right?" Vida asked, helping the woman right herself.

She opened her eyes, blinked as if trying to focus, and drew in a ragged breath.

"You're bleeding," Vida said, alarmed.

Edie touched her nose and then looked at her fingers.

Vida got a wad of napkins from the bar and handed them to her. She looked up appreciatively.

The mosh pit moved closer again. Vida helped her up. "Let's get you out of here. Come on. It's safer on the patio."

Vida grabbed more napkins on the way out. The nosebleed appeared to be subsiding. They sat at one of the picnic tables outside. The waiter came by.

"Want a beer or something?" Vida asked.

Edie nodded.

"They shouldn't allow people to be so rough."

"The rules are, there are no rules," Edie said, pulling the napkins away. "Has it stopped bleeding?"

"I think so," Vida said, studying her nose seriously.

Edie got up and went to drop them in the trash. Vida watched her. She was an attractive woman, slight of frame, dark, but with startling blue eyes, an unusual combination, and she had a nice butt. Vida was a sucker for nice butt, which she knew was a lesbian faux pas—butts were not important—and it was an infantile fixation but one Vida had never managed to outgrow. Kirsten had a nice butt.

She winced a little at the thought of her. Whole weeks would go by when she didn't think of Kirsten and then she'd be in Macy's buying a shirt. She'd remember the two of them going shopping and she'd sit in the dressing room fighting off tears while the concerned salesperson asked her if she had the right size and she'd try really hard not to scream, *It's fine, it's just fucking fine.*

The waiter brought the beers and Edie dug in her pocket for money.

"I got them," Vida said.

"Thanks," Edie said, unaware she'd passed Vida's second test for being an eligible woman by not insisting or assuming that because Vida was pretty she was a femme. Sometimes Vida was jealous of those boyish yet attractive women whom people labeled butch for the easy way their more masculine side was recognized and appreciated, while women like Vida were assumed to be high femme. She would have surprised more than one of her butch suitors with her rather aggressive bedroom tactics. Kirsten had understood that and liked it, teasing her that she was a butch trapped in a femme's body.

"You got hit hard out there," Vida said.

"I haven't been in a mosh pit in a while. They appear to have gotten rougher in my absence."

"You're not a regular?" Vida asked, secretly relieved.

Edie smiled. "In my younger days. Tonight I was kidnapped. Well-meaning friends, you know."

"Me too. I don't like bars."

"They're not my favorite either. Can't say I ever met anyone special in the bar scene, excepting you, my knight in shining armor. Thank you for helping me."

"You're most welcome," Vida said, thinking, *She's flirting with me and for once in a long time I don't find it utterly repulsive.*

The waiter came by and Vida nodded for refills. Edie went for money but took one look at Vida and put her wallet away.

"People always offer to buy you drinks," Edie said.

"They try to," Vida said.

"And you don't like it?"

Vida nodded. Not only was the woman pretty but she was also intuitive.

"Is it an issue of wolf in sheep's clothing?" Edie asked.

Vida laughed.

"You know why. It's because you're pretty. People think lesbians are supposed to be homely. It's hard to be taken seriously as a lesbian if you don't fit the prescription."

"That sounds like something from *Robert's Rules*," Vida replied.

"Actually, it's from a play. *Daughteronomy.*"

"I saw that!"

"Did you like it?"

"Not at first. I thought it was peculiar, not like other plays, and then when I realized what was going on I thought it was beautiful. I don't think I've ever seen anyone capture our lives so well."

"Why did you think it was peculiar?"

"Because it didn't fit my expectations of a play until I realized the very essence of the play seemed about shattering expectations. It was quite the rage," Vida said.

"You should be a theater critic."

"Maybe I am."

"No, you're not."

"How do you know?"

"Because you're too sensitive and intelligent," Edie said.

"You're right. I'm not savage enough to rip things apart like that." Vida lowered her eyes and peeled the label on her beer bottle.

"So how does a sensitive, intelligent woman like yourself spend her time and energy?"

"I just finished school, and a friend of mine got me a job restoring paintings at the Phoenix Art Museum," Vida said.

"So you're a chemist, a painter and an art historian all rolled into one. That must have taken some doing."

"Pretty much. It took a lot of time and energy but I'm really glad I did it," Vida said. "And what is it that holds your interest?"

"Besides you?" Edie said. "I'm sorry, that was really corny."

"No, it was nice. Please don't apologize." The longer she talked the more it occurred to her that they had met before. "Come here for a moment, under the light." Vida pulled her from her seat. The bar and patio were both dimly lit. "It's you!" Vida said, staring at Edie's blue eyes.

"Oh, God, what did I do?" Edie said.

"Are you always this guilty?" Vida chided.

"I'm Catholic."

"We've met before, that day at the university and then later at Petsmart. You helped me with the dog food," Vida said.

"You have an incredible memory. You're Vida."

"And you're Edie."

A large woman clapped her hand on Edie's shoulders. "There you are! I was sent to fetch you. Time for food."

"We just had food, Bear," Edie said.

"That was dinner. This is a midnight snack. We'll get you fat in no time."

"I'll be there in a minute," Edie said.

Bear plucked her out of her chair and over her shoulder. "I was sent to fetch you and fetch you I will."

"Bear, put me down this instant!"

"Say good-bye to the pretty lady," Bear said, swinging her around so she faced Vida.

"Come with us," Edie said.

"I can't," Vida said.

"You never leave with anyone you meet in a bar."

"Right," Vida said.

"Maybe we could talk again sometime," Edie said.

"I'd like that," Vida said, her heart racing.

Their eyes locked until Bear carried her off the patio.

When Bear plopped her down by the car, Edie said, "How am I supposed to meet anyone when you take me away like that?"

"She looked dangerous," Bear said, pushing her in the car.

"Edie met someone?" Sandi said, her eyes lighting up.

"Yes, I did. Someone nice," Edie said.

"Someone nice-looking, too good-looking. Women like that are trouble," Bear said.

Edie eased back in the car seat and mused. "Where are we going to eat?" she asked, suddenly feeling hungry.

143

"The Five and Diner," Sandi said over her shoulder. "Are you okay?" she asked, meeting Edie's gaze.

"Yes, thank you for making me go out."

"You're welcome."

Sandi looked over and smiled at Linden with her *I told you so* look on her face.

"You were right. It is time she met someone new," Linden said.

Monday morning Edie paced the loft, her sneakers making little sucking noises as she went back and forth. She went out for a walk, trying to take in what was beautiful and what was undeniably ugly about living downtown. She wandered aimlessly through the galleries, staring blankly at the artwork, had a beer at Joe's Tavern, fish and chips at the Oyster Bar, and bought magazines that she would never get around to reading at the Kiosk.

Normally, she took these walks in order to ruminate over the play. This walk was about Vida. It had been so long since she'd been interested in a woman she had almost forgotten what it was like. Part of her was content with the relief of not having a lover, of not having to answer to someone, that feeling of being stretched too thin she always had between placating lovers and fulfilling her own great need to be doing something, creating something. Sandi was right—she didn't relax well. It was less complicated to be alone, but the reverse of that coin was not having someone to share all those weird little moments that make up a relationship.

When she found herself standing in front of the Phoenix Art Museum, gazing up at the stark gray pillars and façade, she could no longer deny that she was intrigued with Vida. Because she couldn't go in, couldn't give herself the push she needed to get through the front door, she walked to the corner, found the florist and sent flowers. Maybe tomorrow, Edie told herself.

❧

When Vida got the flowers she nestled her face in them and read Edie's note about how nice it was to meet up again. She smiled. Miranda, her friend and coworker, raised an eyebrow but said nothing. In the afternoon when the second set of flowers came, Miranda inquired.

"A friend," Vida replied coyly. The second note said that Edie would like to see her again. Edie, it appeared, was going to engage in dialogue through flora.

By Tuesday afternoon, with more multiple deliveries, one in the morning and one in the afternoon, Miranda was not to be put off any longer.

"Who is she and why is she sending so many flowers," Miranda asked, her inquisitive blue eyes opening wider with consternation. "I don't get it."

"I think it's something like courting without actually seeing each other," Vida said, smelling the flowers and reading another one of Edie's odd notes about what they might do if they got together sometime.

"What does that mean?" Miranda asked.

"She's afraid to come and ask me out," Vida said matter-of-factly.

"Why?"

"Because she knows I don't date."

"Why don't you date?"

"It's stupid and I don't do it very well."

"How are you supposed to fall in love if you don't date?"

"Instantaneously," Vida replied, picking up her paintbrush and cleaner.

"For someone who doesn't date, you certainly are a hopeless romantic and your secret admirer is just as weird. She sends flowers but doesn't have the guts to ask you for lunch. So who is she anyway?"

"Edie Farnsworth."

Miranda did a double take. "Who?"

"Edie—"

"*The* Edie Farnsworth?"

"I get the sense I'm missing something here," Vida said, puzzled.

"She didn't tell you?"

"Tell me what?"

"I can't believe you don't know who she is," Miranda said.

Vida shrugged, knowing that in three seconds or less Miranda would enlighten her in her usual blurting, overdone way.

"She's that incredibly brilliant playwright."

"I see."

"Remember the play *Daughteronomy*?"

"Yes. I saw it."

"She wrote and directed that, conceived of a new kind of theater really. I can't believe you didn't know that!"

"Does it seriously jeopardize my standing as a human being?"

"It should. Now tell me you won't go on a date with Edie Farnsworth."

"I won't go on a date with Edie Farnsworth."

Miranda threw her hands up in the air.

By Friday afternoon their studio was filled with flowers and Miranda was beside herself.

"I can't believe you haven't talked to her," Miranda said, stuffing her face in a bouquet of calla lilies. The array of flowers was impressive. They sat waiting for the afternoon delivery.

"How am I supposed to talk to her?" Vida said, reading the latest note for the third time. She couldn't deny she was intrigued. But it was Friday and Edie hadn't called. Vida understood her trepidation. It was the same one she felt. And then they heard the click of shoes on linoleum as someone came back toward the studio. Miranda looked over at her. Vida smiled and shrugged.

"She's got to turn up sooner or later. I can't stand the suspense," Miranda said.

Someone walked in the room carrying three dozen roses, someone with very expensive shoes on. Edie peeked around the huge bouquet.

"Funny, you don't look like the usual delivery man," Vida teased.

"I should hope not," Edie said.

"No, you're much prettier," Vida said, flushing slightly. She had thought about Edie incessantly. It was like her image had become an endorphin flowing through Vida's veins, distracting her in a daydream of growing proportions.

"Thank you. Now where would you like these?" Edie asked, surveying the studio filled with a week's worth of flowers. "It looks nice in here, but it does have vestiges of an overdone funeral parlor."

Vida laughed. "It does, so after today no more flowers. But thank you. I've enjoyed them all."

"I'm glad," Edie said, setting the huge vase of roses on Vida's desk, the only available spot.

Edie looked beautiful in her tailored suit, her blue eyes dilated with what Vida suspected was fear. Vida knew at that moment she had fallen in love with Edie . . . instantaneously.

"I know you're not the kind of woman who goes on dates."

"But I'd really like to take you to dinner," Vida said, finishing for her.

"You mean that?"

"I do."

"I'd love to," Edie said.

Edie had changed clothes three times when the buzzer rang. She took a deep breath, threw her jacket on and flew to the elevator and down to the street. When she came out Vida was standing in front of her yellow Land Cruiser holding six equally yellow sunflowers. She smiled.

"You match," Edie said, pointing from the car to the flowers.

"We do," Vida said.

"They're my favorite," Edie said, taking them from her.

"I know," Vida said.

"How?"

"I called the florist on the corner. He said you liked them."

"Those florists, they're sneaky men. I like sunflowers, but I hesitate to give them because not many people are as fond of them as I am," Edie said.

"You like them and Georgia O'Keeffe liked them. I'd say you were in good company."

"I'd kill for that painting she did of the lone sunflower with the incredible blue sky."

"I'll forge one for you," Vida offered.

Edie smiled. "I'm sure you are certainly capable of it."

"Suffice it to say, I've had offers," Vida said.

"But it would be unethical," Edie said, stroking a satiny yellow petal between her thumb and forefinger.

"It would," Vida said.

"And you're not in the least bit unethical."

Vida laughed. "No, I'm pretty by the book."

"I'm glad."

"Would you like to put those in water before we go?"

"Yes, I should," Edie said, hesitating slightly, trying to visualize exactly what shape she'd left the loft in. "Would you like to come up?"

"If it's all right. I don't want to make you uncomfortable."

"Do I look uncomfortable?" Edie asked.

"Maybe just a little," Vida said. "I don't have to."

"No, come up and I'll fix us drinks," Edie said, trying to look nonchalant. She suspected she wasn't pulling it off very well.

"I'd like that."

Edie raised the caged door on the freight elevator and then let it slam with a thud. "It's not as bad as it looks," she said apologetically.

"I don't think it's bad. Isn't this building part of the Art Detour?"

"Yes, the first and second floor. The other two floors are living space."

They reached the third floor and Edie cranked on the door to let them in. She led Vida into the loft. Trying to calculate damage, she scooped up the load of dry cleaning draped across the couch and a stack of reel-to-reel tapes from the loveseat.

She looked at Vida apologetically. "I didn't really have a chance to tidy."

"It's nice, very nice," Vida said, strolling around. "I always liked lofts. I just never knew anyone who had the balls to live in one. They're so urban."

"You like it?" Edie said, incredulous.

"Surprised?" Vida raised an eyebrow.

"I don't think anything about you would surprise me," Edie said. Vida smiled. "Good."

"I had this friend who used to tease me about being so afraid of rural life that I couldn't possibly exist outside an urban environment," Edie said shyly. It felt good to talk to someone about Bia and not get that look of concern that her other friends instantly emitted.

"Could you?" Vida asked.

"As long at it had an oyster bar, a bagel shop and an espresso stand."

"I think I agree with your friend. You are urban. This is nice." Vida pointed to the large painting of a slightly abstracted nude woman.

"It was a birthday gift from the urban woman," Edie said, looking at the painting with Vida. Edie remembered coming to the loft to find it mounted on her wall. She loved it. She loved Bia for giving it to her. When Laura saw it months later she hated the painting. That episode made Edie understand the difference between her lover and her partner, a difference like a chasm, an impassable one. It was then she longed for one woman who could be both. "Would you like a drink?"

"I'd love one," Vida said, turning from the painting to look at Edie.

"Name your poison," Edie said, meeting her gaze with deliberate steadiness. A signature drink told a lot about a woman. Edie instantly hated herself for reverting back to her old habits. She preferred the days when she knew what her lover drank.

"Scotch on the rocks if you have it," Vida said, coming over to where Edie was standing behind the kitchen bar.

Edie stood staring. It was Bia's favorite poison.

"If you don't, that's fine," Vida said.

"No, I've got it," Edie said, getting the Cutty Sark out of the liquor cabinet and pouring them both a glass. Her hand shook as she poured.

"Are you okay?" Vida asked.

"Me? Sure. I didn't have lunch. I probably just need some food, that's all," Edie said, handing Vida her glass.

"So are you a good cook?" Vida asked, running her finger along the base of a hanging copper pan. The heavy, overhead rack was full of pans and utensils.

"I like to cook when I have someone to cook for," Edie replied.

"You like to cook and I like to eat. We'd make great dinner companions. Maybe sometime I could entice you to cook for me."

Edie smiled, thinking there were probably a lot of things Vida could entice her to do. "I'd love to," she said.

Vida walked over to a large table that housed several small models of a theater stage. It was filled with miniature figures and sketches for the scenery. "Latest endeavor?"

Edie blushed and contemplated lying. Before she could answer Vida spoke.

"Edie, why didn't you tell me you wrote *Daughteronomy*?"

"Probably the same reason you didn't tell me that you were a model for Vanessa's Closet," Edie said.

"Match point," Vida said, smiling. "It worked. I thought you were unemployed."

Edie laughed. "Why did you think that?" She found it interesting that Vida would still go out with someone who might have a sketchy financial background.

150

"Because you told me you used to work for a magazine. You neglected to mention you stopped doing that to become a successful playwright."

"I didn't want you to think I was being pretentious. Sometimes people get funny about things like that."

"Or they're unduly impressed and admire the artist rather than the woman," Vida offered.

Edie studied her Scotch glass, clinking the ice cubes. "Precisely. I mean, it's nice that people like what you do, but sometimes it seems that they make more of you than you really are. Writing plays is something I've always wanted to do and I'm thankful that I can, but it doesn't go past that."

"So what's this one about?" Vida asked, pointing to the table.

"Do you really want to know?"

"I do," Vida said, sitting on one stool at the table and pulling the other one over next to her and tapping it. "Tell me."

Edie sat down tentatively. She hadn't counted on this for their first date. She took a deep breath and began. Vida smiled and within an instant Edie forgot to be nervous as she showed her the table of play sketches and models.

A little while later, Edie glanced at the clock. They were late. "We should call the restaurant."

"I made reservations at The Grill," Vida said. "I hope that's all right."

"My favorite," Edie said, picking up the phone and dialing.

"You know the number?" Vida asked.

"I used to frequent it," Edie said. The host picked up.

"The Grill, how may I help you?"

"I need to see if you can hold a reservation," Edie said.

"What name is it under?"

"Sumner or . . . Farnsworth," Edie said.

"Edie, is that you?"

"Joey, are you still there?"

"Girlfriend, where else would I be?"

151

"So if you hold the reservation we can visit," Edie said.

"For you we would wait all night. I'll get you a really good table. New girl?" Joey asked.

"Yes, as a matter of fact."

"Good. It'll be nice to see you," Joey said.

Edie hung up and refilled both their glasses. "We've got time now."

"Good," Vida said.

It ended up being the perfect night, Edie thought as she lay in bed the next morning. She felt kind of guilty for sleeping in several more hours than Vida, who had to go in to work. She and Miranda were pulling an extra shift to get a painting done for an upcoming show. As usual the bigwigs had promised more than they could deliver.

After dinner and more than the usual amount of connective moments, they had ended up slow dancing on the roof of the loft. It was incredible and a little odd how close they had gotten in such a short time, but Edie found herself telling Vida things that she hadn't told anyone in a long time, if ever.

Their bodies fit together nicely, and they danced to the entire CD rather than just the one requested waltz. She wanted to see if Vida could really do it. Edie knew something special was happening.

Edie smiled when she thought of holding Vida's hands after the music clicked off. Vida told her she hoped she wasn't being forward, but she wanted Edie to know that not only was this definitely the longest date of her life but most likely it was the best.

"I don't feel nervous or scared being with you. I just feel good," Vida told her.

Edie had looked at her and then closed her eyes tight for a moment. "I feel the same way."

"Were you saying a little prayer to the universe?" Vida asked.

"How did you know?"

"Because I do the same thing," Vida said.

Edie wanted to do something special for Vida, something that would say what a lovely evening she'd had, something to make up for the fact that Vida had only gotten a couple hours of sleep. It was the strangest thing, but ever since she had met Vida she couldn't get her off her mind. She thought about her smile, her eyes, the way a few loose strands of hair fell across her face, the firm way she held Edie when they danced, the smooth way her hand slid to the small of her back, pulling her closer. If Edie had any balls she would have invited Vida to stay. In the old days they would have made love the rest of the night and woken up in each other's arms. But too many things had happened and Edie knew she didn't have the strength or mental fortitude anymore to be brave in matters of the heart. She desperately hoped Vida would understand this. Somehow Edie sensed she would.

"I could do breakfast," Edie said aloud. She picked up the phone and dialed Options restaurant. Nothing like a catered breakfast to let a girl know how you feel about her, Edie thought smugly. Maybe she could still be good at romance.

She explained her plan to her friend Jeffrey at Options.

He squealed in delight. "Oh, Edie, just like the old times. I miss seeing you and—" He stopped.

"You can say it. You miss seeing Bia."

"Yes," Jeffrey said. "Edie, have you met someone new? Please say it's so. I can't stand the thought of your being exiled in that cage of lesbian celibacy. You're too vivacious and sexy for that."

Edie laughed. "Boy, I should make you my press agent. And yes, there is someone new and special. But last night was our first date, so let's not plan the wedding yet."

"But you like her, I mean, you really like her, right?"

"Very much," Edie said.

"Then promise me I get to do the wedding."

"Jeffrey," Edie warned. "Just send brunch to the Phoenix Art Museum. The works, okay?"

"Consider it done."

Edie hung up thinking she could tell her friend the chef about her new girlfriend, but it would take her months before she could broach the subject with her closest friends.

When the caterer wheeled in the cart, Miranda smiled knowingly at Vida.

"Food is a good thing," Miranda said, rubbing Vida's sore shoulders.

Vida nodded. She tried to tip the caterer but he refused, telling her it had all been taken care of. Miranda was already lifting lids to see what delights they contained.

Vida picked up the phone and dialed Edie's. "Good morning," she chirped. "How are you?"

"Perfectly wonderful. And yourself?" Edie answered.

"About to eat a scrumptious breakfast. Thank you."

"I thought it was the least I could do since I kept you up so late."

"I think it was mutual. I had a lovely time."

"Me too," Edie said.

"I don't suppose I could persuade you to come down and join us in this feast," Vida queried.

"I'm still in bed," Edie replied guiltily.

Vida tried hard not to imagine Edie naked in bed. She wasn't successful. "So come anyway," she said.

"I'm on my way."

"You got her to come over?" Miranda said when Vida hung up.

"Oh, Miranda, she's really nice, and witty and funny and sexy and absolutely beautiful, inside and out."

Miranda raised an eyebrow. "Did you sleep with her?"

"No!" Vida said indignantly.

"Why not?" Miranda was nibbling at a strawberry-filled pastry.

Vida sighed heavily. She didn't really know how to answer Miranda's question. Because Edie wouldn't let her stay, because they'd told each other stories that were enough to scare off the most courageous of lovers. Edie now knew about Kirsten, and Vida knew the tales of Cassandra and then Laura. At one point they both looked at each other with the sad eyes of jaded lovers. But then they'd danced and their bodies forgot the clamorous warnings of the mind, and it seemed like they might have ended up in bed but Edie didn't appear able.

She looked scared and too fragile for Vida to push. So they had hugged their good-byes, and Vida had touched Edie's cheek although she'd she really wanted to kiss her.

"I think we're going to move kind of slow here for a variety of good reasons and be friends first," Vida explained.

"Friends! What is that supposed to mean?" Miranda fairly screeched.

"We're both scared, okay?"

"Oh," Miranda replied. "I'm sorry."

"It's all right. Here, have another croissant." Vida handed her one.

"Why? Do you want my mouth full when she gets here so I don't make any embarrassing remarks?"

"You are an extremely clever woman. Promise?" Vida said nervously.

"I'll be good," Miranda said.

After breakfast Edie and Vida sat on the steps of the museum and basked in the sun like two sleek, happy cats. It was quiet downtown, just a few joggers and slow-paced traffic. The sky was a deep blue and the moon was still barely visible. The moon would be full tonight, Edie thought.

"Ever look at the moon through a telescope?" Edie asked.

Vida opened her eyes. "Can't say I have."

"Me either."

"Hanging out with you is going to make me fat," Vida said, rubbing her pleasantly full tummy.

"Does that mean you won't let me cook you dinner tonight?"

Vida smiled. "I'll go for a run this afternoon. That'll shave off a few pounds."

"Is that a yes?" Edie asked.

"That's definitely a yes."

"Good, then I better get cracking," Edie said, hopping up and grabbing her bike.

"Where are you going?" Vida asked, clearly startled by the sudden action.

"Shopping," Edie replied happily.

"For dinner?"

"For dinner and a telescope," Edie said.

"A telescope?"

"You've never seen the moon through one. It's high time don't you think?" Edie said.

Vida just shook her head and laughed.

Chapter Eleven

Vida slipped into the dimly lit theater. She wasn't a fugitive but she felt like one as she quietly took a seat. Edie had invited her to come down and see the play in its previews so that she would know how much it improved by the time it premiered.

"If it improves," Edie had said as she flipped the pork tenderloin on the grill the previous Sunday afternoon. They had barbecued complete with apron and hats that Edie had bought for the occasion. Edie made everything an event, made everything fun. Vida couldn't remember the last time she had known someone who'd made her laugh and smile as much as Edie did.

Sometimes it amazed her how well she and Edie knew each other already and the immense of amount of time they'd spent together willingly. Edie had been introduced to Vida's pet family and she had been nervous that maybe Edie wouldn't like her furry friends. But when she found Edie on the floor with True, the cat, kneading her chest, and Bertrand, the dog, licking her face while she laughed hysterically, she knew the goddess had sent her the blue-eyed woman of her dreams.

Of course, now as she watched Edie pacing back and forth on stage having a creative shit-fit, she tried to brace herself for another side of Edie: one she didn't know yet. She had been around creative people long enough to know that you pay for your talent with frustration and a bad temper from time to time. Part of her was anxiously waiting to see what Edie was like in the midst of a crisis.

Edie's friend Bear sat down beside her and said, "Hey, pretty lady. I don't think you picked a good day to come see this thing."

Vida nodded. They both watched as Edie flipped into a litany of choice obscenities. The actress dressed in a skintight red leotard sat in the middle of a pool of something red and sticky-looking. A substance Edie did not appear to be happy with.

"It's supposed to be thick and really fucking gooey. This is like red water. Fuck!" Edie screamed. Her nose started to bleed. Edie put her hand up to stop it, quickly covering her fingers. "See, like this, impressive-looking." She waved her bloody hand around. "This is supposed to look like a heart that just imploded, thick, deep red. This is supposed to be a pool of blood and heart tissue—instead it looks like a kid spilled Kool-Aid!"

"Excuse me for a moment," Bear said softly.

Vida watched as Bear climbed onstage and grabbed Edie from behind. Edie was squirming and trying to scream but Bear had her face covered in a Kleenex that was rapidly soaking up blood. She plopped her down in a chair and tilted her head back.

Bear put her hands on Edie's shoulders and physically kept her in the chair. She looked her straight in the eye and said loud enough for Vida to hear, "This is going to be an absolutely incredible play when you're done. This will not happen if you kill yourself first. You need to slow down and relax or you're going to bleed to death. Is that clear?"

Vida had crawled up onstage in the meantime and was feeling the mysterious liquid.

Edie said to Bear, "How long has she been here?"

"Long enough to see you having a huge temper tantrum," Bear said.

"Fuck!"

"Edie, have you tried adding cornstarch to this?" Vida asked.

Edie sat up. "No."

"I'll go get some." Vida went over and squeezed Edie's shoulder. "And by the way, you're beautiful when you're angry." Edie looked stunned.

Vida winked. "Back in a flash."

"Now that's my kind of girlfriend," Edie said, watching Vida leave.

"So is she your girlfriend?" Bear asked.

"I hope so," Edie said.

"What does that mean?"

"Oh, nothing," Edie said, getting up. "Am I free to go now? And when is that creepy little seamstress friend of yours going to show anyway?"

"You're lucky I respect genius," Bear said, straightening her coat. "Soon. I told her tonight or else."

"Good. Only the narrator is nude. The rest of the actors need clothes."

"Yes, ma'am," Bear said, giving Edie a gentle shove.

The cornstarch worked and Edie hugged Vida and danced around the room with her in her arms. "*You're* a fucking genius!" Edie said.

Vida controlled the impulse to hold Edie tight, kiss her ardently and then seduce her right there on the stage. That was the only problem with her dream lover—Edie hadn't touched her. She didn't know how to take this. It didn't make sense, but there were a lot of things about Edie that defied conventional rationalization.

She reminded herself of this daily, which did little to assuage her longing. She would wait until she could stand it no more and then she'd ask. This was not a good method of communication but it was the only one she knew. Half of her didn't want to find out that although they appeared to make great friends, Edie was not inclined to become lovers.

Edie sipped her latte as she waited outside the gym for Sandi, who was always late because she hated working out, although she was convinced she was getting fat from spending all day in a dark theater. Edie had always worked out because she would become a psychotic maniac by afternoon if she didn't work off some of her excess energy. She was thinking about Laura and Bia as she waited.

Their ghosts still wavered in and out of her consciousness when she wasn't expecting it. Most times she kept them well checked. She remembered her time in Belize and the calendar that she put slashes through each day, telling herself in one hundred and twenty days she would be healed. She had chosen that duration because that was how long she had spent in the loony bin when she lost Cassandra. She had decided then it was the amount of time necessary to stop a bleeding heart. On the one hundred and twentieth day she walked into her mother's kitchen and she became a woman with a past but no longer a woman living in the past. She held fast to that distinction. Knowing it made her feel strong, and she clung to it fiercely.

Loving Vida meant opening a door that had long been closed. She felt like she was standing on a diving board but had forgotten how to swim. The water below looked inviting, yet its depth yawned ominously. Each time Edie thought she would jump, fear held her feet tight to the board. Vida would look at her with a puzzled expression and they would move on to the next activity quickly to cover their embarrassment.

Sandi finally arrived and asked, "How are you and Vida doing?"

"Fine," Edie said a little too quickly.

"What's wrong?" Sandi asked.

Edie downed her latte and threw the cup in the trash.

"Don't make me wheedle and whine. Tell me," Sandi demanded as they headed inside the gym.

"I can't seem to get past the friend stage. I know it's good in theory to get to know someone first and not jump right into bed but . . ."

"Not going to bed for a while is okay, Edie. Lots of people date and don't immediately fuck. You play kissy face for a while and kind of lead up to that incredible first night in bed. And Vida's gorgeous body in your bed . . . My God, what are you waiting for?"

"I should probably kiss her first," Edie said shyly.

"What!"

Edie slunk away and pretended to be looking for something in her gym locker.

"You haven't kissed her yet. Most people do that on at least the second date. What's wrong with you? You used to be a master seducer and now you've reverted to some kind of nerdy teenager."

"Sandi, you're not helping," Edie pleaded.

"I'm sorry," Sandi said. "Is it old stuff about Laura or Bia?"

"I don't know," Edie said. "I just feel so rusty."

"Why don't you try self-love?" Sandi said.

"What the hell is that?"

"Masturbation, dummy. Psychoanalysts sometimes treat frigid women by getting them to do it to themselves."

"I'm not frigid!"

"All I'm saying is that your behavior exhibits signs of frigidity." Sandi appeared not in the least bit flustered by Edie's indignation.

"I don't know how to perform self-love," Edie said.

"For shit sake, Edie, you're a lesbian. Think about it. What you do to your lover you can do to yourself. You've never done it?"

"No. If I get the urge I go find someone to fuck."

"Oh, to be so lucky. What if you had an off night?"

Edie was truly baffled. "An off night?"

"Never mind," Sandi said. "Just give it a try."

"I don't think I can do it."

"Do you want to lose Vida?"

"No."

"Well then," Sandi said, pulling Edie off the locker room bench and into an embrace.

Edie started to freak.

"Just relax," Sandi said. She took Edie's face in her hands and kissed her softly. "See, that wasn't so hard, now was it? I'd help you with the rest, but that might be exceeding the bounds of friendship."

"I think we may have already done that," Edie said.

"I won't tell if you don't," Sandi said, smacking her on the butt.

Sandi called later. Edie was taciturn. The whole thing made her horribly uncomfortable.

"Did it work?" Sandi finally blurted out.

"I think so," Edie confessed.

"What do you mean, you think so? Did you get off or you didn't you?"

"Suffice it to say, it wasn't easy," Edie admitted.

"Masturbation isn't like writing a term paper. It's supposed to feel good."

"It was nice, I guess."

"See, I told you it would work," Sandi said.

"But if I can just do that why do I need a girlfriend?" Edie said, anticipating the screech that would follow.

"Edie!"

She smiled.

Edie and Vida lay on a blanket in the park across from the museum. Jansen's huge volume of art history was opened in front of them. Vida was giving Edie a crash course in Renaissance art because

Edie wanted to know something about the kind of paintings Vida was restoring. Vida liked it when Edie came and sat quietly watching her work.

At first Vida was concerned Edie would be instantly bored, but she seemed to find some meditative quality in watching the restoration. Edie would come from the theater and spend the afternoon with Vida. She sensed Edie was only half present. She could tell by the look in Edie's eyes that the wanderlust of her creative mind was taking her elsewhere and that she needed some activity to placate her left brain. Vida didn't mind being that tool if it meant spending time with her.

Edie handed Vida a clump of red grapes from inside the battered wicker picnic basket. When Vida had commented on the uniqueness of the basket, Edie told her that her friend Bia had given it to her.

"Was she a romantic friend?" Vida inquired.

"She was Laura's best friend."

Vida decided she liked the picnic basket even more because it was part of Edie's mysterious past: a past Vida preferred to remain a mystery, not because she entertained visions of Edie's tragic, lost loves, but rather because she sensed the depth of Edie's pain, and contrary to therapeutic notions, she didn't think bringing them to light would repair the damage.

Only new life and experiences could do that kind of work, and Vida desperately wanted to be part of this tender, new life. She welcomed the picnic basket not as an assault of the past on the present but as a gesture from Edie of melding the good times of then with the good times of now.

"Edie, can I ask you something?" Vida said, suddenly deciding this was the moment when she had to know how Edie really felt.

"Sure," Edie said, popping a grape in her mouth with the nonchalance of someone who has no idea that her world is about to be assaulted.

"Do you not think of me sexually?"

Edie instantly choked and then her nose began bleeding. "Shit!" she said, grabbing napkins and plastering them to her face.

"Are you all right?" Vida asked.

"I'm sorry. I'm such a mess sometimes. Let me get cleaned up and I'll be right back."

Vida sat pondering the answer to her question. It didn't make sense. The way Edie looked at her, touched her hair when a stray strand dangled loose, the way she ran her hand down Vida's back when they walked into a restaurant all spoke of a lover's gesture. How could Edie not be in love? Vida knew she was already gone, hook, line and sinker. All she wanted was to touch the woman she loved in the intimate way of lovers. She wanted to wrap her naked body around Edie and feel her inside. She ached with the thought.

Edie stood in the park restroom splashing water on her face. She felt an acute attack of anxiety. It was times like this that made her wish she was still in therapy so that Dr. Kilpatrick, the shrink at the loony bin, could neatly explain her problem with intimacy. She could hear the good doctor's words echoing in her head.

"Edie, you can fuck anyone but you will always have trouble making love until you learn that sex is not intimacy. You need to learn to trust your partner. You must trust that they will not cheat or lie or leave you. That is the power of love. When you believe that then you will understand intimacy."

Edie had told the doctor she did not see how that was possible, considering that her view of love consisted of all of the above.

Edie looked at herself in the stainless-steel-framed mirror and saw a distorted monster staring back at her. Mirrors were frightening things. She wondered if she could get a large enough one to have the character that played Ego in her play look into one, and have it positioned so the audience to see it. It would be a very strong metaphor for the distortion of the ego in how it views itself versus the reality.

She brought herself back to task. Here she was thinking about the play while the woman she loved sat in the park wondering why Edie hadn't touched her yet. Her best friend thought she was frigid and the ghost of her therapist chanted old litanies Edie hadn't improved upon, excepting that she no longer fucked anyone.

She was going to have to get a grip. She had two options. She could step outside her insecurities, trust Vida and fall happily in love, or she could disappear like she'd done a thousand times before. She could learn to take tiny steps toward true intimacy or she could run and keep running in an emotionally void vacuum. She took a deep breath, straightened her shoulders and went to Vida.

Edie sat down behind Vida and put her face against Vida's neck. "Is this okay?"

"Of course. You don't have to ask to touch me. I want you to touch me," Vida said.

"But you always ask," Edie said.

"That's because you always look so uncomfortable," Vida said, turning to face her.

Edie read the pain in her eyes. "I'm sorry. I do want you. I just . . . I don't know. It's been so long since I was with anyone in that way. I'm scared."

"It's just riding a bicycle," Vida replied.

"I know. Sandi suggested I fuck myself to get back in the swing. To learn to feel that way again." Edie tried not to blush. Why did being intimate have to be so embarrassing?

"Did you?" Vida asked, raising an eyebrow.

"I tried. I had a tough time of it but then I thought of you. I hope you're not offended."

"Next time you try, why don't you invite me?"

"I will," Edie said, taking her hand.

"So you'll kiss me?" Vida asked.

"Yes."

"I could kiss you if it would make things easier," Vida said.

"Okay," Edie said. "I love being with you."

Vida smiled and squeezed her hand. "The feeling is mutual."

Edie glanced at her watch. "You need to get back."

"I do," Vida said, helping Edie pack up.

They walked across the street to the museum. It was a fine fall day, one of those not too hot, not too cold days. Edie picked up a fallen leaf from an aspen tree.

"See, we do have autumn here, contrary to Easterners' notions," Edie said.

Vida nodded. "Edie, why do you get so many nosebleeds?"

"It's stress," Edie said, not meeting her gaze.

"You don't have a brain tumor or anything?"

"Why, you wouldn't like me then?"

"I mean it. What's wrong with you?"

Edie got suddenly serious. "I don't know. I've been to see the doctor. She thinks it's from stress, you know, like an anxiety attack."

"That sounds logical," Vida replied, stroking her cheek.

"You'd better go. You're going to be late." Edie took Vida's hand.

"Later?" Vida asked.

"Yes, dinner at Vanucchi's?"

"Please," Vida said. "And take it easy the rest of the day. We don't want to have you in for a blood transfusion."

"I promise," Edie said.

Vida was in the middle of a restoration when Edie showed up again.

"Edie!" Vida said, putting her brushes down.

"I need to talk to you."

"What's wrong?" Vida asked, feeling her heart pump into instant overdrive. She was almost accustomed to this feeling that seemed to happen often in Edie's presence and, like a runner's high, she was finding it addictive.

"When are you going to kiss me?" Edie said, looking straight at her. She resembled a child who had only one request and it had not been granted.

"Is that what's wrong?" Vida asked, trying not to chuckle at the absurdity of two well-worn lovers turned virgins.

"Yes."

"Come here," Vida said, holding out her arms. She kissed her softly.

Edie ran her hand through the back of Vida's hair and pulled her closer. Their bodies touching lightly, Edie kissed her back.

Vida stroked her cheek. "We'll go slow, I promise, but I want to be your lover, not just your playmate."

Edie nodded and held her fast.

The following week, the purr of Edie's Porsche reverberated off the driveway. Vida glanced out the window to see Edie coming up the path. Vida was slowly learning to cook now that she had someone to cook for, and work at the museum had slowed down. Edie opened the door and played with Bertrand, who was very excited to see her. She opened the paper bag she'd brought and handed him his treat, a huge soup bone from the butcher. Vida smiled: only Edie would think to stop and get the dog a treat. Sometimes, Vida would look at Edie and wonder at her good fortune. She would feel elation and then a creeping sense of dread would start to tear at the edges of her happiness.

No one's lover could be so wonderful without turning out to be a serial killer or something akin to one. Vida tried to banish these thoughts and enjoy the pleasantness early love affords. She told herself that it was the phantoms of failed love plaguing her and not anything Edie was doing or going to do. Still, there were times when she longed for the days of companionship, when passion simmered and lazy Sunday afternoons replaced dinner dates. They had been dating for three months now and Vida was getting anxious for more.

Edie came around the corner and kissed her lightly on the cheek. "It smells wonderful in here."

Vida was scorching green peppers over the burner and their pungent aroma filled the kitchen. "Why, thank you." She glanced up. Edie was helping herself to a glass of wine. "Edie, you look like shit," Vida blurted before she had a chance to censor herself.

"Do I? Well, you on the other hand look absolutely stunning," Edie said, wrapping her arms around Vida's waist.

Vida laughed. "You are a charming woman but that doesn't erase the facts," she said, pushing Edie back and taking a good look at her. She looked tired and pale, and judging from the mild euphoria she was experiencing, probably suffering from the early stages of hypoglycemia. Sometimes having a doctor for a father was not a bad thing. Of course, he had done the same thing to her. She'd experienced Edie's kind of high. "Edie, when was the last time you ate something and got some real sleep?"

Edie looked at her and smiled.

"Edie?" Vida prompted.

"What?"

"You didn't answer my question."

Edie poured herself some more wine.

"Well?" Vida said, getting concerned.

"What was the question?"

Vida studied her for a moment, trying to decide if Edie was playing around. "Go sit down." Vida pushed her toward the couch. She got a can of Ensure from the pantry, put it in a highball glass to disguise it and handed it to Edie.

"Contents?" Edie asked.

"Something that's good for you," Vida said.

"It doesn't look like a white Russian," Edie said, sniffing it.

"Drink it anyway."

Edie took a sip and made a face. She gulped the rest of it down. "Do I get a chaser at least?"

Vida handed her a glass of wine. "Did you eat anything today?" she asked.

"Oh, I'm sure I did," Edie replied.

"What?"

"I don't remember. Besides, I'm going to eat shortly, right?"

"Yes, you sit and relax and I'll finish making dinner."

"I'm sorry. I don't mean to disappoint you."

168

"You're not. I'm just concerned that you're driving yourself into the ground. That's not good."

"I know," Edie said.

Vida stuffed the peppers and was in the middle of one of her daily anecdotes when she looked over and watched Edie's head as it slid down the couch in slow motion.

"Edie?" Vida said, alarmed.

Edie was passed out on the couch. Vida touched her cheek. Edie's eyelids fluttered slightly.

"Edie, I'm going to put you to bed. Okay? You need to get some rest."

Edie opened her eyes and nodded, looking up blearily at Vida. Vida got her a nightshirt and another protein drink and put her to bed. Vida sat next to her on the bed. "I'll be up in a little while."

Edie smiled appreciatively. "I'm sorry I ruined dinner."

Vida studied her for a moment. She looked so small and vulnerable, not anything like the woman Vida had come to know, so self-assured and in control.

"You didn't, darling. You need to take better care of yourself. Even someone as magnificent and brilliant as you needs more than Perrier and ether to survive."

She stroked Edie's head until she closed her eyes. She was asleep in a matter of seconds. Vida slipped downstairs and called her father.

"Dad, I'm sorry it's kind of late but I have a question," Vida said, trying to sound calm.

"What's wrong, sweetheart?" Jerome Sumner asked.

Vida explained about Edie.

"It's probably a minor case of hypoglycemia. She's thin, right?"

"Very thin," Vida said.

"Her body doesn't have any reserves so it does what it can with what's left," he explained.

"Does it make you seem high? It seems like she was high but I know she doesn't do drugs. I'm sure of it."

"Yes, her blood sugar gets low, which sets off a variety of chemical imbalances. Has she had any more nosebleeds?"

"Not that I've seen."

"Probably not. Her body is relaxed because she feels high. Make her get some sleep and eat something good. Her body will right itself. It's a form of crash and burn."

"Okay, thanks, Dad," Vida said.

"You really like her?" he inquired.

"I do."

"So when do I get to meet her?"

"Soon."

"Whenever you're ready," he said softly and then rang off.

Vida ate dinner and cleaned the kitchen and then climbed into bed. True, the cat, was already nestled at Edie's feet and Bertrand was nosing around for a spot on the bed.

"No, not tonight. Tonight you're on guard duty," Vida told him. He pouted for a moment and then slumped down heavily at the side of the bed.

She watched Edie sleeping peacefully. This wasn't exactly how she had envisioned their first night in bed together, but having Edie this close was still a delightful sensation. They'd been taking it slow like Vida had promised, but it had more to do with schedule conflicts and no time than it did with physical restraint. Vida nestled in close to Edie, craving her touch, wanting to run her hands across her smooth, warm flesh.

Edie murmured and pulled her closer, running her hand down Vida's backside and then slowly up the front of her nightshirt.

"You're supposed to be sleeping," Vida said, feeling her face getting flushed as Edie's hand found her breast.

"With Aphrodite in my bed, I doubt it," Edie said. She kissed Vida.

Vida ran her hands along Edie's back and pulled her in closer until their half-naked bodies were intertwined. Edie kissed her neck and started to undo the front of her nightshirt.

"Edie, wait!"

"Hmmm . . ."

"Look at me," Vida said. She could see delirium dancing around Edie's eyes. She sighed heavily. "I want you. I have wanted you for so long but I want all of you, when you feel right, not like this, not exhausted and delirious."

Edie touched her face. "I love you."

"Do you understand?" Vida asked.

Edie nodded. She laid her head on Vida's chest and fell back asleep.

Edie opened one eye to see Vida bringing her coffee. "Good morning. Tell me we didn't make incredible love and I missed it," Edie said, sitting up.

Vida handed her the coffee. "Well, first off it's five o'clock in the afternoon and no, we didn't make love, although I can't say you didn't try."

"But you didn't want me to miss the good parts, right?"

Vida watched Edie's face as she slowly registered the second part of the statement.

"What time did you say it was?" Edie said, looking frantically around for a clock.

"It's almost evening. Don't worry, I took care of everything. Well, I called Sandi and she took care of everything. You were greatly missed but the play survived while its creator was getting better."

Edie took a sip of coffee.

"I hope you don't mind. I went to the loft and got you some clothes . . ." Vida said, remembering the fright she'd seen. The loft had showed signs of someone possessed, signs of someone who was living way too fast. Stuff for the play everywhere, stacks of dry cleaning still in the bags, no food, only cases of bottled water.

"It was pretty bad, huh?" Edie said.

"Edie . . ."

171

"I know things are a little out of control at the moment, but I haven't completely lost it."

"Why didn't you say something?"

"Say what?"

"Say you need some help."

"Because young love shouldn't be about that. It's supposed to fun and frivolous and exciting and all that stuff," Edie said.

"I love you," Vida said, taking Edie's face in her hands and kissing her deeply.

"Come here," Edie said.

The doorbell rang. Vida jumped.

"Did you schedule an appointment with the Fuller Brush Man?" Edie asked.

"No, it's Miranda and Sonja. We're all having dinner tonight, remember?" Vida said.

"Yes, of course," Edie said.

"You didn't, did you?"

"No. All right, I need some help. Things are out of control. I'm sorry."

"Don't be. Have a shower and meet us for cocktails," Vida said, kissing her again.

"It shall be done," Edie said.

"You *are* a good Catholic girl," Vida teased.

Edie pinched her.

"Ouch!"

"Behave yourself or I'll make you learn the rosary," Edie said, bounding out of bed.

Vida watched Edie from across the table. She was relieved to see Edie back to her vivacious, witty and entertaining self. She got the impression that running until you drop, falling flat on your face and getting back up again was a cyclical pattern of Edie's. Vida experienced a moment of inner glee at having found out this little quirk. It made her feel closer to Edie and helped to fill in some of the gaps Vida always felt when it came to Edie's past and present habits. There was so much about Edie she didn't know. Part of her didn't want to find out something bad by digging in places she shouldn't go, but another part kept telling her that you can't truly fall in love with an absolute stranger.

Sonja helped Vida clean up while Edie and Miranda discussed childhood antics of their Catholic school days. Vida suddenly understood their affinity toward each other.

"I didn't know you were Catholic," Vida said as she rinsed dishes and Sonja loaded them into the dishwasher.

"I'm not."

"But Miranda?"

"I sent her to Catholic school because I wanted her to get a decent education and to stay away from drugs and boys. Saint Xavier's promised to do that." Sonja smiled benevolently at Vida.

"What are you thinking?" Vida asked, handing her another dish.

"I think Edie is perfectly darling."

"Me too," Vida said shyly.

"You really like her?" Sonja asked.

"I do."

"Good."

"How is Kirsten?" Vida asked. She always felt guilty about Kirsten because of how they had ended.

"She's doing all right. She did ask about you the other day."

"What did she say?"

"I don't know if I should repeat it," Sonja said.

"Go ahead. I can take it."

"She asked how the cheating, lying bitch was doing."

"I guess she is still bitter."

"To say the least."

⊷

173

After Sonja and Miranda left, Vida found Edie rummaging around for her things. "And just where do you think you're going?"

"I should probably go home and get some stuff organized for tomorrow," Edie said, shoving clothes in her duffle and clearly avoiding Vida's gaze.

"Edie . . ." Vida said, pulling her toward the bedroom. "Please don't make me beg."

Edie seemed to waver for a moment and then went willingly. Vida pulled her shirt out of her pants and ran her hand up Edie's back, pulling her close, then Vida undressed her and pushed her gently down on the bed. Vida took her clothes off then eased her body down on Edie and kissed her. Edie wrapped her hands around Vida's butt and drew her in closer. Vida sighed heavily with a mixture of pleasure and relief when she felt Edie quiver and moan beneath her ardent touch. She kissed Edie's stomach and then moved lower, parting Edie's legs and taking her in her mouth. Edie ran her hand through Vida's hair. Vida brought her to climax and then climbed up beside her.

"See, that wasn't so bad after all," Vida said, stroking Edie's cheek.

"No, that was wonderful. Come here," Edie said, pulling Vida on top of her and gently entering her.

Vida thrust hard against her, feeling her own climax coming. She collapsed on top of Edie and whispered, "I love you."

"Then show me again," Edie said, rolling onto her back and waiting for Vida to take her.

The next morning, Edie was still fast asleep and grossly late for work but Vida couldn't bear to wake her up. Instead, she sipped her coffee and let her mind play over last night. Her fears that perhaps Edie might have been slightly lacking in the sexual department and was thus prolonging the revelation were waylaid by some rather startling moments of unbridled physical passion. Vida could only shake her head in joyful disbelief at the ardent talents of her lover. She didn't think she had ever quite been *done* so thoroughly. Finally, she roused herself from her lusty remembrances and went to wake her lover.

She sat on the edge of the bed and stroked Edie's hair back off her face. She was lying diagonal across the bed and that seemed to have been how they both fallen asleep. Vida's face had been pressed up against the footboard. Her neck was sore and her pillow nowhere to be found. The bedclothes were strewn along the floor.

Edie looked up at her. "You stay away from me."

"But I thought you loved me," Vida said, feigning hurt.

"I do. But it doesn't give you the right to abuse me so completely."

"You loved every minute of it," Vida said.

Edie rolled up on her elbow. "I did." She pulled Vida down to her side and began kissing her.

"You're really late," Vida warned.

"I do believe I'm still recuperating. You're my medicine," Edie said, reaching for Vida's breast and sliding her thigh between her legs.

Vida didn't argue.

Chapter Twelve

Vida stood surveying herself in the mirror again.

"You look fine. You look beautiful. I don't know why you're so freaked," Edie counseled.

"They're your *parents*," Vida whined, pulling off the turquoise blouse and exchanging it for the white one.

"Which means they will love you because I love you," Edie said, wrapping her arms around Vida's waist and kissing the back of her neck. She looked at their reflection in the full-length mirror.

"Don't we make a darling couple?" Edie said.

"Sid thinks so. He wants to do some shots and see if he can get us in *Curve* magazine. He is starting to do some freelance stuff," Vida said.

"No way. All my old girlfriends would know where to find me then," Edie said.

"And I bet you had a few."

"That doesn't bother you?" Edie asked, suddenly serious.

"I'm sure had you known I was going to come along you would have remained a virgin," Vida chided.

"I might have had a few liaisons just for practice," Edie said.

"I'm surprised we don't run into more of your liaisons," Vida said, raising an eyebrow.

"I've been underground for so long they've forgotten me. I'm certain of it."

"No one could forget you."

"So you don't mind a woman with a past?" Edie remembered how running into old girlfriends used to drive Laura into a jealous fervor.

"Edie, all I care about is the you standing here with me right this moment. What happened before is none of my concern. I love you for who you are now."

"You should give lessons," Edie said.

"On what?"

"How to be an incredible partner."

"I hope your parents feel the same way," Vida said.

"They will."

When they arrived at her parents' house, Edie introduced Vida to her mother.

"Nice to finally meet you, Vida," Rocelyn said, her voice teasing.

"I told her about you," Edie admitted.

Vida blushed. "It's nice to meet you too."

"You know we haven't eaten a dinner guest alive for at least twenty years," Rocelyn chided.

Vida laughed. "Okay, I will admit to being a little nervous."

"We won't hurt you. We promise. I warned everyone to be on their best behavior," Rocelyn said.

Sal and Corinne sauntered in the kitchen.

"Ah-ha the mystery guest has arrived," Sal said.

"Be nice," Rocelyn warned.

"Have I ever been anything else?" Sal replied.

"On numerous occasions," Edie said, grabbing her arm and twist-

177

ing it behind her back. "I want you to promise. Vida is very dear to my heart."

Sal cocked her head and swore. "Can she come have a cocktail out on the veranda and we'll show her your baby pictures?"

"No," Edie said.

Corrine took Vida's arm and led her away from both Sal and Edie. "We'll go down the hall and you can peer into the family history on the way out back."

"I'd like that," Vida said, looking over her shoulder and winking at Edie.

"You be nice to her and don't tell her little Edie stories. I mean it," Edie said.

"Maybe just a couple," Sal said, taking Vida's other arm.

"Like the one about Edie seducing the little girl next door," Corinne said.

"That's a good one," Sal said.

"She seduced me! Vida, don't believe a word they say. This family is full of pathological liars."

Rocelyn smiled at Edie.

"What?"

"She seems really nice," Rocelyn said.

"Do you like her?" Edie asked, trying not to twitter like a nervous bride-to-be.

"I think a more important question is, do you like her?"

"I love her."

"Good. Now go find your father. He's been more than a little anxious about you."

"Why?"

"Well, what with a new girlfriend and this big play . . . go talk to him."

"Okay," Edie said.

Edie found her father out back talking to Vida. She waited until he was done and then cornered him in his study. This was his usual retreat from all the femaleness of his family. Edie knew she was the closest he'd ever gotten to having a son.

178

She sat down in one of his wingback chairs. "So what do you think about Vida?"

"She's very pretty," Adrian replied.

"And . . ."

"Edie, are you sure she's a . . . you know, one of those?"

"A lesbian, Dad?"

"Well, yes."

"I'm sleeping with her, Dad. I'm sure. I want you to practice saying the word *lesbian*. Just say *thespian, thespian, thespian* and then roll it into *lesbian*. I know you can do it," Edie said.

He did it.

"See, it worked," she said.

"Maybe in my next life I'll be reincarnated as a thespian lesbian and I can have a girlfriend that looks like Vida. She's a beauty," he said.

"She is very pretty."

"Are you thinking about settling down?"

"I'd like to."

"You should, Edie. It's time."

During the course of dinner the cross-examination took place. It wasn't meant to be a cross-examination although it did have the distinct vestiges of a master's examination, Vida thought, only this time she hadn't puked prior to the examination and the board of professors wasn't quite as crusty. Edie helped her field questions and together they made a good team.

It appeared Adrian had known Vida's father during their undergraduate days. He had never met Vida's mother but had heard of her. She was a beautiful young woman and an artist in her own right.

"Your father is still practicing?" Adrian asked.

"Yes, he can't even fathom retirement," Vida said, taking the proffered piece of garlic bread.

"And your mother?" Rocelyn asked before she had picked up the cue from Edie that it wasn't a good question.

"Actually, my mother died of breast cancer when I was eight," Vida said with the practiced ease of someone who had had to say it a hundred times before. She didn't even flinch and Edie wondered if she would ever be so steeled against death. She could barely think Bia's name without choking back tears.

"I'm so sorry," Rocelyn said.

"Don't worry, I've had enough girlfriends in my life who have more than willingly taken on that position," Vida said.

Rocelyn smiled. "Well, you won't be finding that in Edie, will you?"

"No," Vida said, and they both laughed.

"I think we're learning to be each other's partners and not each other's parents," Vida said, looking at Edie warmly.

When Edie and Vida made ready to leave, Rocelyn whispered in Edie's ear as she gave her a hug, "She's a keeper."

"Thanks, Mom," Edie said.

In the car, Edie reached over and took Vida's hand. Vida kissed it and leaned back in her seat with obvious relief.

"Now you know where I get my inquisitive nature," Edie said.

"They *are* a curious lot," Vida said.

"Don't worry, they get easily bored and move on to new topics. Soon you'll be like all the other members of the family, someone to be teased, cajoled and—"

"Pinched, squeezed and overfed," Vida said, finishing the sentence.

"Exactly. Have I told you I love you lately?"

"No, but I expect you to take me home and show me," Vida replied, running her hand up Edie's thigh.

"How did we possibly keep busy before we made love?"

"It was a struggle."

"Do you miss those days?" Edie teased.

"I do not miss being sexually frustrated. You were driving me to distraction, but I am glad that we learned to be friends first. I would have gone to bed with you the first night we went to dinner and danced on the rooftop."

"You would have?"

"If only you'd asked," Vida said, pinching Edie.

"A woman of your character would never succumb to a first date fuck."

"With a woman of your character she most certainly would."

Edie laughed. "Last person to get their clothes off and into bed is forced to make breakfast and bring it to the victor in bed."

"What would your mother say to such gambling?"

"She would lay her wager on the woman with more experience, and in this case that would be you . . . as a model," Edie said, waylaying any inference that Vida had had more lovers than she had. Sometimes Edie wondered about Vida's past but asked no questions, not wanting to expand on her own.

"I would say your mother was a smart woman indeed," Vida said. "Are you fixing me omelets tomorrow? Because if so we need to stop and get eggs."

"Would you like an omelet?"

"I would."

Chapter Thirteen

Vida heard the purr and ping of the Porsche in the drive. Edie's arrival still made her heart leap with anticipation, especially now that the play was in full rehearsal and between Vida's work at the museum and doing a couple of spring shoots for Vanessa's Closet they spent more time apart than they did together. This did nothing to chill the relationship; rather it kept it at a fevered pace despite their having been lovers for five months. Sometimes Vida wondered if, when things settled down, Edie would be bored. She sensed that running at full speed with hardly a moment to breathe was Edie's method of operation and she tried to contemplate a sedate world of dinners at home and life together with no interruption.

She found it hard to imagine. Did Edie do things like trim hedges, watch reruns, lie utterly still in a lawn chair for hours, wait to get her oil changed and read old magazines, do laundry and clean the kitchen floor? It seemed her incredible girlfriend never did anything so banal, yet those things always appeared done. She didn't ask but half suspected some well-paid gofer performed these tasks. She looked for signs of such a person but never found them.

Edie knocked at the door and smiled widely. "My beautiful darling, how have you been?"

"Missing you badly."

"Ditto. Are you prepared for the suburban barbecue?" Edie asked, wrapping her in an embrace.

"Of course. I'm eager to met Sandi's better half and these other friends of yours that I've heard of but have yet to meet," Vida said, pulling her closer and feeling her nether regions ache for her lover's touch. This feeling she hoped future domesticity would not quell.

"It's times like these I wish I hadn't committed us."

"Why?" Vida inquired.

"Because I'd rather spend the day in bed," Edie said, pushing her up against the wall.

"Ditto."

"But we promised."

"Later?" Edie asked, her blue eyes positively sparkling with desire.

"Yes," Vida said, breathing heavily in her ear.

Edie let out a sigh of sexual anticipation.

"Okay let's go so we can come home," Edie said, taking her hand.

Karen and her lover, Mattie, saw Edie's Porsche ahead of them on Squaw Peak Freeway.

"It's Edie," Karen said.

"How do you know?" Mattie asked.

"Look at the license plate, Plan B. It's the personalized plate Laura got for her. She used to say Edie always had a contingency plan," Karen replied.

Mattie nodded. "Who's she got with her?"

"Must be the new girlfriend," Karen said.

"They're sitting awfully close," Mattie said.

"Yes, they are. Bet if you asked the new girlfriend to put both her hands on the dash she couldn't do it."

"What do you mean?" Mattie asked.

"They're fucking, darling," Karen replied flatly.

"Are you serious?"

"Don't look so shocked. It's not like we've never done that," Karen said.

"We have," Mattie said.

"That long drive, straight road, throbbing hormones," Karen said.

"Still they shouldn't be doing that."

"Are you jealous?" Karen teased.

"Maybe a little," Mattie replied.

"We could fix that," Karen said, running her hand up Mattie's thigh.

Mattie blushed.

"Do I still make you feel that way?" Karen asked.

"Yes," Mattie said, removing Karen's hand from between her legs and putting it across her heart. "You are a wonderful woman and I love you dearly."

"And desire?" Karen asked.

"You think too much. Everything is fine," Mattie said.

"You're right, I do think too much," Karen said.

As they passed Edie they honked and waved. Edie looked over at them with a half-witted smile.

"Does she even know it was us?" Mattie asked.

"She'll figure it out and then we can tease her for being a menace on the American highway," Karen said.

Sandi welcomed them while Linden poured drinks. Sandi and Linden had just finished putting a large deck on the back of the house. They gave Karen and Mattie a tour of its accoutrements and told them the stories of home improvement nightmares. Sandi had a mangled thumbnail to show for her efforts.

"At least you're still speaking to each other," Karen said.

"Barely," Linden said.

"Come on, it wasn't that bad. Besides, I needed something to do other than working on the play. The thing was driving me crazy. Thank God it's almost done," Sandi said.

"You say that now," Linden grumbled. "All I could see was that we finished the deck and never got to use it because we were getting divorced."

"I don't think we'll be doing any more home improvements for a while," Sandi said, starting the barbecue. "Are you hungry?"

"Getting there," Karen replied.

"We're just waiting on Edie and Vida," Sandi said.

"We passed them on the way up," Mattie said.

"I wonder where they are," Sandi said.

"Probably fucking in your driveway," Karen said, taking a sip of her Long Island Ice Tea.

"No way!" Sandi said, remembering Edie's apparent frigidity of earlier days.

"Karen is convinced they were fucking in the car as we drove past," Mattie explained.

"I'll be right back," Sandi said.

"Can I go with?" Karen said.

Mattie grabbed her hand, "Don't be crude, sit."

"Good thing we live on two acres, or the neighbors would have called the cops," Linden said, refilling Karen's glass from the large pitcher on the table.

Edie sat back in the seat and exhaled slowly. "My, that was nice."

"Uh-huh . . . I missed you," Vida murmured.

Edie looked around. "I've got an idea," she said, starting the car and backing it up alongside of Karen's Jeep Cherokee. The Porsche was low enough that it was no longer visible from the house. Edie pulled the keys out of the ignition and opened the door. "Come here," she said, smiling mischievously at Vida.

"Are you sure this is okay?" Vida asked, straddling her.

"They can't see us," Edie said, slipping her hands inside Vida's shorts. She was wet and Edie eased inside her slowly, rocking her gently.

Just then Sandi came into view, right in time to see Vida biting Edie's shoulder.

"You are fucking in the driveway!" Sandi said indignantly.

"No, we're done fucking in the driveway," Vida said, still holding Edie tight.

"You two are awful. Now come inside this minute," Sandi lectured.

"All right," Edie said, feeling Vida tighten her cunt, trying to hold Edie fast. Edie raised an eyebrow.

Vida smiled before she got up.

"You're bad," Edie whispered. She stuck her fingers in her mouth and savored them.

"No worse than you," Vida retorted.

"That's why we make such a good pair," Edie said.

Sandi rolled her eyes. "You've obviously been making up for lost time."

Edie stepped on the back of her shoe, flipping it off her foot.

"Hey!" Sandi said, giving Edie a dirty look.

Edie smiled sweetly.

Two weeks later Edie called Vida late at night. She had been at the theater all day. Opening night was fast closing in them.

"I didn't wake you?" Edie asked cautiously.

"No, I was just finishing up some things," Vida said.

"I miss you," Edie said.

"I miss you too. Do you want me to come over?" Vida asked, as if sensing something was wrong.

"No, it's late, I just wanted to call and say good night. We can talk tomorrow."

"Okay. Can you come for dinner?" Vida said.

"Yes."

"Edie, are you all right?"

"Just tired."

"Sleep tight," Vida said softly.

Edie lay on the bed. She was tired . . . tired of not being with Vida, of scheduling dates, of not waking up every morning in bed next to the woman she loved. She wanted them to live together. They had dated long enough. But she wasn't certain Vida wanted the same thing.

They'd never talked about living together, but until now it hadn't been much of an issue. Vida was very busy fulfilling the rest of her contract with Vanessa's Closet and working at the museum.

Edie had tagged along on a few of her locations. Mercedes thought Edie was to die for and understood as only the young can how Vida could give her up for such a woman. Vida didn't mention past liaisons and Mercedes was the picture of decorum. By then she'd fallen madly in love with a fashion designer and they were living happily in a penthouse apartment. Vida and Edie appeared the perfect couple except that they didn't live together. Edie wanted to live together. Get a house, have a yard, buy useful furniture, straighten the linen closet and throw disgusting mysterious things out of the fridge.

The next night Edie cooked them dinner, Brazilian fajitas with an orange slice salad.

"Something new to tantalize your palate," Edie said, slipping Bertrand a piece of cheese.

"Smells incredible," Vida said.

"I don't want you getting bored," Edie said, looking plaintively at Vida as she sat at the kitchen bar.

"With you I don't think that's possible. You don't sit still long enough to get boring."

"What if I wanted to sit still?"

"That would be fine too. Edie, what's wrong?" Vida asked.

"We need to talk," Edie said, her face grown serious. "But alas dinner is prepared and we shouldn't spoil a perfectly good dinner."

"Edie?" Vida said, trying not to appear panicked.

"Come eat," Edie said, not catching her gaze. "It can wait."

Vida tried without success not to worry but each forkful of food was an effort as she felt her stomach tying up in knots.

"You don't like it?" Edie asked.

"No, it's very good. I had a late lunch," Vida said apologetically.

They cleaned up the dinner dishes quietly, each caught up in her own thoughts.

Vida put a CD in and took Edie's hand, pulling her close and letting the music move their bodies. Edie looked at her puzzled.

"This reminds me of our first night together," Vida said.

"It does," Edie said. "Vida, can we talk?"

"Okay, but let me make you feel good first . . . please," Vida said, taking her hands and pulling her toward the bedroom.

Vida ardently seduced Edie, hoping this wouldn't be the last time they made love. Memories of making love with Edie ran through her head and the thought of not being with her anymore made her heart hurt. It wasn't until Edie made her come that they broke the barrier. Vida cried out and then burst into tears.

"Vida, what's wrong?" Edie said, holding her.

"I can't bear it anymore." Vida sobbed.

"Bear what?"

"If you leave me," Vida said.

"Leave you? Where'd you get such a foolish idea? I want to live with you. I want to wake up every morning with you. Buy a house together."

"With a hedge?" Vida said.

"If you want," Edie said.

"Oh, Edie," Vida said, pulling her tight.

"Do you want to live together?" Edie asked.

"More than anything."

"Oh, good," Edie said, breathing a sigh of relief.

"Did you think I didn't?" Vida asked, suddenly grasping the depths of their apparent miscommunication.

"I wasn't sure. We haven't talked about it before."

"I figured when the dust settled we'd set up house."

"Well, you could have told me," Edie said.

"I didn't want to seem pushy. I thought you needed time to unwind."

"I spent all my unwinding time thinking you weren't interested in that kind of a relationship," Edie said.

"Silly you," Vida chided.

Edie got up abruptly.

"Where are you going?" Vida asked, alarmed she had offended her suddenly touchy lover.

"To get my address book," Edie said.

"Right now?" Vida said, rolling up on her elbow.

Edie came back and sat on the edge of the bed. She picked up the phone and dialed.

"Who are you calling?" Vida asked.

"My friend Nicole," Edie said, waiting for the voice messaging to pick up.

"What for?"

"She's a realtor. We need a house, don't we?"

"No time like the present," Vida said, lying back and basking in love.

Edie finished the call and then gathered up Vida's clothes.

"What now?" Vida said as Edie handed them to her.

"We're going shopping," Edie said.

"Right now?"

"You said it yourself—no time like the present," Edie said, putting her pants on.

"Shopping for what?" Vida asked as Edie buttoned up her shirt.

"Furniture," Edie said, tromping off to the bathroom.

"It's Saturday night and it's late," Vida protested.

"Z-Gallery is open until ten. So chop-chop. Let's get a move on."

"What is your hurry? Besides, I think we should find a house, inventory what we already have and then shop for what we need. Don't you think?" Vida asked, pulling herself to the edge of the bed so she could see Edie in the bathroom.

"I don't want you to change your mind," Edie said, poking her head around the bathroom door.

"Edie, come back to bed. I promise I won't change my mind. I just want to hold you naked in my arms and think about how nice it will be to live with you. Please, indulge me," Vida said.

"We'll look at houses tomorrow then."

"I swear," Vida said, pulling her down on the bed.

Edie's friend Nicole must have shown them fifty houses over the next two weeks and not one had been suitable. The problem was Edie. Every house they looked at, Edie liked the one next door or down the block.

"But Edie, those ones are not for sale. This one is," Nicole said, her manner professional and her tone practiced.

"It has to be the perfect house. Besides, when you find it then you get to sell Vida's condo and my loft. Think of the commission," Edie said, obviously pining for the house across the street as she stood looking out the bay window of yet another house.

"I mean, look at that house. It's perfect."

"It's not for sale," Nicole and Vida said in unison.

"I know it's out there," Edie muttered.

The following Sunday Vida drove Edie across town blindfolded. Edie rather liked the blindfold, although it was getting a bit uncomfortable.

"Vida, I don't know if this is going to work. I might get carsick," Edie said, readjusting the blindfold.

"It's the only way. Nicole and I think we have found the perfect house and we don't want you to be distracted by other houses in the area until you have given this one your full attention."

"Really?" Edie said, getting excited.

"Tell me a story. It will take your mind off of it."

"A story?"

"Yes, tell me about the new play."

"Sandi is pulling her hair out, but it's the only way I can let go and have her take over the production. This is going to be a good play. It is a comedy of errors, like Shakespeare's *Midsummer Night's Dream*."

"That sounds like a great play."

"I have a better idea," Edie said, suddenly feeling very comfortable in the darkness of the blindfold. It felt like sitting in the confession booth at church.

"Okay," Vida replied.

"I want to tell you some of the things I've done."

"Why?"

Edie could hear the trepidation in Vida's voice and said, "Because we are moving in together and I don't want you to have any nasty surprises."

"Edie, we don't have to go there."

"These are things I will never do to you."

"All right."

"I'm not a serial killer."

"What have you done?"

"Well, first off, when I was with Cassandra and things started to fall apart I kind of lost it. I went stark raving mad in a public place and the white coats hauled me off to the loony bin for a spell. Just a suggestion: If you're going to lose it do not do it in a public place."

There was silence.

"Vida?"

"I'm listening."

"The second bad thing was that I had an affair with Bia while I was with Laura. The night Bia died I left."

"What do you mean, you left?" Vida asked as she pulled up to the four-way stop sign.

"I left the country for a few months and I didn't tell anyone where I was."

"Oh, Edie, that's not good."

"Which part?" Edie said, pulling up the blindfold and looking over at Vida.

"Put it back on. We're almost there," Vida said, pulling onto Cliffside Drive.

Edie put the blindfold back on.

"You shouldn't have left like that."

"That's the part you're concerned with? What about being a nut job and a cheat?" Edie said.

"That's not that bad. Kirsten left me after she caught me in bed with Mercedes, and the going crazy part, well, haven't we all felt like that before," Vida said matter-of-factly. "But leaving Laura like that, that has a lasting effect on someone."

"I know, but she can't ever know what went on."

"Edie, the truth is a hard thing but it can set you free."

"You sound just like Sandi."

Vida pulled up in front of the house.

Edie felt the car stop. "Are we here?"

"Yes, now take off the blindfold and don't look at anything but the front of the house."

Edie studied the front of a large Spanish Colonial-style house complete with a massive front lawn and a hedge.

"It's perfect for croquet."

"I didn't know you played croquet."

"I don't but I could learn."

"Okay, now stay focused. Don't look at anything else until we get inside," Vida said.

"You slept with Mercedes? She's hot."

"Edie, I want you to concentrate because I'm almost at my wit's end over this house thing," Vida said, guiding her into the large living room that overlooked the lush backyard complete with gazebo and swimming pool.

Edie looked around. "We'll need a lot of furniture for this house."

"Do you like it so far?"

"It's great. Let's see the rest."

"It won't be overload for you?"

"No. Do you still love me despite my confession?"

"Yes. We've both done bad things that have hurt people but we won't do that anymore."

"Okay," Edie said, taking Vida's hand.

When they were done looking over the house, Vida called Nicole and told her they'd take it.

"I think she wet her pants when I told her," Vida said, giving Edie a big hug.

"I can't help it. I'm a picky, cheating nut job."

"You just want everything to be perfect."

"I do."

It was the opening night of Edie's play *Anatomy of a Love Affair*. Sandi was rushing around making sure all the last-minute details were taken care of. Edie was standing in the wings and looking out at the crowd, obviously looking for someone in particular.

"Who is she looking for?" Sandi said. "All the important people are already here."

"She's looking for Laura," Vida said.

"Laura!"

"She invited her to the play."

"At your suggestion?"

"With a little prodding," Vida said, remembering the night when she stood in the kitchen handing Edie the invitations to the play after she had picked them up at the printers.

"Here are the invitations," Vida had said.

"Thanks for picking them up," Edie said.

"And here is Laura's new address," Vida said, handing her a scrap of paper with an address scrawled across it.

"New address?"

"She moved to Sedona."

"Why do I need her address?"

"So you can send her an invitation."

"Have you lost your fucking mind?" Edie said.

"No. It's a nice thing to do and you owe her. You wrote the play for her. She should see it."

Edie had winced. "How did you know that?"

"I just do."

Edie watched as Laura and Isabel took their seats in the front row.

"Oh my God, there she is," Edie said, turning to look at Vida and Sandi.

"Okay, now you know what to do," Vida said.

"I don't think I can do this," Edie said.

Vida took her hand. "When the lights dim . . ."

Laura looked around hoping to see Edie and hoping not to see Edie.

Isabel stroked her cheek. "Are you all right?"

"No. But I think it's important that we came," Laura said stoically.

The lights dimmed. Laura felt someone sidle up next to her in the darkness.

"I wanted you to know that I wrote this play for you," Edie murmured.

"Edie?" Laura whispered.

"I wrote it as a tribute and a tribunal for what we had together," Edie said. She leaned over toward Isabel. "Hi, I'm Edie."

"I'm Isabel."

194

"Nice to meet you. I hope you enjoy the play," Edie said, then she left.

When Edie got back in the wings, Vida said, "See, that wasn't so bad."

"No, it was horrific. But you're right, it needed to be done. Now I need a drink."

"I'm proud of you," Vida said.

Edie smiled sadly. "In my next life I'll be better."

"I know you will. We both will."

Chapter Fourteen

Edie had the new house equipped with a complete gym so that Vida could stay at home instead of having to go to the health club for her workouts. Vida had simply smiled. The new house was perfect. Decorated perfectly, designed perfectly, and now it seemed they were truly living the dream. Except for one thing, Vida thought. Sandi had told her something that Edie had not. Vida finished her last set of crunches, sat up and asked Edie why she hadn't told her about Laura's invitation to a housewarming party for the new house in Sedona.

"I didn't think it was important," Edie said.

"Okay, but Sandi thinks it's important."

"She should mind her own business," Edie replied.

"So you don't want to go because you see no point in seeing Laura."

"Exactly."

"Perfectly understandable," Vida said, getting up.

"That's all right with you?"

"Like I want to spend the weekend with your ex-wife," Vida said, taking her hand.

"I love you," Edie said, looking up at her.

"But I do think you should send a housewarming gift, just to show no hard feelings and all that," Vida said.

"You are a dangerous woman."

"And that's how you like your women. Come have a bath with me."

"I'm there."

Edie bought Laura a housewarming present. That was as far as she was going. She'd spent days freaking quietly on her own and hiding it all from Vida. She knew one thing for certain. She wasn't going to Sedona for the weekend.

Nothing would drag her back to the place where memory lingered in a painful shroud of lost love, of love gone terribly astray, of psycho love. Part of her felt relief wash over her while the other part wanted the weekend to be done so that there remained no possibility of being forced to do things she didn't think herself capable of. She jingled the house keys, unlocked the back door and called out for Vida.

"Vida, I got the stuff," Edie chirped out. "Baby, where are you?"

Edie walked into the living room to find Karen, Sandi, Linden and Mattie looking like a tribunal. Edie felt her nerves begin to stretch taut like a wild thing sensing a trap. She would play it cool but she knew what they wanted.

"Hey, you didn't *all* have to stop by and get the present," Edie said, walking over to a lifesized plastic rendition of E.T., the extra-terrestrial from the movie. She'd purchased it as a housewarming present for Laura. "What do you think?" Edie asked them as she rearranged his white silk scarf and accompanying dark sunglasses.

"I think it will clash with her decor," Karen said matter-of-factly.

"Exactly," Edie said, smiling.

"I don't understand the significance," Mattie said. "Did she like the film or something?"

"Not that I know of, but he is expensive, useless and from another planet, and all he wanted to do was go home. I find that I identify with those particular sentiments, or at least I do in Laura's eyes. Except for the going-home part, I'm one step up on him. I'm staying home."

"Edie, you can't. You've got to go. I promised Laura," Sandi pleaded.

Edie said nothing, trying to buy time and look for the car keys. Where had she set them down?

"You're going. The only reason she's having us up this weekend is to see you. She *needs* to see you."

"Yeah, like I *need* a bad case of hemorrhoids."

"Come on, Edie, let it end," Linden piped up.

"It ended the day Bia died."

"It ended the day you left," Linden corrected.

"Your eye for detail is impeccable."

"Edie, give it a rest," Sandi said.

"I am. I'm not going. It's simple."

"Edie, be reasonable," Sandi pleaded.

"It's not one of my better attributes," Edie said, leaning up against the kitchen bar and slowly sliding the car keys toward her. She felt the hard, cold steel in her hand and slipped them in her pocket. Vida saw her do it but everyone else appeared oblivious.

"You won't go then?" Sandi asked.

"No," Edie said, squeezing the car keys in her pocket: safety and freedom, all she had to do was escape. She now had means.

"You give me no choice then. I'm going to burn your new play page by page until you say you'll go," Sandi said, picking up the first page of the manuscript and a lighter.

"It's only a copy," Edie countered.

"No, it's not. I know you only have the original because you're superstitious, and until it goes to production you retain only one copy," Sandi uttered knowledgably.

Edie flinched, torn between her fear and desire for flight. Was her creative child really about to be sacrificed? She had the notes and some parts of the draft. She could probably reconstruct it but it would take time and she didn't really have that luxury. She needed the play but she needed her sanity more.

Sandi moved the trash can closer and flicked the lighter. She looked at Edie, waiting for a sign. "Make it easy and just go."

"No, I'm not going. You have no idea how difficult this is. It's bigger than you think."

"I know it's hard but you owe her this much," Sandi reasoned.

"No, believe me it'll be better if I don't go."

"You're being a coward," Sandi said.

"No, I'm being more generous and benevolent than you could possibly imagine," Edie replied.

"You walked out of all of our lives, making us frightened and worried, and you didn't even let her say good-bye. Can't you see it torments her? Come on, Edie, just this one time," Sandi said.

"No. I can't."

Sandi lit the first page. The pungent odor of burning paper hit the air. Sandi let the first page fall burning into the empty trash can. She lit the second page.

"Sandi, stop it," Karen said, coming toward her.

Sandi backed up, moving the trash can with her boot. "No."

Vida started to cry. Edie was horrified.

"Oh, for fuck's sake, now look at what you've done," Edie said, going to hold Vida.

"I've done! *You've* done," Sandi said.

"Vida, come on, baby. It's all right," Edie said, wiping her tears.

"But your play . . ." Vida's clear blue eyes filled with more tears.

Edie ran her hands through Vida's long blonde hair, pulling her closer. "I'll write another one."

"Goddamn it, Sandi, that's enough," Karen said, coming toward her. "If she doesn't want to go she doesn't have to. Why are you so invested anyway? Okay, so she cheated on Laura and Laura doesn't know. Big deal. It's over. Some things should be left unsaid. Edie will never confess and clearly you want her to."

Karen reached for the play.

"No, she's going, damn it, or I'll burn the whole fucking thing," Sandi said, struggling with Karen.

Vida started to sob.

"All right, all right. I'll go. Just stop it!" Edie said.

"Good," Sandi said, putting the manuscript in a manila envelope. "We'll take this for safekeeping. You'll get it back at the end of the weekend."

"Glad to see you trust me," Edie said.

"I know how you are, remember," Sandi said. "I hope those weren't crucial pages."

Edie rolled her eyes. "We've got to pack."

"We're already packed," Vida said, pointing to the two leather duffle bags by the door.

Edie handed her a tissue. "You're not to be trusted."

"I'm sorry," Vida said, looking the picture of guilt.

"We made her do it," Linden said.

"I'm sure you did. You've got some making up to do," Edie said, pointing her finger at Vida.

"I'll make it up to you, don't worry," Vida said, pulling her close and sliding her hand across Edie's butt, squeezing one cheek.

"Don't you two ever get tired of each other? It's not like you're newlyweds anymore," Sandi asked.

"It's because she made me wait so long," Vida said, stroking Edie's cheek.

"I didn't want sex to cloud the issue," Edie said.

"What issue?" Vida asked.

"That I loved you, not just your incredible body."

"That's not true," Vida chided.

"No, I was scared shitless," Edie admitted.

"That's better," Vida said.

Karen and Linden grabbed the bags.

Edie whispered to Vida, "I'll be back soon, so wait for me."
Vida nodded.

"Where are you going?" Sandi said.

"For a pee. Vida will help you with the present. He's heavy and I'll be right there. Sedona is a long ride and I have a small bladder."

"All right," Sandi said.

Vida and Sandi waddled E.T. through the door.

"Shit, he's heavy," Sandi muttered. "I'm not doing this to hurt her you know."

"I know. She still doesn't talk about that time if she can avoid it. Sometimes I feel like I'm living with an amnesiac with a gap of five years in her life."

"Are you curious?" Sandi asked as they heaved him in the back seat of Vida's Land Rover.

"Kind of, but I'm also rather anxious. Maybe I don't want to know. The woman I know today is the one I love. Do I really need to see her past?"

Sandi looked straight through her. "That little shit!" She took off running to the back of the house.

Edie splashed water on her face and then studied her face in the mirror. She saw an older, thinner, more vulnerable woman than the one Laura had known. She saw a woman who had been running to forget her past, to forget the best and worst days of her life, to forget a love affair that had almost destroyed her. She wasn't strong enough to do this. She quietly lifted the screen off the bathroom window and crept out. They could burn the manuscript. She didn't care. Getting away was all that mattered now.

Suddenly Sandi grabbed her from behind, sweeping her off her feet.

"I hate being a petite woman," Edie declared.

"I should have known you'd try something like this," Sandi said, pushing Edie to the car.

Edie turned. "Why are you doing this to me?"

"Because I promised Laura. Look, Edie, after all the things that you've done to her I don't think it'll kill you to give back just this once," Sandi said.

Edie nodded.

Linden helped Edie tie down the giant plastic sculpture.

"I guess she could use it for a lawn ornament," Linden said diplomatically.

"Perhaps you should suggest that," Edie replied.

"He sure is ugly, though," Linden replied, securing the final knot.

"You're going to have to help me get him undone," Edie said. "Will you tie his scarf tighter too."

"You're acting like a worried parent," Linden teased.

"I'm practicing."

"Vida's not pregnant?" Linden asked, clearly alarmed.

"One never knows," Edie said, smirking.

"Finger babies," Vida said, laughing and getting in the driver's side.

Sandi came over and handed Edie a beer and two Valiums.

"What do I need these for?" Edie said, getting in the car and studying the pills.

"To relax you," Sandi replied.

"You're so thoughtful," Edie said, cracking the beer. Vida took a sip and they headed out. *A caravan of doomed souls about to meet the lepers of their past*, Edie thought as they headed up Interstate 17 to Sedona. She shoved the two Valiums in E.T.'s mouth and smiled at Vida. "I might want them later."

Vida nodded.

The red rock formations of Sedona approached; today they loomed. Normally, Edie felt immense pleasure at seeing them, at knowing the vortexes that surrounded the town, feeling their energy as she hiked toward them. Today her energy felt like it was being sucked through a black hole. The sheen of her one beer had long worn off. Sandi had offered her more as they made various rest stops, but Edie didn't want to be drunk the first time she saw Laura.

Sandi was another story. She tripped as she got out of Linden's jeep and landed on her face in the soft red dust of the driveway. She groaned and rolled over.

"I think the universe is punishing you for burning my play. You're lucky that wasn't gravel," Edie said, peering over her.

"It wasn't your play. It was Linden's staff meeting notes."

"You slime!" Edie said.

"It doesn't mean I won't burn the original if you don't behave yourself," Sandi advised.

"You didn't say I had to behave myself," Edie said indignantly.

"Like you could," Vida chided.

"You know, Linden, if I were you I'd take advantage of her position. Lesbian bed death could be a myth," Karen said.

Sandi leaned up on one elbow and leered rather lasciviously at Linden.

Linden blushed. She took the dare, easing her body down on Sandi's, breasts touching breasts and thigh touching thigh. She kissed her deeply, making color rise to Sandi's face.

"Oh my," Sandi said, when she came up for air.

Everyone laughed.

Inside the rambling white adobe house, Isabel watched the women in the driveway from the kitchen window.

"I think they're here," she called out.

"What do you mean, *think*?" Laura called out from the living room where, Isabel knew, she was fluffing the cushions on the couch for the hundredth time that afternoon.

"Six women in a variety of sports utility vehicles with six of the seven varieties of lesbian hairdos are in our driveway and two of them are making out in the dirt while the rest watch. I don't think they're Jehovah's Witnesses."

"That's them," Laura said tersely.

"Well, it won't be a dull weekend. Come see," Isabel said.

"I can't," Laura said, clearly dreading the knock on the door.

"Are you going to be all right?" Isabel said, coming and sitting down next to her. She took Laura's hand.

"Don't I look all right?" Laura said, popping up like a jack-in-the-box. She looked in the oval mirror over the fireplace.

"You look beautiful," Isabel said, coming up behind her and sliding her hand around Laura's waist.

"Thank you," Laura said, appreciative. She jumped when the doorbell rang.

Sandi stood admiring the stunning, rambling adobe house. Laura had apparently done quite well for herself.

Linden and Edie worked to get E.T. undone. Karen and Mattie got bags out of the cars.

Edie said, "Vida, you can go in with them. I'll just be a minute. Sandi will take care of you."

Sandi smiled and took Vida's hand. "Laura is a nice woman . . . really."

"Remind me never to date a Navy Seal with a passion for S and M," Edie said as she unwound the rope.

"It's not recommended," Linden said.

Isabel answered the door.

"Mattie and Karen, I'm so glad to see you. You look good," Laura said, giving them each a hug.

"Beautiful house, Laura," Karen said.

"Thank you. And this is my partner, Isabel."

"Nice to finally meet you," Sandi said, shaking Isabel's hand.

204

They were standing in a large living room decorated in Southwest style, a fireplace in the corner.

"And this is Sandi," Laura said, with a pointed glance down at Sandi's hand holding Vida's.

Sandi caught the look and said, "This is Vida."

"Nice to meet you," Laura said cordially.

Linden came in the open door.

"Linden! How nice to see you," Laura said, taking her hand and leading her into the living room. "Did . . . ?"

"She's coming," Linden said, "with a gift."

Sandi heard a few choice obscenities and a swipe of bushes as Edie tried to get the present up the narrow walk to the steps.

"I'd recognize those legs anywhere," Laura chirped, her face reddening.

Edie grunted and set E.T. on the porch. "Fuck, he's heavy. Happy housewarming," she said with a tight smile. Sandi saw her discreetly snatch the Valiums from his mouth and quickly pop them in her own.

"I didn't think you knew about Alex," Laura said.

"Alex?"

"Isabel's daughter."

"Oh, Alex. Well, I hope she likes him," Edie said, recovering quickly.

"She'll adore him," Isabel said.

"Don't I get a hug?" Laura said.

"Do I have to?" Edie said, taking a step backward.

"Edie!" Sandi admonished.

"I have intimacy issues," Edie said, giving Laura a hug.

Laura held her close. "You look good. Thinner, though."

"I believe the term is fashionably lean," Edie said, taking Vida's hand. "Have you met Vida?"

"Yes, I did," Laura said, clearly confused.

"May we see the house?" Sandi asked, hoping to tactfully change the subject.

⁊⁊

After the tour, Edie stood in the kitchen wondering how many more intolerable minutes it would be until the Valiums kicked in. The warm feeling they gave her reminded her of her days in therapy, where she got more drugs than good advice.

"Should we go have cocktails on the back deck?" Laura suggested. "We can sort out rooms and bags later."

Edie made it a point to stay as far away from Laura as she possibly could. At first it seemed like mere logistics but as the afternoon progressed it became evident that although she had agreed to come visit it did not mean she had to be chummy. Seven-year-old Alex proved a good diversion. She loved E.T. and together Alex and Edie whiled away the afternoon. Edie moved E.T. down to the gazebo by the pool where Alex could visit him. They were sitting on the steps of the gazebo when Laura found them.

"I wondered what you two were up to," Laura said good-naturedly.

Alex smiled. "Edie's teaching me to spit."

"Gee that's great."

"I teach all my friends how to spit. It's important to learn how not to get excess saliva on your shoes, especially during sporting events," Edie said.

"Are dirty words next in her education?"

"Yes, I thought we'd start with *cunnilingus*," Edie said.

Laura blanched.

"What's that mean, Mom?"

"She's the lady on the evening news, honey. Why don't you go tell your mom to start the branding iron, I mean barbecue."

They watched her run up to the house.

"When are you going to grow up?" Laura asked, her face getting red.

"I thought you preferred children, or is it teenagers?" Edie said, referring to Isabel and Laura's age difference.

Laura scowled and stormed off.

❧

Laura cornered Edie when she came up to the deck where the barbecue and dinner preparations were beginning. Edie looked at her with a sigh of resignation. That had always been Laura's one big problem. She wouldn't let things come around on their own; she always had to force the issue. Here we go again, Edie thought.

"I don't understand why you're harboring so much animosity," Laura said.

"Like that's anything new," Edie said, spinning around savagely.

"Edie, come on . . ." Sandi tried to interject.

"Why are you here if you're so miserable?" Laura asked.

Pissed off, Edie looked straight at her. "I didn't want to come. I had no choice. I was forced."

"What, they tied you up and brought you here?"

Sandi studied her fingernails. *Coward*, Edie thought.

Laura stared at Sandi. "How forced?" she asked.

Edie looked away.

"Sandi, what did you do to make her come?"

"I burnt part of her play until she got in the car," Sandi said, not meeting Laura's gaze. "You made me promise I'd get her to come. It was the only way."

"It took that much to get you here?"

"I just don't see the point in dragging out the past," Edie replied. "Don't you get it? It didn't work out. I'm sorry. What more do you want from me?"

"I want an explanation. You changed my entire life in one day. Bia died and you got on a plane for God-knows-where. I want to know why."

"I can't explain it."

"Why did you invite me to the play?"

"I owed you that. Sandi made me come here because she's intent on rubbing my face in dog shit for being a horrible human being. She thinks what I did to you was cruel."

"It was."

"Look, I'm sorry. But aren't you better off? I mean, look at her," Edie said, pointing at Isabel. "She's a better partner than I ever was."

"She is not the issue."

"Laura, let it go," Edie pleaded.

"No, you owe me a reason why you loved me once and then you didn't. You are so fucked up."

"I know."

Laura rubbed her forehead. She turned around and went back inside. Vida and Isabel looked rather disturbed. The rest rolled their eyes and shrugged, obviously remembering other stormy days.

"Can I go now?" Edie asked Sandi.

"Not until you fix the mess you've created," Sandi said.

"I'll go talk to her," Karen said.

Edie smiled at Isabel and Vida. "You two look like you just had barium enemas. Come for a walk and I'll tell you stories about worse fights and then you'll understand why we are no longer together." She grabbed the bottle of tequila off the picnic table.

Linden and Mattie sat on the steps and watched them go.

"Only Edie could pull that off," Linden remarked.

"Pull what off?" Mattie said, lighting a cigarette.

"Get the girlfriends laughing, put them at ease after witnessing old lovers' spats. This can't be easy for them."

"What is it with old lovers that makes us seek closure? Why do we care?" Mattie asked. She took a long drag on her cigarette.

"It's a primordial yearning inherent in all lesbians that we must assure ourselves and our lovers that we have not done irreparable damage," Linden replied with a chuckle.

"But we have damaged them, and they us," Mattie said, watching Edie, Isabel and Vida sit in the desert and pass the tequila around.

"Closure is the one last, big apology: the act of forgiving and forgetting," Linden said.

"Do we forgive and forget?" Mattie asked.

"No, lesbians are like elephants. We remember everything but we pretend we don't so we can move on to new lovers," Linden said.

208

"You really liked the play?" Edie asked, looking at Isabel suspiciously. Edie had a perverse disdain for celebrity.

"Yes, I fully expected Medusa to walk out at the end of the play during the encore and instead, such a small woman came out and you looked . . . so vulnerable, like you were asking us if we understood what you were trying to say," Isabel said.

Vida laughed.

"What?" Edie asked.

"You do. You look like the poet about to have her tongue ripped out. It's very powerful."

"I do?"

"You do," they both said.

Edie smiled. "You two are very astute. I didn't realize I was so transparent."

"You are," Vida said.

"It was a great play, Edie, and thanks for making us see it," Isabel said, taking another swig of tequila.

"We're going to have incredible hangovers in the morning," Edie said.

"Do we have a choice on a weekend like this?" Isabel asked.

Edie smiled sadly, thinking Isabel had the prettiest brown eyes she'd seen in a long time. Bia had soft brown eyes like that. Eyes Edie was proud to have never made cry. Not that they hadn't fought, only that they hadn't needed to take it that far. Somehow they understood each other so deeply that an argument ended up seeming like farce. She remembered Bia's dark eyes smiling at her and seeming to say, "Isn't this stupid, let it go." And Edie had let it go, willingly.

"Before I further fuck up this weekend, I'd like you to know . . ." They all waited for her next words. ". . . that I like you," Edie told Isabel.

"Thank you. You're not the demon I thought you'd be," Isabel said.

"Good," Edie said.

"But she thinks you are," Isabel said boldly.

"I know. So why does she want me here? My feelings wouldn't have been hurt if she hadn't invited me," Edie said, getting up. They needed to head back before the search party was gathered up. They were probably already in trouble. Suddenly, Edie didn't envy Isabel. Laura was a hard woman to live with. Living with Vida was easy. They liked being together and the only rule they had was being in love. No head trips, no games, no boundaries, no protocol, just love. And it worked.

"Because she isn't over you," Isabel said.

"Give me the weekend and we'll cure her of that," Edie said with a smile. "This could be fun. Now I have a purpose. I do better with a goal."

"You are very goal-oriented," Vida said amiably.

Edie nodded, helping her to feet. "Why thank you."

"What are you going to do?" Isabel asked, taking Edie's hand to get up.

"Nothing more than being my usual charming self. She'll remember why I was such a pain in the ass to be with and we'll all be cured of our demons. Memory is an evil charmer. Never forget that, ladies," Edie said, pointing her finger at both of them.

"You can charm me any day," Vida said, heading toward the house and looking back over her shoulder at Edie.

Edie smiled as she eyed the comely backside of her lover.

Laura was crying and chopping the veggies into appropriate pieces to be added to marinade and then skewered.

Sandi handed her a tissue and took the long, sharp kitchen knife away from her. She sat her down and poured her a glass of wine. "I want you to relax," she said sternly. She resumed chopping Laura's vegetables.

Laura sipped her wine and didn't protest.

"You know what we really need right now," Sandi said, putting the knife down and grabbing her bag. She pulled out her cigarette case. "A fat one."

"I couldn't," Laura said, drying her eyes.

"You can and you must. Come on, one for old time's sake. It'll make you feel better."

"No, it'll make me silly."

"Better silly than sad," Sandi coached.

"Why is she so cruel to me?"

"Because she's a fucker," Sandi said, taking a long hit off the joint and handing it to Laura, who still looked uncertain.

"She is not a fucker. She's a witty, talented, beautiful woman and I'm still in love with her."

"Yeah, and she's also hell to live with, involved with someone else, and she pushed you away. Why she blames you for anything that went on is her own special psychosis. Let it go."

"I know," Laura said. "It's been so long I know it's stupid to feel this way, and I love Isabel and Alex and I wouldn't want to trade lives but somehow I need to break away and I can't."

"Learn," Sandi said, passing her the joint again.

"And what is going on in here?" Karen said, coming up and taking the joint from Laura. She took a long drag. "Hmm . . . good stuff. I should have known you'd bring some kind of stuff." She took another hit.

"How's the barbecue?" Laura asked.

"Ready, I think. Want me to skewer?" Karen said, nudging Sandi. "Get chopping. You're off task."

"You sound just like the first-grade teacher that you are," Sandi replied.

"I'll go get stuff ready outside," Laura said. Sandi suspected she really wanted to go look for Isabel. Lord only knew where Edie had absconded with her.

"Is she okay?" Karen asked.

"I think so. Closure issues," Sandi replied, trying to get the veggies in a bowl and doing a poor job of it.

"Lesbians suck," Karen said, finishing off the joint.

"You should talk. There are worse things to be."

"Yeah, married and straight," Karen said.

They both made faces and burst out laughing.

"Yuck!" they said in perfect unison like a couple of straight office girls.

Edie and Vida carried the heavy wooden crate marked Merlot up to the deck.

"That's a lot of wine," Linden said, getting up from the step to make room for them to come up.

"False alarm," Edie said. "Perrier, surefire hangover recipe." She cracked off the top of the crate and opened a bottle.

It exploded everywhere and she shot it at Vida, who looked indignant and then grabbed her own bottle. She showered Edie.

"Hey," Edie said, taking a step back. She shot Linden, who was already drunk and didn't even move. She eyed Laura, who stood paralyzed. "I better not. I'm already in trouble," Edie said, taking a swig instead and watching Vida out of the corner of her eye for signs of further retaliation.

"You are," Laura said.

"Perhaps we should call a truce. It'll make dinner less awkward," Edie suggested.

"All right," Laura said, taking Edie's extended hand.

"I'm sorry you had to be forced to come," Laura said.

"Aw, that's just me being afraid of confrontation. Forget it," Edie said, looking at the fully loaded barbecue. "That looks good."

"It will be . . . I hope," Laura said.

"You can cook. You just didn't have to for a while, that's all," Edie said with a smile.

The back deck was lit by candlelight and the Sedona stars did not disappoint. The food worked out and Laura looked relieved. Of course with enough wine anything can be good, Edie reasoned. Laura had always underestimated herself, Edie thought.

"A barbecue extravaganza," Edie said, holding up her wineglass. "A toast to the chef."

"And her helpers," Laura said. Edie could tell the wine had gone to her head. Laura's words were slightly slurred.

"I'll do dishes," Edie said, getting up and gathering plates.

"Me too," Sandi said, helping.

"You guys don't have to," Laura started to protest.

"This is communal living. We want to," Edie said firmly.

"All right," Laura said, easing back in her chair.

Edie and Sandi headed inside.

"You scuttle the dirty ones and I'll start rinsing and loading," Edie said.

"You're not still mad at me, are you?" Sandi asked.

"Not if you have a fat one to smoke," Edie said. "I think I could use one."

"Done," Sandi said, handing her the joint. "I'll be back with more work."

"Hmm . . ." Edie said, taking a long drag, knowing it would make her tired and she wanted to be tired. She wanted to fall into the arms of ether and sleep away the night and not think of where she was and who was here.

When Sandi returned with another load, Edie had done no dishes; instead she had smoked most of the joint and was laughing hysterically as she made faces at herself, seeing her distorted reflection in the bottom of a copper mixing bowl.

"Look, Sandi, it's fucking hilarious," Edie said.

"Jesus, Edie, it's a good thing it's dark out there. You look totally toasted," Sandi said, starting to rinse and handing Edie dishes to put in the dishwasher.

Edie was having logistical concerns about how to best put the dishes in the racks.

213

"Let's switch. You rinse," Sandi said, rolling her eyes at Edie.

"Dish racks are complicated," Edie said, smiling. She couldn't stop giggling.

"No, you're stoned."

Edie smiled. "I forgot how much fun it is."

Edie carried out coffee and Bailey's to the group.

"No sense ruining a good buzz yet," Edie whispered to Sandi.

"Never," Sandi said.

"We were just telling old girlfriend tales and your name popped up," Linden said, smiling and pouring a heavy dose of Bailey's in her coffee.

"You're going to feel like shit tomorrow," Edie said.

"I'm aware of that," Linden said.

"So how did you meet Edie?" Mattie asked Laura. Mattie wasn't around when the infamous couple had been together.

"We both worked at the magazine together. I worked in the advertising department and Edie was a writer, editor, et cetera. They used to call her Edie extraordinaire," Laura said, beaming at Edie.

"Oh, the days at the magazine . . ." Edie said snidely.

"Do you miss it?" Laura asked.

"No, it was a big fucking joke," Edie said.

"Everything's a joke to you," Laura said.

"That remains to be seen. We won't know for certain until the cosmic tally sheet comes in. I might be under par," Edie said, smiling charmingly at Laura, thinking she was still *really* stoned.

Laura apparently took the benevolent smile as an apology, because she smiled back.

"Anyway . . ." Sandi prodded.

"You already know the story," Edie said.

"I know, but I like hearing it," Sandi said.

Linden rolled her eyes.

Sandi had been in love with Edie from the day she met her and nothing Linden or Edie could do would quench the long burning fire of Sandi's infatuation. It was hero worship, Edie knew, and Sandi had admitted it. Edie swore she would outgrow it but this had yet to happen. Linden stopped being offended by it and Edie took Sandi's friendship seriously, so not fucking each other was no longer an issue. They had come close once but Edie stopped it, telling Sandi that she lost her lovers and Sandi was too important to lose. Sandi had smiled at her, disappointed, saying that did little for her desire. Cold shower, Edie suggested. Together? No.

"Sick fuck," Edie said, pinching Sandi's thigh.

"Ow!"

Edie smiled. "You deserve it."

"I think you have an attention deficit disorder," Laura told Edie.

"You *just* figured that out?" Edie said.

"She's trying to sidetrack us," Vida said.

"You stop giving away my tricks," Edie said, gently putting her in a headlock.

"All right, I promise to be quiet," Vida said, trying to extricate herself.

Edie kissed her forehead. "Remember, I trust you with my precious secrets."

"The French say nothing is so burdensome as a secret," Mattie said.

"Is that why you're all so interested in delving into my past? I highly doubt I'm the only one here withholding information."

"No, yours is just so much more interesting," Linden said.

"She's winning . . ." Sandi said. "And when you met Edie . . ."

"This is worse than going home and being subjected to little Edie stories," Edie whined.

"When I met Edie," Laura began, "she was under her desk uttering a stream of obscenities with the word *fuck* being the most commonly used."

"What were you doing?" Vida asked.

"The fucking drawer was stuck and I was trying to pry it out from behind."

"And it wasn't working," Laura added. "Edie says something like

215

'stupid motherfucking piece of shit' and I say 'excuse me' and without getting up she repeats it for me and then inquires into who I am and I'm thinking this will get her up. No, she just keeps swearing and banging until she completely knocks the desk over."

"Don't know my own strength," Edie said, flexing a bicep. "Knocking over the desk did dislodge the drawer, however."

"And made one huge mess," Laura said.

"I saw then that she wasn't one of those stupid muck-a-mucks from downstairs, that she's the new girl they've all been swooning over and, wow, different ball game entirely. Besides, she helped me get my desk back together and she was wearing a short black skirt. Then I found out she worked in advertising and I wanted nothing to do with her."

Laura harrumphed.

"How did you get her to go out with you?" Vida asked.

"She tried lunch, figuring on the lesbian fact that if the date occurs in the daytime it's not a real date," Edie said.

"She still wouldn't go. I had to have the food editor get one of his friends to cater lunch. If she was trapped in her office she'd have to have lunch with me," Laura said.

"And then she got me all enamored and then dropped me like a hot potato," Edie said.

"Why was that?" Mattie asked.

"Because I found out I was one of her fifteen other girlfriends," Laura said.

"I did not have fifteen," Edie declared emphatically, watching Vida's face closely.

"Suffice it say you had more than one?" Laura inquired with a raised eyebrow.

"Well, yes, more than one but . . ."

"More than one and less than fifteen," Sandi chided.

"I don't think this is pertinent information," Edie said, looking at Vida and wishing she wasn't hearing this. Edie liked feeling in con-

216

trol and right now she felt only vulnerability and the intense need for strict damage control.

"So you didn't want to go out with Edie after that?" Isabel asked.

"Of course I did. I still thought she was wonderful. She was smart and attractive," Laura replied without hesitation.

"Then why didn't you?" Isabel asked.

"Because she was a slut," Laura replied.

"Laura!" Isabel said, clearly embarrassed.

"Why thank you, darling," Edie said.

"Edie, you have to admit you slept around a lot," Laura said.

"It was the fashion. People did that," Edie said, trying to gauge and measure Vida's response.

"Nonetheless, she got rid of the girlfriends and we went to dinner," Laura said, pouring another glass of wine for her and Edie.

"And you liked dinner?" Mattie asked.

Karen looked at her girlfriend and smiled. "You're a hopeless romantic."

"I am," Mattie said, taking Karen's hand.

"I did," Laura said, looking hard at Edie.

Edie looked away.

"And just how was it that the illustrious Ms. Farnsworth walked into your life?" Laura asked Vida.

"She came flying out of a mosh pit at the Crowbar. She hit the wall and sank to the floor with a bloody nose," Vida said, smiling at Edie.

"Vida got me a wad of napkins," Edie said.

"Great introduction. Edie, you're too old to be in mosh pits," Laura said.

"You're never too old for mosh pits," Edie said indignantly.

Vida smiled, then related the rest of the story.

Laura was surprised at how their first meeting ended. Edie read it in her face.

"I don't go to bed with everyone I meet on the first date," Edie said by way of explanation.

"That happened much later, didn't it, Edie," Sandi chided.

"I don't think we need to go into that," Edie said.

"Edie had a difficult time getting up to the first date," Sandi said.

"I find that hard to believe," Laura asked.

"It's true," Vida said.

"I was too intimidated to go see her so I did a lot of walking . . . and buying flowers," Edie said, looking at Vida and remembering how hard it was finally getting up the nerve to ask her out. "There was a florist at the end of the block and I'd end up at the museum where Vida worked, but I couldn't go in, so I'd walk to the florist and send flowers instead," Edie said, looking intensely at Vida.

"Twice a day," Vida chimed in.

"That's Edie," Laura said.

"Which drove my coworker Miranda perfectly mad with curiosity. Of course, Edie had neglected to mention that she was a playwright of some notoriety. I learned this from Miranda," Vida said.

Vida finished the rest of the story and looked over fondly at Edie.

"I don't understand lesbians. The ones you want to go out with don't want to go out, and the ones you could care less about chase you. It doesn't make sense. The chasers should go after the chasers and the rest should go hang out where lesbians who don't like lesbians hang out. The world would be much simpler," Edie said, giving them all a terse grin.

"See now, that wasn't so bad. You got it all out in the open," Sandi said.

"What? Now we all know how each other got into the other's pants. What's that supposed to mean?" Edie said, getting up abruptly.

"No, I just think it's good that you two talk, that's all," Sandi said.

"Where are you going?" Laura asked.

"To bed before things start getting ugly," Edie said, pulling out Vida's chair.

"I think that's a good idea, get everyone settled," Isabel chimed in.

❧

218

Later on, Laura sat thinking. She was still rather shocked by the change in Edie. Edie was right, although she hated admitting that, but talking about old times and how things had changed was more cruel than necessary. This weekend was about healing, but Laura wasn't sure how they were to go about doing it. She only knew she couldn't live one hundred and twenty miles from Edie and not see her at least once more. This would all be so much easier if Edie hadn't disappeared. Edie never let her say good-bye and Laura knew she needed that.

She was sitting on the bed, brushing her hair and listening to the bathwater fill when Edie went streaking by.

"Edie, wait up a minute," Laura said.

Edie was holding a quart of Perrier and looked perturbed. "You're not going to torture me any more this evening are you?" she asked, looking suspicious.

"No, I just want to talk to you," Laura said, patting the bed. "Come, please."

Edie looked around. "Where's Isabel?" she asked, obviously uncomfortable in Laura's bedroom.

"She went to get Alex at the neighbors'. Edie, I just want to talk to you," Laura said, trying not to get upset.

"Why?"

"Because I wanted to tell you that I'm glad to see you, that I missed you," Laura said, touching Edie's face and running her fingers through her hair.

Edie looked at her askance. "I don't understand what you want."

"Edie. We were in love once."

"Once."

"You disappeared and we still had so much to say."

"Like what? What a shit I was."

"I couldn't find you, Edie," Laura said, the old hurt returning.

"There was a reason for that."

"One I wish I knew."

"Look, I suck as a partner."

219

"No, you don't."

"Well, I'm sure after this weekend I'll remind you of what you didn't like about me. Give me seventy-two hours and you'll remember it all!"

"Edie, stop it!"

"No. Isn't this what you want? Isn't this why we're all here, so you can remember, substantiate all that you had grown to despise about me?"

"No, this is about closure."

"Close what?" Edie said, standing up.

"Edie, stop it!"

"Stop what? Being what you hated," Edie said, glaring.

"I never hated you."

Laura grabbed her, pulled her close, held her and then kissed deeply, an almost pathological response, like the addict to the drug. Edie kissed her back in the same craving, needful manner.

"Don't ever do that again!" Edie said, pulling away and running from the room.

Toweling her hair dry, Vida came out of the bathroom to find Edie sitting on the bed.

"This was a mistake," Edie said, running her fingers through her hair.

"No, it's not," Vida said, rubbing Edie's shoulders and neck, gently nibbling at her ear. "This is a vacation," she said, unbuttoning Edie's shirt and running her finger around her nipple.

Edie turned to look at her. "You have a very sick idea of a vacation."

Vida smiled and continued to undress Edie.

Isabel was tucking Alex in when Laura found them.

"There you are," Laura said, sitting down on the bed next to Alex.

"Were you looking for me?" Isabel teased.

"Of course."

"Because you missed us, right?" Alex piped up.

"Why yes, darling," Laura said, a little surprised by the seven-year-old's excitement.

Isabel kissed Alex's forehead. "Now, you get some rest, remember you're going to West World tomorrow with Sheila to ride the horses."

"Yeah!" Alex said.

Her mother smiled at her indulgently. "Okay, now sleep," Isabel said.

"Laura, can you stay for a minute?" Alex asked, seriousness clouding her young face.

"Sure," Laura said, sitting back down on the side of the bed. She looked up at Isabel. "I'll be right there."

Isabel nodded and left them alone.

"What's up, little one?" Laura asked.

"I was just wondering about Edie," Alex said.

"What were you wondering?"

"You loved her once, right?"

"Yes," Laura replied, trying to read where this was going.

"Do you still love her?"

"Not like I love your mom. Edie's an old friend."

"But you don't want to be with her anymore, do you?"

Laura brushed Alex's cheek. "Is that what you're worried about?"

"Kind of . . . I mean, I don't want you to leave us," Alex blurted, "'cause you know grownups do that sometimes. They say they won't leave and then they do," Alex said, her blue eyes filled with an old hurt. Laura could see it.

"No, baby. I would never leave you two. I love you and I love your mom. I'm not going anywhere. Edie's a nice lady but I want to be with you two, okay?"

Alex nodded. Laura put out her arms and the little girl fell into them.

"I won't ever leave you, sweetheart," Laura said, feeling her chest ache with the swelling of her heart. "Never ever."

Alex smiled.

"Now you rest. You've got a big day ahead of you."

"I love you."

"I love you too."

Laura tucked her in and turned off the light. She wandered past Edie's room, feeling guilty for kissing her, for making them both uncomfortable and for abusing the trust of Isabel and Alex. Hoping she could apologize for her indiscretion, she started to knock, seeing the light on from beneath the door. She heard noises, sounds of love. She rested her head against the door and felt sad and confused.

"I smell coffee," Edie said, opening one eye, hoping she'd drunk enough Perrier to stave off most of the bad effects of a hangover. After last night she should have a hangover. She sat up and adjusted her pillow. She smiled. "How did I get so lucky?" Edie said, taking her coffee.

"I'd venture to say the Astral Goddess likes you," Vida replied.

Edie sipped her coffee wondering if the Astral Goddess invented coffee as the nectar of the gods. "Are we ready for yet another fun-filled day?"

"We are," Vida said, sitting on the side of the bed.

"Hmm . . . come here," Edie said, remembering last night.

Vida straddled her. Edie felt her naked body beneath her long T-shirt.

"I hope no one saw you get coffee in this outfit," Edie said, running her hands around Vida's waist and starting to go lower.

"Just Sandi."

"Who was ecstatic, I'm sure. You should have flashed her."

"I did. A well-timed moon shot."

"She probably went into cardiac arrest," Edie said, laughing.

"I think she spilled her orange juice," Vida replied, slowly closing her eyes as Edie stroked her and then slipped inside her. "We're supposed to be down for breakfast in a half an hour."

"Uh-huh," Edie said, removing Vida's shirt and kissing her breasts. "Let them wait." They rocked in unison.

"Tell me when you're ready. I want to do it together," Vida said.

"Almost there," Edie said, feeling Vida's nails gently scraping down her back in slow, sweet agony. She felt them both quiver and pull tight, letting out a simultaneous sigh.

Edie eased her back and took Vida in her mouth, feeling Vida run her fingers through her hair.

"We're going to be late for breakfast," Vida admonished.

"Do you care?" Edie said, looking up.

"Under normal circumstances I wouldn't but this time . . ." Vida tittered, clearly on the brink of pleasure and obligation.

"Because of Laura?"

"Yes, now come have a shower with me."

Vida came down first for breakfast. The table was set and she smelled food.

"Hungry?" Isabel asked.

"Very," Vida said. "Need some help?"

"Sure," Isabel said, getting her started with slicing strawberries.

"I thought you were getting Edie up?" Sandi asked as she dipped into the batter and started another batch of pancakes.

"I did."

"So where is she?"

"She's coming," Vida said, smiling sweetly.

"Without you?" Sandi chided.

"Very funny. Edie's not an easy one to get up."

"Oh, I think she's easy to get up all right. It's just hard to get her out of bed," Sandi said.

❧

223

Laura tried hard not to frown as she reached behind Vida to get a cup of coffee.

"Sandi, you're embarrassing Vida," Linden said.

"Vida, you look familiar. Where are you from?" Laura asked.

"Cleveland originally, but I've been around," Vida said.

Laura refrained from saying *I bet*, but she felt it quivering in her gut. *It's because she's sleeping with your ex, that is why you feel this animosity*, her therapist voice counseled.

"I know where you know her from," Sandi said. "Got any catalogues?"

"Sandi, no. Don't go there," Vida said.

"They're on the front table," Isabel said.

Sandi came back with the culprit happily in hand.

Vida sipped her coffee and kept glancing at the door. Probably watching for Edie, Laura thought.

Sandi flipped through the catalogue until she found a picture of Vida modeling a sweatshirt and shorts.

"Thank God," Vida muttered.

"Look familiar?" Sandi said, pointing to the page as Linden, Laura and Isabel aborted breakfast to lean over and solve the mystery.

Edie appeared out of nowhere and leaned over to peruse with the rest. "It appears your secret life has caught up with you."

"With no help from you-know-who," Vida said.

Sandi thumbed through the catalogue until she found the lingerie part. "My personal favorite," she said, pointing to a rather provocative photo of Vida.

Vida blushed. The group peered.

"Lovely," Sandi crooned.

"Give me that!" Vida said, trying to snatch the catalogue.

"Not yet," Sandi said, slamming her hand down on the page. She looked closely at the ad. "Doesn't she have incredible breasts?"

"Yes, she does," Linden said.

"Not that you can tell in that outfit," Sandi said, pointing at Vida's oversized shirt.

"You do have lovely breasts, darling," Edie said. "And yes, I will testify that they are real."

Vida grabbed the catalogue and pitched it in the trash.

"You weren't thinking of ordering anything, were you?" Vida asked.

Edie got more coffee, grabbed a muffin and sat down. "Well, what are we going to do for fun today?" she said.

"I thought we'd hang out by the pool," Laura said.

"Oh good," Sandi said.

"I brought a really tasteful bathing suit," Vida said.

"Shit!"

Edie laughed.

Later that afternoon, Linden and Karen had gone into town and the rest of them were sipping cocktails around the pool. Laura watched Edie get out of the pool, her gaze running across Edie's shoulders and down her slim waist. She knew if the Goddess had asked on the pain of death did she still desire Edie she would have to say yes. Laura saw the even stripes of reddened flesh down Edie's lower back. What were they doing to each other? Edie didn't use to be like that. She was regular like the rest of us, Laura thought, sipping the last of her drink and wondering how long she could wait before having another.

Vida snapped Edie with a towel and Edie tackled her on the lawn. They were laughing and kissing each other. Laura tried to keep her disapproval hidden behind her dark sunglasses.

Laura watched them as they whispered to each other. She could feel Isabel eyeing her, but she didn't say anything.

"I think we're going to go take a little nap," Edie said.

"Okay," Laura said.

"And none of that funny stuff," Sandi said, looking up from her book.

"Yes, Mother," Edie said.

"You'll thank me later," Sandi reassured her.

Edie rolled her eyes and took Vida's hand.

Laura could hear them thumping and laughing as they ran up the stairs. Laura prayed they'd have enough common courtesy to close their bedroom window so the rest of them wouldn't have to hear the two of them coming into the wild blue yonder. It was difficult enough sitting by the pool and knowing they were fucking each other's brains out just up the stairs.

Vida ran the bath. Edie came in and smiled as she watched Vida draw the shade, light candles and put something very aromatic in the bathwater.

"You make sex a fine art," Edie said.

"Why?"

"Because you travel with accoutrements," Edie said.

"How about you get us a couple cocktails," Vida said, clicking a CD into the player.

"Be right back," Edie said.

Edie ran smack into Laura as she came flying around the corner. She backed away instantly.

"I'm not going to bite you," Laura said, more than slightly affronted by Edie's behavior.

"I know," Edie said, averting her eyes and making her way to the fridge.

"I thought you were going to have a nap."

"We are."

"With beer?" Laura asked, watching Edie open the bottles.

"Beer, bath and then nap," Edie said.

"Edie, are you all right?"

"Sure, why?"

"Well, you know, this morning."

"Oh, that. It's just getting older, I guess. Your body doesn't bounce back like it used to."

"Does she hurt you?" Laura asked, concerned.

"I'm a consenting adult."

"I don't understand it."

"Understand what?" Edie snapped.

"The weird shit you two are into."

"It's not weird. It's called making love, showing love, feeling love."

"Does it have to be painful to be good?" Laura asked.

"It's not painful."

Laura pressed on the red nail marks on Edie's back. Edie cried out. "What's this then?"

"I don't have to explain myself to you anymore."

"Like you ever did explain yourself. That's one of the reasons we fell apart. You wouldn't tell me anything," Laura said, feeling herself grow angry.

"Look, what I do is my concern. We have different tastes now, that's all. I'm not trying to piss you off and I'm sorry if you don't like me anymore but I can't help that."

"I don't know you anymore."

"I'm afraid you don't. What did you expect? That you could walk back into our lives and everything would be the same? People change."

"Edie . . ." Laura could feel herself start to cry.

"We'll talk later," Edie said as she left.

Laura went up to her room to cry quietly. She went into the bathroom, trying to straighten herself up before she faced the others, especially Isabel. She knew this was hard on her too. She washed her face and then heard noises from next door. Sounds of splashing water and mixed with lovemaking. She muffled her sobs with a towel. It was too much. It was all too much. Why was she doing this? Was it to see what her life could have been?

❧

227

Laura was making herself another drink in the kitchen when Sandi came in. Laura was trying to calculate how many ounces of gin she'd had already today divided by the number of ounces of tonic water, which served to stave off dehydration, and whether she should call out for dinner. She was beginning to have serious reservations about her ability to cook in such an inebriated state.

Sandi seemed to have picked up on her mood. "Are you all right?"

"I'm stinking wonderful. And yourself?" Laura said, secretly thanking God it was Sandi she was abusing and not Isabel.

"I'm fine."

"Why didn't you talk me out of this insane weekend?"

Sandi poured herself a gin and tonic. "Because for some insane reason you wanted it."

"I should have known better."

"Be careful what you ask for—you might just get it," Sandi said.

"So just what exactly do they do to each other?"

"Who?"

"You know who, the two upstairs busy fucking each other's brains out, that's who."

"I don't think it's for me to say."

"Sandi, if you don't tell me, I'll conjure all manner and fashion of atrocity. Please tell me. It's not S and M, is it?"

"Depends on your definition."

"Oh, my God!"

"Not really. I wouldn't put it past them though."

"Seriously?" Laura asked.

"They just like to fuck each other, that's all."

"I see."

"Well then . . ." Sandi said, picking up the menu for the local Chinese restaurant. "Perhaps we should get an order together for dinner."

"Let's," Laura said, grabbing a pen.

After they had decided on an order to call in later that evening,

Laura went back outside. She sat down on the chaise lounge and tried to smile at Isabel when what she really wanted to do was burst into tears and fall into her lap, begging forgiveness for wanting things that were too far gone to be attainable. Isabel took her hand and gently kissed it.

"I love you," Isabel whispered in her ear.

Laura smiled, thinking, *if it's the last thing I do tonight I'm going to make love to you. I'm going to make you feel me, all of me this time.*

Laura kissed her deeply. Isabel blushed.

"Maybe we should go to bed early," Isabel said.

Laura smiled. "I'd like that."

"Good."

Sandi walked by the bedroom door, which was cracked open. Snoozles, the cat, was sleeping soundly between Edie and Vida. They looked like two Greek goddesses intertwined and Sandi found herself staring. Vida rolled over and looked up. She smiled at Sandi. Sandi stood mortified.

"Were you spying?" Vida chided.

"No, really, the cat opened the door, I swear," Sandi said.

Edie open one eye, looked over and saw Sandi. "Come here, my little voyeur," she said, "and we'll show you a really good time."

Sandi put her hands on her hips. "Not likely."

"Don't bet on it. Come here, darling," Edie said, patting the bed. "I dare you."

Sandi came in and sat down on the bed.

"You've never done three-ways have you?" Vida raised an inquiring eyebrow.

"Suffice it to say I was young and still in my school uniform. Can't trust those Catholic girls," Edie said, smiling as Vida ran her hand up Edie's her inner thigh.

Sandi watched her. "All hands on deck."

"Relax," Edie said, pulling her down on the bed.

"I find that difficult in this situation," Sandi said, unable to suppress the urge to straighten out Edie's messy hair.

"See, it's nice. Come snuggle. It'll make you feel better," Edie teased.

She's calculating, Sandi thought. She wondered what Vida thought about all this, but Vida appeared only interested in getting her fingers inside Edie. Sandi heard footsteps and started to get up. Edie grabbed her and kissed her fiercely. When Sandi pulled away, she looked over to see Isabel standing stunned in the doorway. Vida gave a knowing smile.

"Hi," Vida said. She had successfully entered Ediem, whose face had that sudden look of *oh my*. She'd figured out Edie's game, only she was one up on her. Sandi tried to get up quickly, her embarrassment making her look guilty.

"Hi, uh. Laura," Isabel stammered, pointing downstairs, "she wants to know if you want to . . . go to town with her."

"Beer run?" Edie said.

"I think that's a great idea," Sandi said, standing up. "Ouch!"

Edie had pinched her butt and was smiling lasciviously at her.

"I mean, if you want to . . . or if you're busy . . ." Isabel said, blushing head to toe.

"She'll go," Sandi answered, scrambling to get out of the room.

"Tell her I have to have a shower first because I smell like sex," Edie called out loudly after them.

Vida laughed.

Isabel stood shaking as Laura looked up at her inquiringly.

"What's wrong? What did she do to you?" Laura asked, her antennae immediately sensing trouble.

"Nothing," Isabel said, sitting at the bar and turning the shopping list round and round.

"It must have been something. You're acting strange. Tell me."

"I can't."

"Well, I'll guess I'll have to go see for myself."

"No," Isabel said, panicking and grabbing her arm.

"What is it then?"

"The three of them . . . in bed . . . together."

"What three?"

"Vida, Edie and Sandi."

"You saw them?"

"The door was open."

"That does it!"

"Where are you going?"

Laura didn't answer. She stood at the base of the stairs and screamed, "I will not have three-ways in my house!"

Isabel buried her head in her hands.

"Damn it, Edie get out of bed and come to the store with me before I come up there and throttle you."

Edie laughed and called out, "I'm coming, Mother."

"I am really," Edie said, feeling her body convulse under Vida's able hands. "You are bad," she said when she could think again. Vida pulled her tight.

"No, worse than you. You counted on that happening."

"I did," Edie said. "Laura thinks our sexual practices are disgusting so I just thought I'd really give her something to chew on."

Vida stroked her cheek and looked deeply into her eyes. "I love you."

"I know you do, sweetheart. I don't know what I'd do without you. No worries, okay?"

Vida nodded. "You better go. She's waiting."

"Promise me something nice when I get back. To get me through," Edie said, heading for the shower.

Vida thought for a moment, her hands behind her head. "Why don't you pick us up some *fruit* at the store."

Edie smiled. "I like that."

Vida blew her a kiss.

"We're bad," Edie said.

"Perfectly awful," Vida replied. "Wait." She called out, "Sandi, Sandi, where are you? Edie's leaving."

They burst into furtive giggles.

Edie got in the car.

"I don't know what you were doing but don't do it again. You really gave Isabel a turn and that's not nice," Laura lectured.

"Boy, this brings back memories," Edie said, slinking down in the seat.

"You wouldn't force me to do this if you'd stop acting like a juvenile delinquent. Now put your seatbelt on."

"Is this why you wanted me to go to town, so we could fight all the way there?" Edie said, meeting Laura's gaze.

Laura touched her face. Edie didn't pull away.

"I'd forgotten how pretty your eyes are," Laura said, softly.

Edie took her hand and patted it between her own. "Why do we always fight?"

"I don't know. I wish we didn't," Laura said sadly.

They rode in silence.

Laura broke the spell. "Edie, why do you hate me?"

"I don't hate you," Edie said, surprised. "Why do you think that?"

"That animosity thing, for starters," Laura replied, gliding deftly into the first parking spot she saw.

"Back forty as usual," Edie said, referring to Laura's old habit of parking way out in the lot.

"Some things never change," Laura teased back.

"I don't hate you. It's just hard to see you now. It hurts," Edie said.

Laura nodded.

232

Edie grabbed a cart and they headed directly to the liquor section.

"We are definitely a thirsty bunch," Edie said, smiling and feeling like a naughty teenager.

"I think it might be stress-related," Laura said, loading things in the cart.

"Do we need food?"

"Maybe some breakfast things," Laura said, looking at her list.

"What about dinner?"

"This afternoon when I was drunk I thought we'd order out but now maybe . . ."

"You were drunk?"

Laura smiled. "I've been known to get drunk. I wasn't a hazard to public safety."

"All right then."

"So maybe we should cook," Laura said, her ability to concentrate clearly taking hold.

"How about grilled pork tenderloin and some fixings? For old time's sake?" Edie said.

"Perfect."

"Would you be offended if I cooked? Take some pressure off of you."

"No, I'd like that," Laura said, her eyes full of appreciation. "You can be so sweet sometimes . . ."

"And the other times?"

"I want to kill you," Laura replied.

Edie immediately flipped into gourmand mode and got all the necessary items for the dinner extravaganza. They stood in the checkout line and then started to argue over who was going to pay.

"I mean it. Let me," Edie said. She felt it was the least she could do.

"No, you're a guest."

"I want to."

"I don't want you to. You always pick up the tab."

"Because I like to," Edie said, attempting to snatch Laura's ATM card out of her hand.

"Edie, don't. Now stop it. You always overdo. I won't let you this time."

"I don't overdo it. I do things because I want to," Edie said, suddenly noticing the line of people watching their dispute. Laura caught her gaze and their audience. She blushed. "Please," Edie said, putting her hands gently on Laura's hips and moving her aside.

"Just this once," Laura said with a shrug.

"That's fair. Thank you," Edie said, their eyes meeting. Edie felt color in her face and she knew she was starting to feel things she shouldn't. The clerk was more than glad to see them go.

The sky had turned from high overcast to ominous black. The promised afternoon storm had set in quickly. Laura looked up, worried. They barely got the groceries in the Grand Cherokee when the downpour started. Laura flicked on the wipers and got them out of the quickly flooding parking lot.

"I'll never get used to how sudden these storms set in," she said.

Edie nodded. The raindrops bounced off the now sodden earth. The road was covered in water and Laura could hardly see.

"Maybe we should pull over and wait it out," Edie suggested. "It'll stop soon. We've got time. We'll talk and I'll promise to be nice."

Laura found the first road off of State Route 89 and pulled over. Her knuckles relaxed on the steering wheel.

"At least we have snacks," Laura said, watching the deluge continue with no immediate relief in sight.

Edie handed her the cell phone. "Why don't you call home and tell them we're going to wait it out so they don't worry."

Laura called and told Isabel not to worry.

They both sat back and listened to the pounding rain. Edie dug them out a beer.

"I'm sorry about earlier," Edie started to say.

"Don't. It's all right."

Edie nodded and handed Laura the Cheetos.

"These are horrible for you."

"Nuclear snacks. Old age is never certain. Live a little."

Laura took one. "Oh, Edie . . . how did we let it get this far?"

"I'm sorry," Edie said, looking out the side window.

"I just don't understand what went so wrong."

Edie took a long swig of beer. "It was just that whole thing with Bia . . ."

"You still miss her, don't you?"

"She was an incredible woman," Edie said, tears welling in her eyes. She quickly brushed them away.

"I know that was hard on you."

"And you," Edie said.

"I felt like you blamed me."

"It wasn't your fault."

"I know, but I don't think I was as helpful as I should have been. I felt so disconnected from you both. I didn't know what to do. I wanted to help."

"You did. I was a real basket case," Edie said, looking straight at her.

"I wanted . . . I wanted you and you wouldn't let me near. You made me feel so, I don't know, undesirable, and I didn't know how to get you back. I wanted you back . . . so badly," Laura said, starting to cry.

"Please don't cry. It wasn't you. It wasn't. I swear," Edie pleaded.

"Edie . . ." Laura started to sob.

Edie pulled her close. "Laura, please," Edie said, wiping away her tears. "I didn't want anyone."

"I missed you. I just wanted you to touch me like you used to and you wouldn't."

"Shhh . . ."

"Why wouldn't you touch me?"

"Because I couldn't."

"Why not?"

"It wasn't you. It wasn't," Edie said, kissing her gently on the cheek.

Laura pulled her close. "What was it?"

"I can't explain," Edie said, brushing her tears away.

"Edie . . ."

Edie kissed her, softly. Laura kissed her back, a lover's kiss. Edie fell into it. She started to pull away.

"I'm sorry," Laura said, looking deeply into Edie's eyes.

"Don't be, please don't be," Edie said, looking sad and vulnerable, looking more beautiful than Laura remembered.

They held each other until the rain stopped.

Edie kissed her cheek. "We should go. They'll be worried."

Laura nodded and started the car.

When they pulled in the driveway Vida and the others went out to meet them. As soon as Edie saw Vida she freaked, her eyes wild, and ran past them up into the house and her room.

"What happened?" Sandi said.

"Nothing," Laura said lightly. "We talked about Bia."

Sandi looked at Vida who caught her cue.

They helped Laura unload the groceries. Vida got a Valium from Sandi and took Edie a brandy.

Edie was lying in the fetal position on the bed.

"Are you okay?" Vida asked, sitting on the edge of bed.

Edie had been crying. She nodded.

"Take this," Vida said, handing her the Valium and the brandy snifter.

Edie obeyed. She crumpled in Vida's arms and cried profusely. Vida held her until she was done.

"I know this is hard for you, but when it's over you'll be a free woman and that's a good thing," Vida said, stroking her hair.

"I didn't want you to see or know about these things," Edie said, looking up at her.

"They're part of you. It's all right," Vida said, kissing her forehead.

Laura finished putting the groceries away. When Vida returned, Isabel shyly inquired about Edie.

"She's just a little overwhelmed by all this. I don't think she's thought a lot about all this old stuff in a while."

"Is she lying down?" Isabel asked as Laura handed her stuff to put in the fridge.

"Yes. She'll be okay," Vida said, more to herself than Isabel, Laura thought.

"You should have known better than to talk about Bia," Sandi said.

"I thought time would have healed some of that. She was my best friend too. Edie wasn't the only one that lost her," Laura replied.

"I know," Sandi said softly.

"I'm going to go see if she's all right. Will you start the grill? I think we all need to eat," Laura said.

"Be nice," Sandi warned.

"I will." Laura gently tapped on Edie's door. "Edie, are you all right?"

"You can come in," Edie said. She was sitting on the bed putting her shoes on. She patted the bed. Laura sat down. "I'm fine. Sorry, I just sort of freaked. I'm better now," Edie assured her.

"Are you sure?" Laura asked.

"Yeah," Edie said, smiling at her.

But Laura knew that smile, it was the one designed to fool people, the one that spoke of nonchalance while deep emotional issues were being hidden. Edie's love was back in place and Laura knew she'd lost her.

"Okay, well, I've got Sandi starting the grill and then we can start dinner," Laura said.

"Do I still get to cook or does being emotionally unstable revoke my rights?" Edie asked, standing up and offering Laura her hand.

"No, it doesn't. Edie, I just wish you could talk to me," Laura pleaded.

"I know. I don't talk to anyone . . . I might someday," Edie said, looking away.

Laura nodded.

"Maybe after dinner we should all go for a walk up Schnebly Hill and watch the sunset," Edie suggested. "It's a beautiful view from up there."

"That sounds wonderful," Laura replied, finding herself breathing a little easier.

Isabel came outside with the rest of the food to be put on the grill. They were neat little tin-foil packages of baby red potatoes and fresh green beans. She handed them to Edie. Edie turned to look at her, knowing that her nosebleeds were back. If she could help it, she didn't want Isabel to see, but her hand and upper lip were already full of blood.

"Edie, are you all right?"

Edie nodded.

Isabel went inside and got a roll of paper towels. Edie took a wad and smashed them against her face.

"You should sit down and lean your head back," Isabel instructed.

"But dinner . . ." Edie started to say.

"I'll put them on," Isabel offered.

Vida looked out the window and saw Edie with her head back and blood staining the white towel. She let out a heavy sigh. She'd been doing so well, not having them since the early days of the play, and then they'd stopped altogether. Vida was relieved that Edie had slowed down and relaxed enough to avoid them. She went outside and sat next to Edie. Edie looked at her apologetically.

"They're back," Vida said.

"Just a slight relapse," Edie said, pulling the towel away. "Is it done?"

"No," Vida said, handing her more towels and tilting her head back. She took the old ones inside.

"What happened?" Laura asked, looking at the blood-soaked towels.

"It's Edie," Vida said. "Her nose is bleeding."

"I see," Laura said. "I can't believe she still gets them."

"Only under duress," Vida said, going back outside to find the rest of the group crowded around Edie, who was struggling to get free.

"Jesus Christ! It's a fucking nosebleed. I'm fine," Edie said, getting up.

"Edie, calm down," Vida said, taking her hand. "Let's go for a walk, okay?"

Edie looked uncertain.

"I'll watch the grill," Isabel said.

"All right," Edie said, following Vida off the deck. They went and sat at the gazebo.

"We've just got to get through tonight," Vida counseled Edie.

"I know. I'm sorry. Now do you understand why I didn't want to come? It's always like this when we're together."

"I know, sweetie."

Edie put her head on Vida's shoulder and Vida hoped the worst was over.

After dinner they hiked up Schnebly Hill and watched the sun turn from a fierce white fireball into a gentle orange disc settling into the horizon. They smoked one of Sandi's fat joints. It was almost like the old days when everyone got along, Edie thought as she looked at her friends benevolently. She watched the couples settling peacefully into each other. Linden smiled at her and Edie felt a little better about the world.

"Time for beers?" Edie said, feeling cottonmouth setting in and wanting to stop her stoned paranoia from taking over.

"Definitely," Karen said, helping Mattie off the giant orange stone monolith they were sitting on.

"I still can't believe how beautiful this place is," Mattie said, scanning the horizon.

"Sedona is incredible," Karen said. "You forget places like this when you live in the city."

"Well, you'll all have to come up again soon. Anytime really," Laura offered.

Edie stopped herself from shuddering but Sandi caught her vibe and gave her a cautionary look. Edie smiled innocently.

Edie and the others were sitting around the kitchen table having a midnight snack except it was only eight-thirty. Alex was staying over at a friend's house and Edie was behaving herself.

"It's a good thing I don't smoke dope," Laura said, her mouth full of Oreo cookies.

"Oh, you don't, do you. Then why do you have the munchies?" Sandi said.

They all laughed.

"It's fun spending time with all my old friends," Laura said.

"Just like the old times," Sandi said.

"Older, wilder times," Edie said.

"Like you've slowed down," Sandi chided.

"I have slowed down," Edie said indignantly. "I got slow when I lived with Laura. Didn't I?"

"Perfectly bloody domestic," Laura said.

"I don't know about that," Sandi said, taking another shot of tequila. Edie was keeping count—that was five.

"Did I not do all the grownup things? I was the perfect little woman, house in the suburbs, charming wife, steady career," Edie said. "I think that was my most settled period."

Vida nodded in agreement. "She's not like that now."

Edie looked at Sandi smugly.

"I'll give you that. So I guess with the exception of your interludes with Bia you were a pretty settled partner," Sandi said.

Edie shot her a look. Sandi blanched, realizing her mistake.

"I thought you two talked about Bia on the way to the store. I thought that was why you were so upset," Sandi said, trying to backpedal as fast as she could.

"What do you mean, the interludes with Bia?" Laura asked.

Sandi was quickly trying to collect her drunken self. Edie felt like the sacrificial lamb: revered and yet about to be slaughtered.

Sandi scrambled. "You know how Edie and Bia used to go out and get wild."

"No, I didn't know. Why don't you tell me?" Laura said.

Sandi started to say something but Edie had come up behind and clapped her hand across Sandi's mouth. She whispered in her ear, "Let's you and I go have a little talk outside and see if we can fix this mess you've gotten us into."

Sandi nodded.

"Sandi and I are going to go get some air."

"She's not going anywhere until one of you tells me what happened," Laura said, putting her hand firmly on Sandi's shoulder.

"What does it matter?" Edie said. "It's over and done with."

"It matters to me," Laura said. "Bia was my friend and you were my partner. I have a right to know."

"Karen, can I have a cigarette?" Edie said.

"No smoking in the house," Laura said.

"We'll smoke outside," Edie said.

"Not until you tell me about Bia," Laura demanded.

"How about we stand by the arcadia door and blow the smoke outside. I have the distinct feeling things are going to get ugly. Smoking might keep me from getting a nosebleed."

"I thought you gave up smoking," Laura said.

"I did until you got ahold of me," Edie retorted.

"Let her have a cigarette," Karen said, handing her one.

"All right, one," Laura said.

Karen got up and lit them both one.

"How many have you got?" Edie whispered.

"About half a pack," Karen replied.

Edie looked at Sandi, who was more composed now that she had time to think.

But Laura was not so easily distracted. "Tell me about Bia."

"There's nothing to tell. I was just messing around. You already knew that they hung out together. That was nothing new and they didn't hide that from you," Sandi replied, tracing the wood designs in the table and avoiding Laura's gaze.

"What *did* they hide from me?" Laura asked.

Edie watched Laura's face, knowing she was slowly putting events together.

"Did you sleep with Bia?"

Everyone was staring at Edie. She took a drag of her cigarette and contemplated lying, knowing it would be easier but wondering if it would really work. Laura obviously suspected something.

"Why do you think that?" Edie asked, keeping her voice even.

"That's not the question," Laura said, as if sensing the answer.

Edie looked at Sandi. "Tell her what you saw that day."

"Why do I have to tell her?" Sandi whined.

"Because you opened this can of worms," Edie replied.

"Tell me," Laura screeched.

There was a long pause before Sandi answered. "I found them in bed together one afternoon at the loft."

Laura took a deep breath. "So you slept with Bia once, twice . . ."

"What does it matter?" Edie said.

"Sandy said interludes, how many interludes?" Laura demanded.

"Your grammar is impeccable," Edie replied.

"You slept with my best friend. I can't fucking believe you!"

"Don't ask questions if you don't like the answers," Edie retorted, lighting her second cigarette from the end of the first.

"How long did you two sleep together?" Laura asked.

"For a while," Edie replied.

"How long?"

"Six months after they moved to Phoenix until the day she died," Edie replied, graciously abstaining from getting down to hours and minutes.

Laura ran her hands across her face. "Do you fuck around on Vida too? Got another fuck buddy in the wings?"

"No, I don't, nor do I want one," Edie said, staring intently at Vida.

"So Bia was the only one you condescended to having as a fuck buddy."

"Don't call her that!" Edie said, her face getting hot.

"What was she then?" Laura taunted.

"All the things you weren't," Edie said, losing her temper and lashing out.

"Like a whore and a cheat."

"Don't say that! Don't ever say that!" Edie said, moving dangerously close to Laura.

"I suppose you loved her," Laura said.

Edie studied her, knowing the weight of the words she was about to speak. The room was silent in apprehension of Edie's bringing down the house of cards that masqueraded as a relationship.

"Yes, I loved her very much," Edie said.

"Then why didn't you leave me? Why not run off together instead of sneaking around all those years? Where did that put Julie and me? On the outskirts, while you two were so madly in love. How could you do that to me? How could you do that to Julie?" Laura ranted.

Edie looked away. "Julie knew."

"Oh, that's just great! And she didn't care? Why didn't she throw her out?"

"Bia made me swear not to tell you. If I left you then she wouldn't see me anymore. I didn't know she was dying. She didn't tell me that until later. She didn't want me to be alone and she didn't want to hurt you."

"I suppose you all knew! And not one of you had the balls to tell me," Laura said, looking around at the suddenly guilty parties seated at the table.

"We thought you knew," Karen said quietly.

"You thought I knew. If I knew do you think I'd stand for that!"

Edie looked away.

"God, this is a fucking nightmare! I can't believe it. All that time I spent with you I was just filling up space until you could be with Bia again. I loved you. I thought you loved me," Laura said.

"I did love you," Edie said.

"Just not as much as you loved Bia. You can't love two people," Laura said.

"It was a different kind of love," Edie said.

"Oh, I get it. We were roommates that occasionally slept together and Bia was the love of your life," Laura said.

Edie looked away and didn't answer.

"You fucking cunt!" Laura said, kicking Edie in the shin.

Edie went down while Laura dashed for the door.

"Edie! Are you all right?" Sandi said, jumping up.

Edie grimaced and righted herself. It hurt like hell. She nodded. "I suppose I deserved that." She looked at the somber group. "I wish I had some incredibly wise and witty thing to say to you, to her, to make things right, but I'm afraid I'll have to disappoint you all." Edie limped outside.

"Edie . . ." Sandi started to say.

Edie put her hand up and went outside. She sat on the porch step. She knew she couldn't say anything to make this right, to make Laura not feel so bad.

Vida came out and sat by her.

"Do you hate me too?" Edie said, looking at her.

Vida stroked her cheek. "No, I don't."

"You probably should," Edie said, studying her hands.

"I couldn't. I know things are hard right now but you told her the truth and she needed to hear it. She needed to know."

"So she can let go?" Edie asked.

"Yes," Vida said.

Laura came walking into the porch light. She watched Vida and Edie talking. Vida had her arm around Edie's shoulder. Vida got up.

"You two should talk . . . without an audience this time," Vida said.

"Thank you," Laura said softly. She stuck her hands in her pockets and rocked back on her heels. "I'm sorry I hurt you. Are you all right?"

"I'm sure it was a mere pindrop compared to what I've done to you. Come sit. We should talk," Edie said, patting the steps.

Laura sat, trying to do so without trepidation. She took a deep breath.

"I wanted to tell you. I wanted to let you go, to say I was sorry for falling in love with someone else. It wasn't something we planned. It just happened. I wanted to make it honest. But Bia . . ." Edie said.

"That was selfish . . . even for someone who was *dying*," Laura said.

"I know. I hated myself for doing that to you," Edie said, looking away.

"But not enough to come clean."

"You know how hard it is to let go. You loved me like I loved Bia."

"Edie, you lived with me as the perfect partner and now I have to resolve the fact that it was lie. Do you know how hard that is? Why it's so hard to let go? I thought you were madly in love with me, and then when Bia died you walked away. Do you have any idea what that does to a person? How difficult it makes it? I have only been able to give half of myself to Isabel because the other half is still very much in love with you," Laura said, wiping away a tear.

Edie studied the ground. "I'm sorry. I never meant to hurt you."

"You know that doesn't really cut it."

"I know."

"How am I supposed to go on with my life thinking that part of my life was a total farce, that what I thought was love wasn't true?" Laura said, trying to make some sense of it all.

"You got me there. I did love you. I still loved you even when I was with Bia. It just got so complicated and I didn't know what to do."

"But it was love out of obligation, not passion. It was half love and half responsibility," Laura said.

"Isn't that what you've been doing with Isabel?" Edie said.

Laura thought for a moment. "I suppose you're right."

"Do you want it to be different? Do you want to be free to love her completely, without ghosts, without a sense of guilt for not loving her enough because you're still in love with someone else?" Edie said.

"More than anything," Laura said.

"Does the thing with Bia make more sense? If she hadn't been dying I hope that we would have come clean. I begged her to be able to do that, but it wasn't in the cards, so we did the best we could, but you have that chance with Isabel. You can come clean and love her with all of you, without guilt, without obligation, and isn't that better?"

"You should have been a lawyer," Laura said, stroking Edie's hair out of her eyes, knowing this time would be the last time.

"I know you're convinced that you can't love two people at the same time but you can. *You've been doing it*. I never regretted the time we were together and I did love you. Please don't ever forget that," Edie said, pulling her close. "You made me think and feel things I never thought myself capable of and for that I thank you."

"You never cease to amaze me. How I can hate you one moment and think you're wonderful in the next?"

"Ditto," Edie said.

She kissed Laura's forehead and felt the giant weight that had been clinging to both their ankles like shackles for all these years take flight, like the Phoenix from the flame.

ABOUT THE AUTHOR

Saxon Bennett lives in the mountains of New Mexico with her partner and their two cats and two dogs and a tractor named Minnie. She
is currently trying to cure herself of her four lifelong phobias:
rodents, children under thirty-six inches, cat tracks on ski hills, and
drive-thru windows.

Publications from
BELLA BOOKS, INC.
The best in contemporary lesbian fiction

P.O. Box 10543, Tallahassee, FL 32302
Phone: 800 729 4992
www.bellabooks.com

SURVIVAL OF LOVE by Frankie J. Jones. 236 pp. What will Jody do when she falls in love with her best friend's daughter? ISBN 1-931513-55-4 $12.95

LESSONS IN MURDER by Claire McNab. 184 pp. 1st Detective Inspector Carol Ashton Mystery ISBN 1-931513-65-1 $12.95

DEATH BY DEATH by Claire McNab. 167 pp. 5th Denise Cleever Thriller.
ISBN 1-931513-34-1 $12.95

CAUGHT IN THE NET by Jessica Thomas. 188 pp. A wickedly observant story of mystery, danger, and love in Provincetown. ISBN 1-931513-54-6 $12.95

DREAMS FOUND by Lyn Denison. Australian Riley embarks on a journey to meet her birth mother . . . and gains not just a family, but the love of her life.
ISBN 1-931513-58-9 $12.95

A MOMENT'S INDISCRETION by Peggy J. Herring. 154 pp. Jackie is torn between her better judgment and the overwhelming attraction she feels for Valerie.
ISBN 1-931513-59-7 $12.95

IN EVERY PORT by Karin Kallmaker. 224 pp. Jessica's sexy, adventuresome travels.
ISBN 1-931513-36-8 $12.95

TOUCHWOOD by Karin Kallmaker. 240 pp. Loving May/December romance.
ISBN 1-931513-37-6 $12.95

WATERMARK by Karin Kallmaker. 248 pp. One burning question . . . how to lead her back to love? ISBN 1-931513-38-4 $12.95

EMBRACE IN MOTION by Karin Kallmaker. 240 pp. A whirlwind love affair.
ISBN 1-931513-39-2 $12.95

ONE DEGREE OF SEPARATION by Karin Kallmaker. 232 pp. Can an Iowa City librarian find love and passion when a California girl surfs into the close-knit dyke capital of the Midwest? ISBN 1-931513-30-9 $12.95

CRY HAVOC A Detective Franco Mystery by Baxter Clare. 240 pp. A dead hustler with a headless rooster in his lap sends Lt. L.A. Franco headfirst against Mother Love.
ISBN 1-931513931-7 $12.95

DISTANT THUNDER by Peggy J. Herring. 294 pp. Bankrobbing drifter Cordy awakens strange new feelings in Leo in this romantic tale set in the Old West.
ISBN 1-931513-28-7 $12.95

COP OUT by Claire McNab. 216 pp. 4th Detective Inspector Carol Ashton Mystery.
ISBN 1-931513-29-5 $12.95

BLOOD LINK by Claire McNab. 159 pp. 15th Detective Inspector Carol Ashton Mystery. Is Carol unwittingly playing into a deadly plan? ISBN 1-931513-27-9 $12.95

TALK OF THE TOWN by Saxon Bennett. 239 pp. With enough beer, barbecue and B.S., anything is possible! ISBN 1-931513-18-X $12.95

MAYBE NEXT TIME by Karin Kallmaker. 256 pp. Sabrina Starling has it all: fame, money, women—and pain. Nothing hurts like the one that got away. ISBN 1-931513-26-0 $12.95

WHEN GOOD GIRLS GO BAD: A Motor City Thriller by Therese Szymanski. 230 pp. Brett, Randi, and Allie join forces to stop a serial killer. ISBN 1-931513-11-2 $12.95

A DAY TOO LONG: A Helen Black Mystery by Pat Welch. 328 pp. This time Helen's fate is in her own hands. ISBN 1-931513-22-8 $12.95

THE RED LINE OF YARMALD by Diana Rivers. 256 pp. The Hadra's only hope lies in a magical red line . . . climactic sequel to *Clouds of War.* ISBN 1-931513-23-6 $12.95

OUTSIDE THE FLOCK by Jackie Calhoun. 224 pp. Jo embraces her new love and life. ISBN 1-931513-13-9 $12.95

LEGACY OF LOVE by Marianne K. Martin. 224 pp. Read the whole Sage Bristo story. ISBN 1-931513-15-5 $12.95

STREET RULES: A Detective Franco Mystery by Baxter Clare. 304 pp. Gritty, fast-paced mystery with compelling Detective L.A. Franco ISBN 1-931513-14-7 $12.95

RECOGNITION FACTOR: 4th Denise Cleever Thriller by Claire McNab. 176 pp. Denise Cleever tracks a notorious terrorist to America. ISBN 1-931513-24-4 $12.95

NORA AND LIZ by Nancy Garden. 296 pp. Lesbian romance by the author of *Annie on My Mind.* ISBN 1931513-20-1 $12.95

MIDAS TOUCH by Frankie J. Jones. 208 pp. Sandra had everything but love. ISBN 1-931513-21-X $12.95

BEYOND ALL REASON by Peggy J. Herring. 240 pp. A romance hotter than Texas. ISBN 1-9513-25-2 $12.95

ACCIDENTAL MURDER: 14th Detective Inspector Carol Ashton Mystery by Claire McNab. 208 pp. Carol Ashton tracks an elusive killer. ISBN 1-931513-16-3 $12.95

SEEDS OF FIRE: Tunnel of Light Trilogy, Book 2 by Karin Kallmaker writing as Laura Adams. 274 pp. Intriguing sequel to *Sleight of Hand.* ISBN 1-931513-19-8 $12.95

DRIFTING AT THE BOTTOM OF THE WORLD by Auden Bailey. 288 pp. Beautifully written first novel set in Antarctica. ISBN 1-931513-17-1 $12.95

CLOUDS OF WAR by Diana Rivers. 288 pp. Women unite to defend Zelindar! ISBN 1-931513-12-0 $12.95

DEATHS OF JOCASTA: 2nd Micky Knight Mystery by J.M. Redmann. 408 pp. Sexy and intriguing Lambda Literary Award-nominated mystery. ISBN 1-931513-10-4 $12.95

LOVE IN THE BALANCE by Marianne K. Martin. 256 pp. The classic lesbian love story, back in print! ISBN 1-931513-08-2 $12.95

THE COMFORT OF STRANGERS by Peggy J. Herring. 272 pp. Lela's work was her passion . . . until now. ISBN 1-931513-09-0 $12.95

CHICKEN by Paula Martinac. 208 pp. Lynn finds that the only thing harder than being in a lesbian relationship is ending one. ISBN 1-931513-07-4 $11.95

TAMARACK CREEK by Jackie Calhoun. 208 pp. An intriguing story of love and danger. ISBN 1-931513-06-6 $11.95

DEATH BY THE RIVERSIDE: 1st Micky Knight Mystery by J.M. Redmann. 320 pp. Finally back in print, the book that launched the Lambda Literary Award–winning Micky Knight mystery series. ISBN 1-931513-05-8 $11.95